# THE
# FREED
# CHURCH
# BOY

# OTHER BOOKS BY THE AUTHOR

The Dog Catcher
Tricks for a Trade
The Best Possible Angle

# THE FREED CHURCH BOY

A NOVEL

LLOYD JOHNSON

Diamond Lake Publishing

DISCLAIMER

This book is a work of fiction. Names, characters, businesses, organizations, places, events, and incidents either are the product of the author's imagination or are used fictitiously. Any resemblance to actual persons, living or dead, events, or locales is entirely coincidental.

Copyright © 2020 Lloyd Johnson

DEDICATION

For Lyle, the love of my life

# ACKNOWLEDGMENTS

I would like to first and foremost thank God for putting ideas in my head and the will to see them turned into stories. I also thank my partner, Lyle, for believing in my talent and not forcing me to dim my creative light; my family for their continued encouragement; my youngest brother, Phil, for giving me a good-talking-to whenever I get a case of the lazies; Jean Benton for her friendship and planting the seed in my head to do a "sequel" to my novel *The Dog Catcher,* which turned out to be this book. I'd also like to thank my editor Donald Weise and my cover designer James from GoOnWrite.com. Last but not least, I thank the readers both old and new. You continue to inspire me to do what I do.

# THE FREED CHURCH BOY

# ONE

October 25, 2016

Minneapolis, Minnesota

Okay, I'm officially drunk, which is nothing new. Most evenings end this way.

"C'mon, folks! Let's go! Finish 'em up," the bouncer shouts at us as though we're meandering cattle.

I hate this time of night; the inevitable moment when the club's house lights come on and the hit dance-mix du jour playing over the sound system fades to zero decibels. It means the party is over.

Hands down, Sparkles Nightclub is my home away from home. Some of the staff joke since I'm often here until closing, I may as well keep a sleeping bag stashed to pull out after closing time. They have me pegged correctly; I am here most evenings, squandering my hard-earned cash. I figure the amount of money I've blown over the years could easily pay for two four-year college degrees. I waste money tipping drag queens and club staff who don't give two-shits about me. The bartenders especially are like bees to my honey. They keep the liquor flowing, usually beyond my tolerance level. And because I'm such a great tipper, they listen to me bitch about whatever has my briefs in a bunch on any given day. However, once they announce last call, they lose interest, turning on me like a fair-weathered friend. Now, as the bar closes, I have only my mundane existence to look forward to, which I'm certain is waiting outside where I left it.

"Let's go, people! You don't have to go home, but you can't stay here!" the same asshole shouts as the club vomits us onto the sidewalk like we're chunks of nothing.

I wander through an inebriated throng, many of whom hide their own misery behind drunken smiles. They aren't difficult to spot. After all, like attracts like.

I search for my friend and presumed ride home, Kenyatta…last seen canoodling in a dark corner, stuffing his hand down the crotch of some stranger's pants. Now I can't find him or his latest conquest.

*So much for the ride home.*

Getting pissed about it won't make Kenyatta magically appear, but his lack of consideration does piss me off. I shouldn't have allowed him to talk me into going out for two-for-one, especially since he barely has two nickels to rub together… ever. But after my day from hell (including my car breaking down on the way to work and rude customers working my nerves at the restaurant), I welcomed the opportunity to unwind.

People say when someone shows you who they are, you need to believe them the first time. Kenyatta's behavior isn't surprising. In fact, he behaves true to form, which I consider tantamount to being a shitty friend. From the time I've known him, he's always been flighty, the kind of person who tentatively commits to things while keeping his options open for better offers. That said, ditching a friend to go bouncing on some random guy's penis is a new low, and indicative of the way I've allowed Kenyatta to treat me.

We met as teenaged church boys. Each guessed the other was gay before either of us was able or willing to accept it in ourselves. But, despite every unhelpful thing our pastor said about gays, it was our presumed homosexuality that drew us together.

However, while Kenyatta's bourgeoning sexuality fit him like a glove, I struggled with mine. So much so that I attended a Christian college in America's heartland. The intention was to meet an acceptable Christian girl to rid me of this "homosexual spirit" as my grandmother called it, or at the very least throw off any scent that I liked guys. Before heading off to school, Kenyatta and I fooled around. I wanted my first and last same-sex experience to rise to the "fuck of the century" level had by Michael Douglas and Sharon Stone in *Basic Instinct*. Unfortunately, because of our inexperience, the encounter culminated in mutually unsatisfying blowjobs. Now, whenever I mention it, Kenyatta's recollection is willfully different.

"A blowjob? I don't remember anything about giving you any blowjob! Now, we might've jacked off..." he says.

Back before I went away for spiritual fixing, we were close. However, as we grow as men, Kenyatta prefers to keep our relationship transactional. He only calls when he wants to complain about his life, though he's never shown any interest in changing the things he has problems with. Sometimes (which is often) he calls to suggest a fabulous night out on the town, which begins with an expensive meal at my favorite restaurant, Palomino. Afterward, when I'm sufficiently lubricated with wine and sentimentality, Kenyatta begs for a small loan to get him through until his SSI checks arrive. Of course, I foolishly give him the money, though I no longer hold any expectation of repayment.

I zip up my jacket, shielding myself from the crisp, autumn night air. In four months, I will beg for the balminess of summer.

The "Sidewalk Sale" is about to start. That's what we call the post-club gathering out front to admire the talent pool of guys and to close the deal on potential hookups. Weekends offer the crème de la creme of male specimens, however, on any night you can usually find someone to go home with. If you're lucky, the guy you've spent all evening following around the club is as sexy in natural light, has all of his teeth, and doesn't have psychological problems.

As I take my usual spot against the wall, the best place to check out the after-bar shenanigans, my cell phone vibrates inside my back pocket. A text reads: *Busy tonight?* followed by triple heart emojis. I scowl and slip the phone away before the temptation to reply wins out.

Drunk gay men continue spilling out onto the pavement, splintering into predictable cliques... homo thugs to the left, bitchy twinks to the right. An elderly interracial couple, who probably remembers Sparkles from its heyday, stands in the middle of the after-club frolic, no doubt overwhelmed by how many things have changed.

Conventionally attractive, white, thirty-somethings walk past with an air of aesthetic superiority. A black guy tags along, sticking out like a token, brown-skinned clone. The men are conservatively dressed in sport coats, khakis, and designer eyewear. I lock eyes with the black guy and offer a "brother to brother" smile and nod. But his frosty response informs me he is uninterested in being my "brother." Unfortunately, he isn't the first black man willing to snub other black men to stand with the white paragon of beauty, nor will he be the last. Sadly, I expect this treatment from the people whose approval "brotherman" seeks, but the affront is especially hurtful when it comes from another black person.

Disappointed, I shift my focus towards a butch lesbian dragging her femme girlfriend by the wrist as they exit the club.

"You better bring your drunk ass on before you get left!" she says.

Embarrassment covers her girlfriend's face the moment she notices me watching them.

"Nita, will you please calm down? People are staring," she replies, hoping to shame the stud into behaving.

I continue watching them until their quarreling voices fade in the distance.

Brianna, one of my favorite drag performers, bursts through an alternative club exit, touching a wet streak of red running down the side of her terrified face. Hobbling to the curb, she sparkles beneath the streetlights, wearing a black catsuit bejeweled with rhinestones. She wears a glittering, ankle-strappy stiletto pump on her left foot while barefooted on the right. She frantically waves at a school of cabs whizzing by.

"Taxi!"

Northbound traffic slows to a halt at the red light. A fleet of car windows lower in unison to the halfway point. Then the insults begin…

"What a bunch of freaks!"

"Fuckin' faggots!"

"Yo, check out the butt pirates!"

"Eww, look at the tranny!"

"Y'all need to repent before Christ returns. Read your Bible!"

I've heard them all before. Random homophobic outbursts are the new normal… a referendum on PC culture and basic civility. The troublemakers resent the hard-won progress made by the LGBTQ community, wanting instead to return to an era when gays, and trans people, in particular, were the butt of jokes and made easy targets.

"All of y'all can go suck a dirty dick!" Brianna hollers back, swinging her enormous purse overhead as if to dare someone to a brawl.

Undaunted by the drag queen's retort, the bigots continue their vitriol until the traffic light turns green, and the waiting traffic leans into their horns. Car windows rise to a close, and the hateful caravan speeds off.

A taxi pulls up to the curb. Brianna swiftly opens the back passenger door.

A second drag queen named Donesha exits the club, brandishing Brianna's missing pump in one hand and a box cutter in the other. She dazzles in a silver, cinch-waisted sequined gown.

She radiates a grandness that commands those of us watching to move out of her way.

"Gimme my wig, you ol' raggedy bitch! I already done busted you upside the head with your shoe. Don't make me cut yo' ass too!"

Brianna can easily dive into the back seat of the taxi, shut the door, and be on her way. Instead, she cowers against the vehicle, the fear of God etched into her face. She obediently removes the black, asymmetrically cut wig in question from her head, revealing a tattered stocking cap beneath it. Embarrassed, she wags the fake hair at arm's length like a surrender flag.

"I'm sorry! Here, take it!"

Donesha snatches it from her, rewarding Brianna with a slap to the face. "That's for stealing my shit!"

"Whoa! Whoa! Whoa!" the taxi driver yells from inside the taxi.

"Aww, shut the hell up before I slap the shit outta you too!" Donesha warns.

Spectators standby, their mouths agape in shock. They bellow "Oooohs" as though watching a gladiator being mauled by a lion.

Donesha follows up the slap with a high-heeled kick to her drag nemesis's midsection, sending Brianna tumbling into the taxi's open backseat; her limp legs hanging from it.

"And that's for making me chase your dumb ass!" Donesha says, panting heavily. She stuffs the thieving queen's legs into the cab and slams the door. The taxi drives away.

Once upon a time, street theater like this: a pair of sparring drag queens or quarreling, jealous lovers amused me. But, after a while, it has become needless and tacky… a symptom of Sparkles' decline.

The same bouncer comes outside, too late to do anything, of course. "Yo, you can't congregate out here! Let's keep it moving, folks. C'mon!"

The crowd disperses like flies being swatted from a picnic basket. A few lonely men remain, determined to go home with someone... *anyone*.

I walk to the curb to hail myself a cab, unencumbered by my usual worry of being gay-bashed on the way back to my car. Lately, going out to have some fun is akin to taking my life into my hands.

*The fun times...* I remember them well. Some might say I drown my sorrows in the past. But I see nothing wrong with cherishing fond memories.

In the mid-1990s, I was a precocious man-child stumbling through life. Those few euphoric years allowed me a freedom that, until then, I hadn't known existed, which was to feel one-hundred percent right in my skin as a gay person. It was no minor feat considering the albatross of religion around my neck. The Bible verses are drilled into my brain. Leviticus 18:22 and 1 Corinthians 6:9 still follow me...no matter how hard I try to forget them. The holy rollers often pull these scriptures from their tool kits to remind gays that God has given us over to our sinful ways; that He no longer hears our prayers. Some days I believe that. Some days I don't. But I'm not completely sure I'm ready to give up on God, even though I'm told He has every reason to give up on me.

Back in the day, I ran away from religion and found refuge at Sparkles, watching the writhing bodies of shirtless, sweaty men dance with sexual abandon. I yearned to be a part of that brotherhood. However, in years to come, those crowds of brawny, handsome men would shrink away. Back then, AIDS still threatened the community and claimed the lives of many. As death swung its mighty scythe, I lived under a staggering fear of contracting HIV. Times were changing; many gay men began to want more from their lives than a slew of colossal dicks and seductive smiles. Guys disappeared from the scene, found love and monogamy, and settled into domestic life.

I'm unsure whether I still believe in love. That ship has sailed with a fine-ass brother named Byron Ross steering the wheel. His name still lingers like a burn on my tongue. Whenever he's in my life, I become bereft of common sense. He remains a hard-learned lesson I need to remind myself of, and the one thing stopping me from responding to text messages better left unanswered.

Byron is the straight-but-curious type I enjoy from time to time, despite his being too much emotional baggage for anyone in their right mind to deal with.

His modus operandi is simple: hit me up for drunken sex after arguing with a supposed estranged wife. Then, after screwing me senseless, he sits regretfully on the edge of my bed, his body still warm from our sex. Like clockwork, he raps his knuckles against his temples as his spent dick hangs between his open, muscular thighs, and has the nerve to ask me why I make him do the things he does to me.

As I wait at the curb, traffic passes, and a memory of my last time with Byron hits like a sudden punch to my gut...

That night, Byron's dick raged long and solid. It gleamed at the tip. His eyes were penetrating as he sexily dragged his tongue from one corner of his mouth to the other.

"Can I hit some of this pussy?" he asked, scooping an abundance of my firm ass into his enormous hands.

Pussy. I usually hated the word. However, I loved the lustful way in which it fell from Byron's lips. Aroused by the sound of his deep voice, I could only nod my desire.

"No. I want you to tell me," Byron whispered, brushing his soft lips against mine. We had not kissed up to that point. He had refused to do so, considering it the line separating "punks" from the *real* men who occasionally "got down." To Byron, kissing was a sign of affection. It meant he cared. He swore he would never allow himself to care for another man... until now.

"Tell me I can have this pussy," he said, sandwiching each word between deep, wet, encompassing kisses; each rolling beautifully into the next. His smile warmed me like an area heater. And his willingness to defy himself and break his own rule made me special.

"You can have it," I said, lost within an unquenchable yearning that caused my voice to crack like a pubescent boy.

Byron twiddled my right earlobe with his long tongue, saying, "You're gonna give me what I want, aren't you?"

His tongue descended in playful swirls along my neck. Rapturous tingles ignited my body as Byron's mouth returned to unite with mine. My vessel wanted to float away, but my stiffening dick anchored me.

Byron's natural scent smelled of boozy leather and cocoa. Every whiff of him was a gift, and I was grateful to be in the presence of a black Herculean god-made flesh. But then…

"I can't do this," he said, pulling away.

"What's wrong?" I tried to meet his eyes, but disgust shone on Byron's face, making him a stranger to me.

"I can't be doing this. I'm a married man," he said, picking his scattered clothes from off the floor.

"I thought you were getting a divorce."

"Trina called me today. She wants to work it out."

He knew the rule. I warned him before never to utter her name. I didn't want to know anything about her. She was a phantom to me. If she was as insignificant as he led me to believe, I wanted her to remain inconsequential. However, the utterance of her name gave her texture and validity.

"I almost forgot. She calls, and you come running," I said.

"Don't start with that."

*How else am I supposed to react?* "Fine, let's talk about you kissing me today."

"Big deal!"

"Big deal? You've never kissed me before."

Byron looked down at the clothes in his hands. "Yeah, and I shouldn't have done it," he said with regret.

"You shouldn't be playing games with me, either."

"I'm not playing games. Yes, I have feelings for you, but what I have with my wife is morally right. Besides, you can't argue with God, and He says Trina and I belong together."

"You really think God told you that?"

"Don't make jokes about my faith. And don't act like I made a secret of how important God is to me."

"He's important to me too."

"Then you should understand what I'm saying. God has given me another chance to pull this... this thorn out of my flesh."

My eyes pooled with tears. Never had I felt so expendable... worse, like being tossed away like garbage. "Let me guess... I'm the thorn, right?"

Byron busied himself getting dressed. "I never lied to you. I've been honest from the jump that this is a struggle for me."

"I wasn't aware it was such a struggle to be honest with yourself."

"I've told you a thousand times, I ain't like you! I ain't no..." his words fell away.

"Don't stop now. You're not a what?"

"Fine," he said, a coldness entering his eyes. "You want me to say it? *I ain't no faggot!*"

"Hey, buddy! Do ya wanna cab or not?" a brusque-sounding voice asks, bringing me back to the present moment. I open my eyes to a new cab driver's impatient gaze. I hop into the car.

"Sorry, my mind was somewhere else."

"Yeah, yeah. Where we goin'?"

I slur out an address, hoping it is my own. As the driver starts the meter, my cell phone hums again against my butt.

*Can I hit some of that pussy tonight?* Byron's text says.

Being in charge of employees at the restaurant every day makes me long to submit to someone in other areas of my life. My bedroom is my chosen area to do so, and Byron is usually the person I submit to.

A pic of his erect penis fills the length of the screen with a caption that reads, *I want to be inside you!* His mating call charges old and pleasant memories, spurring life inside the crotch of my pants.

My choices are simple: let Byron's texts go unanswered; take my drunk ass home and stay up late chasing an elusive orgasm with my calloused hand. Or allow Byron to come over and use me as a respite from yet another bout of marital strife and sexual confusion.

I bite the corner of my bottom lip. My fingers spring into action, taking on a life of their own, tapping out a response to Byron's proposition. The driver glances at me through the rear-view mirror, no doubt smelling my desperation from the backseat.

There was a time when self-respect kept me from groveling at the feet of any man. But I'm drunk and horny. There will be plenty of time later to regret what I'm about to do tonight.

# TWO

The red, blurry, digital numbers on the alarm clock read 11:11. I put an open palm over my squinting eyes and lower my throbbing head (imagine your head being squeezed between a vice grip) back onto the pillow. A heavy aftertaste of stale cigarettes and beer coats my parched tongue. I lay here for a while, my jumbled thoughts seeking order inside my brain.

I didn't sleep well if you can call it that. My younger, less mature self would plot excuses to call out of work. But the grownup version of me is better than that. I live by the rule to play is to pay.

A morning chill prickles my exposed abdomen, turning it into gooseflesh. I reach across the bed for Byron, but my hand falls over an empty space where his body once lay. Disappointing, yes, but I got exactly what I expected... phenomenal sex and a reminder of why it could never work between us. I pull towards me the pillow that only hours before cushioned Byron's head. Now his fading scent will have to be enough.

I swing around to the edge of my bed, planting my socked feet onto the hardwood floor. My tired eyes focus on the *Paris Is Burning* movie poster on the wall as my feet send empty beer bottles skittering towards a pair of dumbbells I haven't used for months.

After putting on a T-shirt and jogging pants, I give the dumbbells another groggy glance. Before my guilt from not exercising sets in, I follow a welcoming and savory scent of cinnamon and bacon to the kitchen.

My roommate and best friend, LaSaundra, has taken it upon herself to open every drape to flood the house with sunlight. Lucky me I'm not a vampire, otherwise, I'd burst into flames.

I enter the kitchen and sit down in my usual corner spot at the breakfast nook. LaSaundra walks about in slow, exhausted movements, dragging the soles of her gray, furry slippers across the floor. She appears comfortable in her favorite pink and gray flannel pajamas, and her shoulder-length hair is still wrapped in a yellow and blue scarf. The moment our eyes meet, I can tell she's pissed with me about something.

"Glad to see you're finally awake," she says with more attitude than I need to start my day with. She slaps a plate of French toast down in front of me, topping it with an angry sprinkle of powdered sugar.

"What's wrong?" I ask.

LaSaundra drops a small plate of bacon on the table hard enough to make the bacon bounce from the plate.

"Nothing."

"You could've fooled me," I reply, eyeing the syrup.

She shrugs, sits down. Her ample bosom flattens against the table's edge as she reaches for the juice pitcher.

I wait a few seconds for an answer. She gives me nothing. I'm familiar with LaSaundra's moods. She intends to make me work for her response. But I'm too hungover to work this hard. I give up and proceed to enjoy my breakfast. The first bite of French toast is divine, and the crispy bacon delivers the perfect crunch.

"Do you like it?" she asks, watching my every bite and chew.

I want to say no, to prove I can be bitchy in the morning too. My mouth is too stuffed to respond anyway. But I nod my approval. After washing it all down with two swallows of juice, I say, "Oh, the mechanic said my car won't be ready for at least another couple of days. Do you think you can drive me to work?"

After a long pause, she says, "I suppose."

"Are you sure? If it's too much trouble, I can take the light rail or Uber."

"Sounds like you have it all figured out. You don't need me."

"Will you please tell me what's wrong?"

"You came home drunk again last night."

Although I'm satisfied she's finally telling me what's bothering her, my defensiveness kicks in. I push the remaining pieces of French toast around the plate with my fork. "Yeah, so?"

"And from the sound of it, you had company."

"Yeah?"

LaSaundra exhales a long, exasperated sigh. "Why do I even bother trying to have an adult conversation with you?" She turns away to conceal her rising frustration. "I'm going in early today, so if you want a ride, you'd better get ready now." She gets up from her seat, tosses her napkin on the table, and leaves the room.

I'm used to LaSaundra's sanctimony. I usually let her sententious comments pass without responding. I would never tell her so, but figure it easier for her to be holier-than-thou when her own sex life is DOA.

Part of me thinks she might still be pissed over what happened the time she dared me to have sex with her. It was during one of my bouts of religious guilt over being gay, and yet another example of a drunken lapse in judgment. That night, she asked if I'd ever been with a woman, followed by the age-old question, "How do you know you don't like it unless you try it?" She reminded me of the countless times I said if I was straight, the two of us would be perfect together. After killing half a bottle of tequila between us, I attempted to slide my unresponsive dick inside her, slipping out three times before giving up. It was all the evidence I needed to confirm I wasn't sexually drawn to women. LaSaundra, however, took it as a personal rejection, and I spent the rest of the evening comforting her wounded ego as though it were my fault her vagina wasn't the elixir she thought it would be to "turn" me straight. I explained it was no one's fault, and if she thought about it, we probably make better friends than lovers.

As my best friend, I put up with her sticking her nose into things that don't concern her (like my sex life). She's certain my love of sex is bordering on addiction, rooted in some kind of childhood trauma. LaSaundra is always trying to put me in touch with my feelings. But I've told her a thousand times that feelings are overrated. Feelings trump common sense. She means well, but I loathe her intrusiveness.

Whenever I don't agree with her analysis of why I behave the way I do, she accuses me of withholding, one of her favorite words. It almost makes her sound like she knows what the hell she's talking about. But Iyanla Vanzant, she's not, nor is she anywhere close to fixing my life.

*****

The ride to work is an exercise in awkward quiet. I'm officially on LaSaundra's shit list, making me the lucky recipient of her patented silent treatment. She likes to think it matters, but it doesn't bother me. In fact, her refusal to speak is a win because it allows me to peacefully enjoy the magic of autumn happening outside my passenger window.

I love autumn… the abundance of sunshine passing between naked tree branches. I love the wind catching the leaves and how they quilt the ground. I adore the crunch of dead leaves and the snap of desiccated twigs beneath my feet.

However, my serenity is short-lived, vanishing the moment we enter the freeway. Asphalt, cement, and colored fleets of fast-moving steel replace the autumn splendor.

Aggressive drivers refuse to let LaSaundra merge into the flow of traffic, compounding her stormy mood. By the time someone finally lets her in, traffic slows to a snail's pace.

I crane my neck to see what's causing the traffic snafu. Only after passing a spectacle of tangled steel, shattered glass, and crushed plastic of an accident does traffic begin to move again. LaSaundra speeds up to make up time.

"Don't worry about it," I tell her, trying to massage her frustration. "We'll be there in plenty of time."

"Easy for you to say, you're not the one running late!"

"If you want to take the next exit, I can find the light rail that goes to the airport."

"Yeah, right, so you can tell people what a bitch I am?"

"You've been beefing at me since I woke up. Is this how you're going to behave for the rest of the ride? If so, you can put me out right here and I'll take my chances walking!"

LaSaundra grips the steering wheel, delighting in making me wait for an answer.

"Are you going to answer me?" I ask.

"I could ask you the same question. What's going on with you?"

"Nothing's going on with me."

"I disagree. Seems to me you're on your way to self-destruction. Well, I ain't gonna sit around and watch it happen."

"Who's self-destructing? I had too much to drink last night. Big deal, it happens. And I'm paying for it today, but I'll be fine."

When LaSaundra glares, her eyes are like knives. If looks could kill, I'd be a mutilated corpse slumped next to her. "And from the sound of it, you brought some strange man into our home. We've talked about this. If you won't take your own safety into consideration, at the very least take mine!"

"Oh, I see. You think giving me a ride entitles you to lecture me?"

"No lecture. I'm expressing concern." She leaves it there and doesn't speak for the rest of the ride, though I sense there is plenty more she wants to say.

We arrive on the Departures Level at the airport. I unbuckle my seatbelt and open the door. I place one foot onto the curb and thank her for the ride. I also tell her I hope she gets to work on time.

"Are you going out after work?" she asks, her tone tinged with judgment.

"I'm thinking about it."

"Of course, you are, Lawrence. Well, do me a favor. Try not to drink yourself into oblivion. We still have some things to discuss."

"I doubt I'll be in the mood later. Just say what you need to say and be done with it."

"I'm serious about what I said about you bringing your strays home. It isn't safe."

I pull my foot back inside the car. "I didn't bring a stray home last night."

"Then who was it?"

Staring at the curbside is preferable to meeting LaSaundra's gaze. An elderly black couple checks their luggage with a skycap I recognize from the restaurant. As the wife speaks to the skycap, the husband stares adoringly at her. I guess mature, ripened, black love is possible after all. It forces me to smile, despite LaSaundra's question, which still requires an answer.

"You're going to be pissed," I finally say.

"I'm already pissed."

"I meant more pissed."

"Tell me who it was," she repeats.

"Byron."

Her eyes practically jump off her face. "You brought *him* home?"

I inhale deeply, making certain to choose my words carefully as to avoid stirring her fury. "He's been texting me."

"And you couldn't ignore him?"

"Apparently not. Anyway, I took one look at the man and a bunch of unresolved crap I thought I was over came out."

"Oh yeah? Did he ever resolve the fact he's married?"

"Don't go there, LaSaundra."

"My mistake. It was better when I only thought you were an irresponsible drunk. I shouldn't have forced you to confirm it just now."

"Is that what you think of me?"

"Get out of my car."

"No! Is that what you think of me?"

"I told you he's bad news. You can go down the same rabbit hole again if you want to. But you're not dragging me down there with you!"

I exit the car, slamming the door on every accurate word she said. My stubbornness won't allow me to listen to any more of her rant. After all, I'm a grown-ass man with needs. Byron just so happens to be one of them.

# THREE

"Hi, may I help you?" I ask the burly, lumberjack-looking man at the counter.

He doesn't acknowledge me. Instead, he rolls his meaty neck and scratches his beard. His eyes, black and shiny like tiny, wet pebbles, are fixed on the menu.

"May I help you?" I ask again.

"Gimme a sec, will ya?" he replies, sounding like someone who gets a hard-on whenever he thinks about food.

"Call me when you're ready." I smile to thaw the sarcasm in my voice. A wasted effort. He pays me no attention.

I walk over to the beeping fryer to pull a metal basket of dark, shredded potatoes from the oil, making a mental note to have someone change the oil later.

"Hey, you! I'm ready to order now," the customer says, adding an unnecessary and spectacularly rude snap of his fingers to catch my attention, the lowly fast-food worker he believes me to be.

For every disagreeable customer I serve, a part of me dies. As it is, I regret most of my earlier life choices. Not taking my high school studies seriously charts high on the list. Doing better in school would've enabled me to go to a reputable college and major in something viable to forge a career I could love and flourish in. Instead, I've settled into a dead-end job I doubt I'll ever have the balls to quit. Still, I hold on to the possibility there is more to life than serving ingrates like the one waiting for me at the front counter.

I take my time returning to the register. Getting there too quickly will only empower his arrogance. Sure, I'm being petty, but I have to take back my power wherever I can.

I'm in the crosshairs of the customer's heated gaze. He puts his beefy paw-like hands onto the counter. His splayed, dirty fingers reveal fingernails chewed to the nub.

*He probably doesn't wash his hands after taking a piss, much less before eating,* I say to myself. Part of me wishes I'd said it aloud.

"What would you like?" I ask, my phony smile flickering on.

"Yeah, gimme a deluxe burger combo. Upsize everything."

"And what would you like to drink with that?"

"Diet whatever you have."

"Sure thing."

"And make it snappy," Mr. Personality says with the enthusiasm of addressing someone he considers beneath him. He pulls two crumpled bills from his pocket and tosses them onto the counter. He sneeringly watches me uncrumple the money.

My co-worker, Sameer, appears at my side like a superhero arriving on the scene to dispense justice.

"You have a telephone call," he says, moving in to take over the transaction.

Grateful, I leave him to handle the difficult customer. The business phone lays off the hook on the counter in the office. I pick up and say hello.

"Lawrence?"

The sound of Ma's voice causes my stomach to spasm. I thought by changing my cellphone number she would catch the hint I don't want to be bothered. I have no idea why she's called me at work, hell, called me at all. I have nothing to say to the woman. When her new husband called me an abomination, she said nothing to defend me. Unfortunately, it isn't the first time Ma has failed to protect me from the slew of homophobic men she brought into our lives. Also, a long-running point of contention between us is her waffling acceptance of me being gay. One minute she's cool with it, the next she isn't.

"What do you want?" I ask as rudely as I can. She deserves my rudeness. If she's forgotten why, then I have no problem reminding her.

"Grandma's gone," she says, her voice sounding dreamily remote.

*Grandma. Gone.* At first, the two words don't register. I stare up at the gigantic clock mounted on the wall. It reads 3:33. Suddenly, I go all cottonmouth, and the phone slips from my numb fingers.

Ever since learning Grandma's prognosis, I've tried envisioning what it would be like when she died. Where would I be when I received the news? How would I react? I've watched plenty of TV to witness fictional characters bulldozed by their grief. But it doesn't happen for me. Instead, I'm frozen in a moment, bracing for an enormous wave of emotion to knock me about like ravers in a mosh pit. Any emotions I expect to experience are MIA.

There is no shrieking or dramatic swooning. No compulsion to curse God. Only when I stare down at my shoes am I once again aware of the greasy texture of the floor. I pace the room until the office becomes narrow and confining. I hold my hands crisscrossed over my mouth, too embarrassed by my paltry display of grief for a woman I love more than my mother. It was Grandma who took me in (much to the consternation of my grandfather) when my parents kicked me out of the house. She was stiflingly old school but showered me with the unconditional love her Christian faith spoke of.

*Grandma. Gone.* The two words hover inside my brain like static. I struggle to put them together. Needing a distraction, I poke my head outside the office door.

Everything is business as usual in the restaurant. Many of the sights and sounds are familiar. A cash register drawer slams shut. The fryer timer beeps. Burger patties sizzle. A customer orders two burger combos without onions or mustard. Someone requests fries without salt. Another substitutes a soft drink with a strawberry shake. The cranky lumberjack sits alone and angry with the world, ravaging his hamburger like a lion ripping flesh from its doomed prey.

However, the phone beckons me back inside the office, suspended by an infinity of pale-yellow cord where I left it. I pick up the phone again and put the receiver to my ear. But in my mind, I implore God to make Ma take back what she just told me.

"What do you mean she's gone?" I ask finally.

"She's gone. Died a half hour ago."

"Who's there now?"

"Just me, Daddy, Marva, and Auntie Daphne. Can you come by the house? I think the family should be together at a time like this."

The request makes my skin itch from dread. I don't want to see Grandma lying there… dead. I need an excuse. I should tell Ma I'm the only manager on duty, and there is no one else available to close the restaurant. Why see Grandma dead today when I can attend both the wake and funeral later, once the shock wears off? *If it wears off.*

"Son, did you hear me? Can you come by?"

"My car's been acting up. I had to put it in the shop." A cringe-worthy excuse even if it's true. I wish I'd gone with the only manager on-board story. Sounds more urgent. The ensuing silence from Ma's end of the line riles my nerves. I fumble around for something less ridiculous to say.

"Uh, I guess I could take the light rail. Better yet, I'll hire a cab or Uber."

"Don't be silly. I'll come pick you up." There is a finality in her voice that suggests declining isn't an option.

"Yeah, okay," I reply absentmindedly. It's too late to take it back, even if I want to.

"I'll be there in about fifteen minutes."

"Okay, fine. See you later."

Sameer appears in the doorway as I hang up. His exotic musk oil scent enters the room before he does.

"My grandma just died."

He gives me an obligatory pat on the shoulder. "Aw, man, I'm sorry."

"Thanks. Happened a half hour ago."

The bastard doesn't believe me. I can tell from the way he scans my face as if checking it for appropriate traces of distress. I'm not surprised. Despite sharing the position of salary manager, I've never gotten the sense Sameer considers me his equal. And the way he takes his sweet time checking the shift setup, no doubt coming up with reasons not to let me go, only stokes my unease.

"I assume you need to go?" Sameer's accusatory tone matches the brewing intensity in his eyes.

I clear my throat. Who does he think he is? He doesn't have a choice in the matter. "Uh, yeah. She died at home. My mother's picking me up to take me by the house."

"Go ahead. We'll be fine," he says, dialing back the exasperation in his voice, though his vexed expression remains intact.

"You sure?"

"Yeah. We're fine. I'll give Quish a heads up."

"Thanks. I appreciate it."

Outside on Departures Level, I pull a cigarette from a vintage, silver cigarette case LaSaundra gave me for my fortieth birthday. My hands shake terribly. It takes six attempts to light the damn match. Once I light my cigarette, I reward my efforts with a long, self-congratulatory drag.

Cigarette ash flutters into an ever-expanding Newport smoke cloud. I sit down on a steel bench, avoiding the annoyed glares from the anti-smokers surrounding me as I wait for my ride.

I call LaSaundra. Her phone rings repeatedly. I assume she isn't answering on purpose. I leave a message on her voicemail, informing her of what happened, and that I'm heading to my grandmother's house.

Freddie, an older black man who shines shoes across from the restaurant, joins me on the bench. He stretches his legs and exhales a long sigh as though relieved to be off his feet. He eyes the cigarette hanging from my mouth.

"Say, young blood. Let me have one," he says, palming his hand over the vast ripples of gray wavy hair on his head.

The request puzzles me. I heard from several airport employees with whom I'm friendly that he has a terminal illness. Not wanting to contribute to his demise, I give silent protest with my eyes.

Freddie shrugs. "Too late now. Damage is already done."

Reluctantly, I extend my cigarette case.

"Well, I'll be good and goddamned. Ain't you fancy?" he snorts, pinching a cigarette between bony fingers that are inked with black shoe polish.

I offer him the waning embers from my cigarette to light up. After Freddie hands it back, I drop it to the ground, mashing it into the pavement with my heel. I don't want to share Freddie's fate.

"Here, knock yourself out." I give him the remaining four cigarettes from the case. He accepts them merrily, either in denial of the severity of his condition or having made peace with his impermanence.

An attractive chocolate sister wearing a festive orange dress walks past. She smiles brightly. Her dreadlocks cascade majestically over the front of one shoulder. She welcomes the flirtatious glint in Freddie's gaze and executes a saucy shake of her hip, leaving exquisitely perfumed air in her wake.

"Damn, I bet she got a nice, wet, meaty pussy," Freddie says, lowering his chin in the sad resignation he will never find out.

I ignore much of what he says next as a deepening sadness fills my spirit. The woman's dress reminds me of the orange sherbet I enjoyed as a kid at Grandma's house. She used to serve the creamy scoops in ugly, pumpkin-colored Tupperware bowls, scarred by cigarette burns. I hated the way the melting sherbet oozed over the blackened flecks of warped plastic.

My memory drifts on to her spicy Thanksgiving dressing complementing the turkey Granddaddy cooked on the Weber grill. And I can almost taste the creaminess of her potato salad and sweet potato pies. Those memories conjure my first tears since getting the news of Grandma's passing.

From behind a swirl of cigarette smoke, Freddie stares at me, confused. But I can't explain the reason I'm crying. The words are stuck in my throat.

He pulls a tarnished copper flask from his apron and unscrews the cap. He helps himself to a deep swig, then shudders.

"You look like you could use some of this medicine, son," he says, offering me the flask.

"What is it?"

"Cognac."

I accept the flask and sip from it. A comforting warmth spreads across my chest as I hand it back.

"Young blood, this here is my good shit. I don't give it to just anyone," he says, dropping it into the black of his apron's pocket.

"Guess I should consider myself lucky."

Ma's red Mazda pulls up to the curb. She sits on the passenger side. Her husband Tyrell Murphy is in the driver's seat. From where I stand, I see she's been crying. I give Freddie a nod of gratitude and a wave before heading towards the car.

"Be strong, young blood!" the old man yells to me. I crawl into the backseat and close the door.

No one speaks, which is fine by me. I don't want to be forced to compare my grief with anyone else's. If Ma is hoping for an emotional breakthrough between us, she'll be waiting a long time. As far as I'm concerned, the deterioration of our relationship is her fault.

When she divorced her first husband, Plez Jackson, she was a broken woman. Years of physical, mental, and emotional abuse left her without self-esteem. Thankfully, Dino Taraborrelli, a man she dated for a long time, treated her like a queen and helped restore her self-worth. The relationship ended when she became uneasy at the prospect of marrying again and having more children. I long suspected she broke up with him because she could not handle the barrage of judgment she received for being involved in an interracial relationship with an Italian man. I saw firsthand the effect Dino's leaving had on her. I adored Dino, who, unlike my former stepfather, didn't show favoritism towards Junior and didn't mind me being gay. The only person happy to see Dino gone was Junior, who despises anyone who isn't his father.

After Dino, Ma dated a slew of losers. Then, out of the blue, she decided to re-dedicate her life to Christ and started attending church service. She met Tyrell, pastor of the church. Next thing anyone knew, they married at the downtown courthouse and Ma fell back into the old habit of allowing a no-good man to control her.

I buckle myself in. Once the seatbelt clicks, my emotions betray me, and I break down sobbing. Ma reaches behind her seat to offer her hand, but I flick it away. I'd rather choke on my tears than take her hand. She's let me down more times than I care to remember, and I want nothing from her.

We arrive at Ma's house. The next-door neighbor blows leaves to the edge of his yard with a leaf blower. He waves as we're getting out of the car. I'm the only one who waves back. Not watching where I'm going, I trip. Ma grabs hold of my arm before I stumble to the ground. "Pastor," as I bitterly refer to her husband, continues on (unmoved by my near wipeout) to unlock the front door. I would bet money had it been just the two of us, Pastor would've let me drop.

Inside the house, I collapse, emotionally spent, into an oversized, patchwork chair by the front door.

"Anyone want a soda?" Ma asks.

*No! I want something strong enough to help me cope with the loss of Grandma and the annoyance of having to be there with you and your fake holy man,* I say to myself while simultaneously nodding yes to her offer.

She hesitates, rethinking the wisdom of leaving me alone with Pastor, the combustible elements we are. She waits until she receives an affirming nod from her husband before her shoulders drop and the worry lines vanish from her face. Then she leaves us to ourselves.

Pastor takes a seat on an ugly watermelon-colored sofa he moved in with after marrying my mother. He crosses his long, slender legs in a way he probably thinks to be debonair. His wrists hang limply, crisscrossed over his knee. Rings made from chunk gold and diamonds adorn his expertly manicured hands. I'm unimpressed.

We sit quietly for a time. Dust particles float inside the streaks of sunlight shining through the living room window. I mostly avoid my stepfather's reptilian-like gaze, looking instead towards a tall, glass cabinet housing Ma's collection of black dolls. From there my eyes move to a big potted plant dying in the far corner.

"Look," Pastor begins testily, "I understand you and your mama aren't exactly on the best of terms right now, but she needs you. She's torn up about losing her mother."

Why isn't she telling me this? I smell an ambush.

"Yeah, like you're so concerned," I reply, rolling my eyes. "No need to be fake about it. You're thrilled to have me and my brother out of the picture. Now you get to control her any way you want."

"I think you're giving me way too much credit. Actually, Junior is always welcome here. You'd be too if you weren't so intent on dishonoring your mother with your lifestyle."

There it is. The word so many Christians pull from their arsenal to draw distinctions between themselves and those of us they deem to be sinful deviants. *Lifestyle* suggests there is a one size fits all expression of homosexuality.

"Cheryl didn't have a problem with my 'lifestyle' until you came around," I say, smirking. I always refer to my mother by her first name when I'm unhappy with her. The dig is an easy show of disrespect.

"Boy, in this house, you will respect your mama and refer to her as such!"

"First of all, there's no boy sitting in front of you. I'm a grown-ass man. And second, I will continue calling her by her first name until she earns the respect to be called anything else!"

"You wouldn't be here if it weren't for her and your daddy's seed. Don't think she didn't tell me all about Mr. Diallo Washington, the man who wanted nothing to do with you when he realized what an abomination you were. And you're sadly mistaken if you think my wife is proud to have a fa... homosexual for a son."

"Wow. You were about to call me a faggot, weren't you? How Christian of you."

"I'm not going to argue with what the Bible says."

"The Bible says a lot of things. Last I checked, there was something in there about not judging people."

Pastor scoffs. "The first thing you people think when anyone calls out your perversion is someone is judging you."

"You can keep that bullshit to yourself. People like you are the reason I don't go to church. You don't give two-shits about my salvation. You enjoy sitting on your high horse, telling people they're going to hell. You get off on it. But I've got news for you, Mr. Man of God... you have neither a heaven nor a hell to put me in."

Pastor leans forward, his piercing eyes turning cold. "I get no pleasure from telling people they're going to hell. If anything, I pity you."

"Pity me? What a joke."

"Eternal damnation is nothing to laugh at. My heart aches only because you refuse to see the truth."

"You religious folks crack me up. You think you have it all figured out. You think someone somewhere gave you the moral authority to tell people where they will spend eternity. Yet, you have no clue where you're even going on the day of judgment."

"Oh, I know for certain where I'm going. I'll be spending eternity with my Lord and Savior."

"Are you sure? All of your paperwork is in order?"

"My paperwork is the Word of God," he says, his smile stretching eerily across his face.

"You're so full of shit. But don't worry, I see you for what you truly are. One day Cheryl will see it too."

"You think you're gonna convince her to leave me? Fat chance."

Ma returns holding three sodas close to her chest. She hands one to me, taking notice of my anger.

"What's the matter?"

I shoot Pastor a look but open the can of soda without saying a word. I don't want to give Ma yet another opportunity to pick his side over mine.

"Son, I understand you gotta find your villain in all this, but I'm not trying to take your father's place. All I want is to see you and your mother come together again. If that makes me a bad guy because of it, so be it."

He pats the cushion next to him, beckoning Ma to join him like some damn lapdog. The gesture illustrates his dominion over her, which is difficult to witness. The Cheryl Greene who raised me is youthful, even as she almost touches sixty years old. But this woman, with her sunken disposition, is a shell of my mother.

The doorbell rings half a ring before Junior lets himself inside the house. His wife, Nadine, trails behind, holding their two-year-old daughter, LaTavia. The child, adorable and innocent, leaps from her mother's grasp and into her grandmother's embrace.

A pall of negativity hangs over the couple like bad mistletoe. My guess is they were arguing prior to entering the house. Nadine's smile is fake, intended to disabuse us of thinking something is wrong. It fails miserably because the purplish, black splotch under her right eye tells a different story.

"What's with the two of you?" I ask, already knowing the answer.

Flustered, Nadine turns to my brother for some sign as to how she should respond. But Junior leaves her hanging.

"LaTavia's been such a handful lately. She doesn't sit still. When I went to pick her up, she was moving around so much she accidentally socked me in the eye," Nadine says, nervously running her words together.

*Girl, please.* No idea who she thinks she's fooling. "Mmm-hmm," I say snidely.

"You need to mind your own fuckin' business," Junior snaps.

"Don't send your baby's mama out the house with bruises and maybe I will," I reply, matching my brother's glare with one of my own.

"Why don't you *both* shut the fuck up!" Ma screams, startling everyone into stillness.

"Sorry, Mama," Junior says, his eyes red and full of contrition. I realize he's been crying. The last time I saw him cry was when his father wound up in the hospital after being severely beaten over a gambling debt.

"I mean it, damn it! I have enough to deal with; I don't need this dumb shit from either of you!" she screams to us the way she did whenever we stressed her out as children.

Pastor's right eyebrow arches in an almost feminine way. He runs his finger along his pencil-thin mustache and clears his throat. Then, he squeezes Ma's hand. "This is a Christian household. I'm sure you can find other words to make your point."

Ma pulls her hand away and massages the ache. She drops her head, and her despondent eyes drift back and forth. "You're right, Daddy. You're right."

# FOUR

Daphne, my great-aunt, greets us by the back door of Grandma's house. She taps her cigarette ashes into a clear, plastic cup, filled with smoked butts floating at the top of dark liquid.

She's a tiny, almost brittle woman, wearing a powder-blue jogging suit and a huge Maxine Waters-inspired wig overwhelms her small head.

"She's upstairs in the bed," Daphne rattles in a deep, twangy smoker's voice.

Inside, familiar scents of the house stir my memories of Christmases past and summer vacations. My eyes tear up again from the sensory overload.

Ma's sister, Marva, is slouched in a corner, folding one of Grandma's quilts. Her facial expression carries its usual scowl, pursed lips, and arched eyebrows. We used to be close, but that changed when I stopped going to church. One day after years of estrangement, I reached out to her...

"I've explained the issue I have with you, so I don't understand why you think we need to have this conversation," she said over the phone.

"You shouldn't throw family away over pettiness."

"No, my reasons for removing you from my life aren't petty. You turned your back on God. So, unfortunately, I have to turn my back on you."

It was Classic Marva... unapologetic, in-your-face self-righteousness. Her version of events portrayed me as the sole reason for our ruined relationship. As long as I "chose" to live my life openly, there was no going back; no chance for redemption, no making amends.

It isn't my first exposure to Marva's religious fanaticism. There was also the time when Ma found herself the focus of her sister's ire.

Years ago, when Ma was still with Dino, he sometimes spent the night at the house. Junior, out of spite, told Grandma about the "strange white man" sneaking out of Ma's bedroom in the morning before he went to school. A day later, Marva showed up at the house, armed with her Bible and prayer cloth. Crazy-eyed, she thumbed through the pages of the Bible, shouting scriptures with the fervor of a priest exorcising demons.

"Cheryl, you better repent right now! You're in here layin' up with some man you ain't married to! What kind of example are you setting for the boys? You weren't raised this way!"

"Marva, you're my little sister, and I love you. But don't come in my house telling me how to live my life. I don't live for you."

Marva snapped the Bible shut before pounding her fist into it. "You're absolutely right. I am your sister. Why else am I here begging you to turn from your wickedness?"

It took little effort to work herself into a sweat. "You ain't the only one who needs cleansing," she said, pointing in my direction. "The devil is already working his evil on your son. This poor child walks around as soft as he pleases. Being filled with depravity as we speak!"

All eyes were suddenly upon me. My face warmed from self-consciousness. *Why is she bringing me into this?* I thought to myself.

"Ain't nothing wrong with my child! Take your foolishness someplace else," Ma said.

Marva dropped her Bible on the floor. She clasped her hands together, head bowed, micro-braided wig shaking as she spoke.

"Sweet Jesus! Rock of Ages! The Master is displeased by the way y'all been living!"

"No, it displeases the Master when you bring that bullshit to my house."

Marva dropped to her knees, forcing her sister down by her wrists. "Cheryl, please! I don't want to see the three of you burn for eternity. Please, before it's too late! Make these children pray with you for forgiveness!"

Despite the awkwardness the memory brings to the present, I give Marva a hug, hoping our shared loss will soften her heart. However, she's stiff in my embrace and just as sanctimonious as the night she came to pray us out of our iniquity.

Granddaddy appears at the bottom of the stairs. His overall manner is stoic. I haven't seen him since the last time I came to visit Grandma. I'll never forgive him for the way he treated her, ordering his sick wife out of bed to fix him a plate of food. When I offered to do it, he told me to go sit my faggot-ass down.

"Go on up," he says.

The stairs creak as I ascend them. A portrait of my grandparents in happier times hangs high on the wall past the white iron banister. I step into the bedroom, a room my mother and aunt shared as children. Everything is old and unchanged. Same matted pink shag carpet that is worn through in some areas of the floor. Same funky retro, red and white diamond patterned wallpaper. The room smells like death. Not decomposition, but the absence of a newly departed soul.

There is an oval dressing mirror facing the entrance to the room. It reflects Grandma's favorite Sunday wig resting on a Styrofoam wig head on the vanity… and her lifeless body on the bed.

This is my first time near a corpse. As I approach, she looks different from what I imagined a dead person would look like. Her real hair, chemically untreated for some time, is little more than braided gray wisps on her head. Her face is cool to my touch and void of the peacefulness people often associate with someone who passes from a terminal illness. I'm particularly disturbed her right eye remains open, staring out at nothingness. I attempt to close it. I've seen it done hundreds of times on TV, but her eye flicks open like a sinister doll's glass eye. TV writers got it all wrong. Dead people's eyes don't close with the swipe of the living's hand.

I crumble to my knees with grief. "Oh, God!" I cry out with no idea what I'm crying for. Am I crying because Grandma is dead or because I've neglected to visit her when I should've? Or am I crying because her right eye won't close?

Ma and Daphne notify family and friends that Grandma is gone. Locals show up at the house to spend last moments with her before we call the funeral home. For the next few hours, people stroll through like this is a museum exhibit for them to satisfy their morbid curiosities. Equally infuriating are the well-meaning comments about how peaceful Grandma appears. How can they not see the same gaunt, evacuated corpse I see? Others describe her passing away as a blessing in disguise because it means she's in a better place, no longer suffering. People tell themselves this to feel better about death, but none of it makes me feel any better.

There is a lot going on... too much for me to handle. It annoys me when people ask (good-naturedly) how am I holding up. How do they expect me to be holding up?

Before I say something I might regret, I hide out in the bathroom to compose myself. I gaze at my reflection in the mirror. I detest the face staring back at me. I loathe every inch of weathered flesh, the effect, I imagine, from chronic unhappiness. It doesn't help that my diet is crap, and I guzzle more booze than I should. Aside from my non-existent love life, the stress of my job no doubt also contributes to my misery. The rude, demanding customers I deal with every day gave me every premature gray hair I have.

After rinsing my face, I call Kenyatta. I could use a friend, however superficial, but he isn't answering his phone. I haven't heard from him since Tuesday night. By now I should've heard how amazing the dick was he left me high and dry for. Assuming he isn't dead and stuffed under a bed somewhere. I consider texting him to tell him I'm hiding out in a bathroom, watching the faucet drip while my grandmother is dead in the next room. Should be dramatic enough to elicit a reply.

Downstairs, I find LaSaundra waiting for me on the piano bench, reminding me of the time she enjoyed Thanksgiving dinner with me and my grandparents. Afterward, she played Grandma's favorite song, "His Eye Is On The Sparrow." Now, instead of playing the piano, she patiently listens to whatever gibberish Marva is telling her. Despite our unresolved issues, I can't be happier to see her.

"Hey, kiddo. I came from work as soon as I got your message. I'm so sorry," she says, getting up quickly as if relieved that I've rescued her from Marva's rambling. She rewards me with one of her best hugs.

"Thanks for coming."

Marva rocks gently and stares at an old photo album. She runs her fingertips gingerly over each photo, cherishing memories each picture evokes. When she waves me over, I break my embrace with LaSaundra.

"I remember when Mama braided my hair, she'd let me hold my dolly because she knew I was tender-headed," she says, giggling in a little girl's voice.

The regression of my religious zealot aunt is both fascinating and sad. I imagine both she and Ma running through the house as children, their heads adorned with rows of freshly braided plaits, and dollies swinging from their playful hands.

"How are you holding up?" LaSaundra asks. Only because she's the one asking, I don't bristle at the question. Instead, I shrug, too confused to explain such a mashup of emotions.

"Sorry I was a complete asshole this morning," she says.

"No, I'm the asshole. I shouldn't have brought you-know-who home with me. Besides, he doesn't particularly enrich my life in any way."

"Then why do you bother giving him the time of day?"

"Loneliness makes people do foolish things."

"Not me. I can do bad all by myself. Don't need any help, thank you very much."

The funeral home employees arrive to take Grandma away. They're polite and orderly in their handling of her body. I wait for them to close her eye, but they make no attempt. Instead, they place her into a body bag, zip it closed, and lift her onto a gurney. Granddaddy chooses this moment to make a scene.

"Oh, my dear God! Why'd You take my wife away from me? You ain't right, Lord! You ain't right!" he yells, letting rip the histrionics. Spittle flies from his mouth as he mock convulses on the floor. What a shame to work himself into a sweat and yet, not a single tear falls from his eyes.

He thinks he's slick, trying to fool us with his amateur performance, but he's incapable of mourning the loss of a woman as devoted as my grandmother. If there's any truth in his sadness, it's only because he no longer has anyone to cook, clean, or run errands for him.

A familiar, husky voice floats over the three or four voices closest to me. I follow it to the den where I come face to face with Ma's first husband, Plez Darnell Jackson, the living embodiment of a distant and unpleasant past.

Time hasn't been kind to him. His outer appearance never fully recovered from being beaten for failing to pay off his debt to a local gangster. His attractiveness was once his currency; to let him tell it, no woman could resist him. He used to be mistaken for the singer Johnny Mathis. But no more. Now he's a broken and bloated man, clothed in a maroon and tan velour tracksuit riding up over his distended belly. Thick, tinted bifocals partially conceal a crossed eye.

We stare at each other, once figments of each other's lives. I'm suddenly filled with crippling anxiety familiar to my childhood when he beat me for the first time...

"Lawrence! Bring your little ass in here!"

I stood in the doorway of Ma's bedroom, but she wasn't the one calling me.

"Did you take my money?" Giant Plez bellowed, his eyes blazing. Why was he asking that? He already knew I took his stupid coins from the dresser. They were just sitting there in a pile, getting bigger each time he came to spend the night. I figured I needed the coins to fill my little blue safe, a gift from Granddaddy.

"Look at me when I'm talkin' to you! Did you take my money?" Giant Plez throws me onto Ma's bed.

She pounded on his chest. "Plez, are you crazy? Don't put your hands on my child! He's five years old!"

He grabbed her wrists and pushed her against the wall. "Oh, you done lost your fucking mind! You don't put your hands on *me*, do you understand?"

"Leave my mommy alone!" I yelled from the edge of the bed. As I cried, I swung my tiny fists into the air, jumped from the bed, and charged at Giant Plez. Still swinging my fists, I channeled the courage of my favorite TV superhero, Wonder Woman. I hit him on his calves, which were solid like cantaloupes. He laughed at me like I was as insignificant as an ant crawling on his foot. I screamed louder, "Leave my mommy alone!" and kept hitting his legs with all of my might.

The belt came out of nowhere. It was a long, weathered, leather blackstrap lined with rows of metal holes. Giant Plez caught me by the wrist and connected the strap to my kicking legs. Each hot lick stung worse than the one before it. I cried and leaped about on tippy-toes to avoid being hit.

"Nigga, don't you ever raise your hands to me again! Do you understand me?"

I grabbed the belt as it came down mid-swing.

"Let go of it!" he said.

"No! You're gonna beat me with it!"

"You're damn right I am! You're gonna learn how to respect me!" Giant Plez said. He yanked the belt away from my grasp with one big tug, causing me to fall to the floor.

He held me by the ankle, but I continued kicking and thrashing until the belt came down, landing differently than before. An explosion of white light blinded me as an excruciating pain seized my body. I folded into myself, cupping my hands over my privates. I screamed as though my mouth blazed fire, until the sound dried up and nothing was left except the gasps caught in the back of my throat.

Giant Plez stumbled away from me, sweaty and terrified as he watched me writhe on the floor. It was the first time the man had ever shown actual fear.

"Why did you beat him like that?" Ma yelled.

"What's wrong with him?" he asked.

She ignored him and took me into the bathroom. Ma gently lowered my pants. Speckles of blood dotted the crotch of my underoos. Blood dripped from my urethra. The top of my wee-wee ached.

"Is he all right?"

"Get out of my house, Plez!" Ma shouted.

"Is he all right?" he asked again.

"Hell no, he ain't all right! You cut his fucking dick! You don't do that to a child!"

Now, as an adult, I panic, and back away before Plez raises his feeble arm to wave hello. Pastor moves in to speak to the very man who once broke a beer bottle over Ma's head. The idea of two demons sharing the same space is unsettling and gives me the perfect reason to leave.

I put on my jacket and grab LaSaundra by the hand. As we're about to sneak out the backdoor, Junior enters the kitchen.

"Where y'all going?" he asks.

"Who invited *him*?" I reply.

"Who invited who?"

His smirk tells me he knows exactly who I'm talking about. Unamused with his game playing, I glare at him. "Your father."

"I did."

"You think that's wise?"

"Why wouldn't it be? He used to be Grandma's son-in-law."

"Emphasis on used to be."

"He has every right to be here."

"Fine. We're out."

Junior eyes LaSaundra briefly before glancing back at me. "Did you say bye to Mom?"

My body is tingling and warm. Anxiety sets in. I'm ready to leave. "For what?"

"Because it's the right thing to do. Besides, she needs us right now."

"I showed up. Considering where our relationship is at the moment, she ought to be grateful I'm here at all."

"I don't believe this shit."

"Believe it. Anyway, why are you worried about it? Between you all being here, she should be fine."

"Why're you being so petty?"

"I'm removing myself from an unnecessarily stressful situation that I'm not being paid to endure. If *that's* petty, so be it."

"You're saying your family stresses you out?"

"I sure am."

"That's messed up."

"If you say so. LaSaundra, let's go." I open the backdoor to usher her through it.

"Listen, I'm not sure what crawled up your ass and died, but you need to squash the bullshit and be here for our mother. Have some respect for the woman who gave us life! Your black ass ought to stay here!"

The only way I'll stay is if he literally ties me to a chair. "Tell you what, when you stop knocking your wife around, I'll be more than happy to listen to you school me on how I should conduct myself!"

"Nigga, what did you say?" Junior asks, puffing out his broad chest. His six-four dwarfs my five-ten. He clenches his fists, ready to pummel my face.

"My name isn't Nadine. I'm not scared of you!" I say, surprised by my bravado.

Junior squints his demon-red eyes, nostrils flaring. "Talk shit again!"

"Whatever. Stop beating women. It didn't work for your daddy, what makes you think it'll work for you?" I walk out into the night, slamming the door behind me, and hoping he doesn't follow.

"What was that about?" LaSaundra asks.

But I'm too flustered to come up with an answer to adequately explain the years of acrimony that exists between my brother and me.

"Wanna go somewhere for a drink, kiddo?"

This question I understand and have an answer for. But after the day I've had, she shouldn't have to ask.

# FIVE

We pack the church for Clarice Greene's homegoing. However, I don't recognize the woman lying on pink satin inside of the burgundy casket. The makeup colors Dudley's Funeral Home used on her are wrong. The foundation is at least two shades darker than Grandma's skin, and the gold and bronze eyeshadows and lipstick are colors she never would've worn. Have they ever worked on dead black people before?

The funeral home dressed her in a navy-blue skirted suit and cream silk blouse the family provided them with. But the clothes are ill-fitting because of her dramatic weight loss. Someone also had the bright idea to accessorize Grandma's ensemble with a pillbox hat with a piece of netting clipped on like a veil and a jeweled cameo on her neck, neither of which she would've worn. It's like someone picked through a theater prop box and used the first random items they pulled out.

"Oh, she's never looked more beautiful!"

"She looks so peaceful like she's sleeping!"

"They did a wonderful job on her, didn't they?"

How can these people lie like this? How can they possibly look into the casket and not see what I see? Grandma looks horrible!

Great-aunt Daphne walks up to the casket and collapses from despair. "Oh, my sister! My poor, sweet sister!" she wails loud enough for those walking past outside to hear. Choking back sobs, she lets out a gasp before passing out. An usher rushes over to place smelling salt under her nose to revive her.

Daphne's outburst green lights everyone else's carrying on. To my left, Granddaddy cradles a bawling Marva against his chest as though she's a three-year-old.

"Not my mama," Ma sobs, pounding her fists into her lap. "Not my mama!"

Pastor puts his arm around her, playing his role of the dutiful, supportive husband. When he tries to leave to deliver the eulogy, Ma holds fast to his suited arm, unwilling to let go. The ensuing struggle lands Ma on the floor. Pastor finally pries loose her fingers. She pulls herself back up onto the pew, and he heads to the podium.

Louise, another of Grandma's sisters, nudges her way onto the pew where LaSaundra and I are sitting.

"Baby, scoot over a little and let your auntie have a seat," she says. Her demeanor is strangely cheerful amid all the mourning going on around her. "How y'all doin' this morning?"

"Hello, Auntie," I reply, sliding down to make room for her.

Louise fans herself with the service program, craning her neck for a better view of who's sitting where and doing what. As Pastor gives the eulogy, she interjects with spirited amens and praise Gods. She wiggles her shoulders and arms, broadening their span.

"Excuse me, y'all, but can you inch over a tad bit more?"

I pass LaSaundra an exasperated glance before moving as far over as I can without ending up on her lap. Louise closes her eyes, takes a deep breath as though preparing to go into a deep meditation. Her wrinkled face tightens as though inflicted with sudden pain. She bites the tip of her index fingernail and sways her head from side to side, letting out a guttural caw. Raising her arms, she shrieks, "You ain't right, Lord! You ain't right!"

Louise gets up again and dramatically stumbles into the center aisle to crawl her way toward the casket. Once there, she gets up from the floor, peers inside the casket, looking horrified by what she sees.

"Aw, Lord, no! Why you do us like this, Lord?" Louise exclaims, clawing at the air before falling away. The same usher springs into action, waving smelling salts like burning sage and revives her. Louise is escorted to the front pew to pull herself together.

"Brothers and sisters, please calm down! I beg you to have some respect for the dead! Sister Clarice wouldn't want any sadness. Not today. Why? Because our sister is going up yonder to be with our Lord. Yes, God called our dear sister-in-Christ home, but our job is not done. In fact, we've only just begun!" Pastor thunders from the pulpit.

He locks eyes with me and says, "Day in and day out, the will of God is being challenged by the depravity of man! We got men layin' up with other men, women layin' up with other women! People dressin' up in clothes intended for the opposite gender! And y'all wonder why we got classroom shootings, climate change, and all these natural disasters... God is saying, 'Enough!'"

Pastor smirks boldly; each of his spoken words is a personal indictment of me. As Pastor continues to stare at me, some attendees, curious who Pastor is looking at, follow his gaze.

"What the hell does any of this have to do with my grandmother?" Junior mutters, frowning his displeasure. "Since when did this become Sunday morning service?"

Nadine, wearing heavy eye makeup to cover the shiner he gave her, rubs his arm soothingly.

After Pastor finishes his diatribe, he steps away from the podium, satisfied by the sea of glowering faces he's created at my expense. It's impossible to avoid the judgmental stares coming from otherwise kind faces.

The choir sings an off-key rendition of "In the Garden" as pallbearers prepare to take Grandma's casket outside to the hearse. Although I'm quiet as everyone else wails, my anger towards Pastor's grandstanding matches my brother's.

Afterward, congregants bombard our family with hugs and words of condolence. Many of the people who mean-mugged me earlier have maneuvered around me to give attention and solace to Ma, Junior, Granddaddy, and the aunties. I call it well-intentioned Christian chaos at its best. There is still the burial, but I have neither the strength nor the desire to go.

Everyone moves solemnly towards the exit. Ma, in a show of family solidarity, links her arm with mine. I'm not interested in playing along with the phoniness but am too emotionally worn out to protest.

"Can you please explain to me what just happened?" LaSaundra asks.

"What, you've never seen black folks act a fool at a funeral before?" I reply.

"No, I meant your step-father turning his eulogy into a sermon?"

"My mama devoted her life to Christian living," Ma says, jumping in. "Given everything happening in the world, we needed to hear every anointed word."

Her putting God's name on everything is unnatural and ironic considering she used to complain when Grandma did the same thing to her. It makes me sad to witness Pastor hook his talons into my mother. Now, she blindly follows his lead with no idea of where she's going or where she'll end up. Sadly, I no longer recognize this woman.

Pastor waits by the doorway to accompany Ma to the designated limo that will shuttle them to the gravesite.

"Oh, honey, I was telling Lawrence how much I enjoyed your eulogy," she gushes.

"You don't say."

"He and his friend weren't sure what to make of it." Ma winks playfully at me, but Pastor says nothing else to acknowledge mine or LaSaundra's presence. As he whisks Ma away, my misgivings about him set fire to my gut.

"Are you okay?" LaSaundra asks, prodding me to keep moving.

"No, I'm not," I respond, still watching the fake display of chivalry when Pastor holds the car door open for Ma.

"She's grown, kiddo. She's allowed to live her life… make her own choices… and mistakes."

I nod half-heartedly, but LaSaundra's words are cold comfort. Pastor isn't fooling me. How is it possible others can look into his eyes and not see the devil staring back at them?

# SIX

I should've called out from work. I woke up feeling as though I barely survived an assault. It's proved difficult to shake off how traumatic the funeral was, reminding me of the familial animosities and fragmented relationships occupying my life. The family is as divided and messed up after Grandma's funeral as it was before she died.

Returning to work, my mind is in a million different places. For much of the day, I'm certain Quish is watching me. Besides occasionally asking whether I'm doing okay, she doesn't speak much to me. And when she asks, it's as though she already knows the answer regardless of what I tell her. Still, I respond with some variation of, "I'm doing well. So glad to be back at work. Being here is the best thing for me right now." What else am I going to say?

Customers are rude with a vengeance. A group of airline baggage handlers goes off on me because I refuse to allow them to redeem expired complimentary meal cards.

"Who cares about a couple of days? I'm talking about a burger and fries, not a mortgage payment," one of them says.

Ordinarily, I would honor the cards, but today I resent their sense of entitlement. I went to high school with guys like them, the ones who stick out their chests, sneer, and bully to get their way. They always travel in groups with an appointed leader.

"With all due respect, imagine if a customer tried boarding a flight with a ticket from two days ago. The airlines you work for wouldn't allow it, right?" I say, giving them a business smile.

"What's your point?"

"My point is that I can't honor these cards. If I do it for you, then I'll have to do it for everyone. I can't set that precedent."

The men exchange glances between themselves, snickering like a modern-day Three Stooges.

"Who are you to tell us no? We own you," says one, stepping forward to show his preeminence in the group. Dark, sweaty curls hedge his pink coarsened face.

"I'm afraid not. We pay rent to the airport, not the airlines. You don't share our profit."

"No, you idiot! Our airlines drive eighty percent of the business that comes through here!" he yells, his face turning crimson. He flings his expired card at me, and his sidekicks, wanting to please their master, do likewise.

"Can you believe it? The one job this faggot can probably get, and he can't even do it right!"

Unfortunately, I'm bound by the "customer is always right" rule, which precludes me from saying the kinds of things I *really* want to say. Imagine being spat upon, but not allowed to wipe away the spit. These men, the sorry lot that they are, don't deserve the satisfaction of seeing me cry. And yet, the tears show up like inconvenient truths.

"Let's hit it, guys. Way better food over in the food court," their leader says, tapping his underlings on their shoulders. They walk away, guffawing arrogantly.

And here I am, alone in my humiliation, sweat beading my brow and drenching my armpits. I hope for sympathy from the waiting customers, but receive only impatient expressions staring back at me.

I wish I could disappear. Better yet, I want to teleport home, curl up on the sofa, and weep into my favorite chocolate-brown throw pillow before devouring a carton of butter pecan ice cream.

The reality hits me, I'm not ready to return to work. I have no idea what possessed me to think I was. Although most of my coworkers have been supportive, it isn't enough to make any of this professional struggle easy or worthwhile. The hardest part is letting down the rest of the team.

Sameer is running the lunch shift. I requested to work someplace out of the way like the grill area but he put me upfront on a register. He promised he'd have my back if we got busy or if there were unhappy customers needing assistance. But, when the long-gone airline employees gave me a hard time, Sameer was nowhere to be found. Now that the coast is clear he's come out of hiding.

"I'm taking over when you finish this transaction," he announces.

"Where am I going?" I ask.

"To talk to Quish, I guess."

I smile my relief, the first time I've smiled all day, and head to the office to speak to Quish. She whirls around in a swivel chair. For the first time, I notice that she's cut her hair. It reminds me of the short cut Angela Bassett wore in *Waiting to Exhale*. "Hey, you got a minute?" she asks.

"Sure."

"I appreciate you coming in today, but I've been watching you most of your shift, and regardless of what you say, I don't think you're ready to be here."

My stomach drops as Quish's words yanks the facade from my face. "I really thought I was."

"I bet you did, but you're definitely not on your game. I think you need more time off."

"How much time are we talking here?" I ask, my anxiety kicking in.

"At least another week. That should give you time to sort everything out. Because if you're going to be here, I need you focused."

After seeing the worry in my face, her eyes soften. She adds, "Don't think of it as a punishment. Think of it as self-care."

I listen and smile, pretending to be grateful she's taking my well-being into such consideration. I should be flattered she cares so much. Unfortunately, my fear of not having a job to come back to is greater than Quish's flattery, and just getting started.

# SEVEN

On my way to the airport taxi stand, I receive a call from the mechanic that my blue Acura is ready. The great news massages the blow I received from having just been sent home. However, the positivity is short-lived when the mechanic informs me that he had to replace the fuel pump, and it sets me back six hundred bucks. I instruct my cab driver to take me to the auto garage.

Later at home, I make myself a turkey sandwich. Trying to avoid cutting the inside of my mouth on ciabatta bread, I ponder Quish's real reason for placing me on a mandatory break. Has she run out of patience? Have I become a problem she no longer wants to deal with? Is she looking for a way to phase me out? After eating, I shower, then crawl into bed for a nap.

By the time I wake up a few hours later, the house is dark. There are none of the usual dinner-time aromas wafting through the house, a sign that LaSaundra still isn't home.

I check my phone for missed calls or texts, informing me she's running late. There aren't any. Nothing from Kenyatta either, which isn't surprising but bothersome nonetheless. After leaving four voice messages on Byron's phone, I hoped for a response from him, too. I stopped at four messages because any more might appear obsessive. Maybe I should've left texts since no one answers their damn phones anymore.

Sometimes I fantasize about Byron coming over to bless me with pity sex, something to take my mind off my troubles. Eventually, I stop filling my daydreams with him. I ask myself at what point did I become so utterly desperate and pathetic, reduced to chasing a man whose actions shout that I'm nothing more than an occasional piece of ass to spice up his hetero-normative existence?

Just when I'm about to plunge into the abyss of worthlessness and self-pity, I receive a text from my dear friend, Doug. It reads: *Hey doll! Back from Rome! Having a meeting tonight. I know it's last minute. Come by if you can!*

Doug and I met in our twenties, back when we were both fixtures at Sparkles. He's one of the few guys I've known from that time who enjoys conversation and getting to know people without the expectation of sex. As our friendship grew, I found out he's also experienced traumas at the hands of the church. A Catholic priest molested him. The abuse began when Doug was ten and lasted until he turned thirteen. It ended suddenly when the priest transferred to a different parish. Years later, Doug discovered that not only were there other victims, but the priest put in for the transfer upon learning several parents planned to report him. Until meeting Doug, I wasn't aware black Catholics existed.

Thankfully, my trauma isn't sexual. Mine is years' worth of good-old-fashioned hate speech disguised as the Word of God. When I was sixteen, a guest pastor told my home congregation that homosexuals weren't just abominations, they were the most disgusting life form ever to exist, worse than the feces pigs roll around in. He said God did the world a favor when he destroyed Sodom and Gomorrah, but apparently sodomites were like roaches, difficult to get rid of completely. Hearing that, coupled with the bullying I received in high school, I tried to commit suicide by swallowing a bunch of Sudafed. Fortunately, the worst thing to happen was it cleared my nasal passages out and I had a headache, but when Ma found out she was livid.

"What the fuck is wrong with you?" she screamed. "You've got these white people up at that school thinking I'm a terrible mother!" When I tried to explain how I felt after the pastor's sermon, she replied, "I told you a long time ago, you're too soft!

Man up! Do you have any idea how shameful it is to have church folk whispering that my son is a sissy?"

It bewildered me that upon hearing of my suicide attempt, her humiliation was most concerning to her. I replied, "Then it would've been better if I succeeded. That way you won't have to worry about what other people think."

But she was unmoved by my plight. "What's gonna happen one day when you're supposed to be watching your brother and you get it in your head to kill yourself? How am I gonna find another babysitter when you know my money is funny?"

My relationship with the church died after that. I still went because Ma made it clear that as long as I lived under her roof, I was required to go. But I was a mere empty shell taking up a pew seat, And I never forgot how she treated me after my suicide attempt.

Years later, in my thirties, Doug told me he created a group called "The Freed Church Boys." It is a judgment-free space primarily for gay men reconciling their belief in God with their sexuality. Every member has a story of spiritual trauma, some more horrific than others. For many of us, our parents raised us with fire and brimstone interpretations of the Bible that we struggle to break free from. It's difficult to hold on to faith without the accompanying religious dogma and man-made traditions.

Over the years, the number of members has dwindled, and while we still speak on spiritual matters when we get together, the Freed Church Boys meetings have now become an excuse to meet up, drink wine, and spill tea.

It's been a while since our last get-together, but with all the friction happening between my family and me, Doug's text is a welcomed distraction.

Before heading out, I select a bottle of wine to bring to Doug's and his partner Alvin's house. The selection is a far cry from the fancy stuff they swill, but no doubt better than showing up empty-handed.

*****

Doug and Alvin live in a mid-century-modern-style home in an expensive part of Edina. Their house is an angular glass box on full display, thanks to curtain-free, floor-to-ceiling windows. I always feel exposed whenever I visit. Still, the house is lovely, decked out with expensive high-end minimalist furniture and sleek appliances. Soft earth tones offset the hard edges and lines throughout the home. Beneath the sophisticated track lighting stands strategically placed African sculptures Doug bought in Cape Town.

"Oh, how cute," Alvin says, dripping sarcasm as he takes the bottle of wine from me at the door. From his usual resting bitch face to the way he makes himself scarce during our meetings, I think he resents having us meet in his home.

Alvin is a bougie SOB; the stuck-up one in the couple whose tastes the house most closely reflects. He's a good-looking, entitled Morehouse College dropout who lives off his family's wealth and relishes his light skin and "good hair" privilege. Doug is a community college graduate. His mystically dark skin, square jaw, and romantic eyes give him a foreign mystique despite being born and raised in Minneapolis. He's down to earth and unaffected by his partner's pretentious and materialistic nature.

"Small group tonight. Why don't you join them in the living room, and I'll bring you a glass of wine?" Alvin says.

Upon entering the house, I proceed to walk away, but there is a sound of a coarsely clearing throat behind me. I turn back to Alvin, who eyes me with the sternness of a schoolmarm.

"Yes?"

He says nothing. His lips purse tightly as his gaze falls to my feet the way Meryl Streep's did to Anne Hathaway in *The Devil Wears Prada*.

"Sorry." I bend over to untie my shoes. When I raise up after slipping out of them, Alvin is gone.

I follow Doug's piercing voice down a long hallway of gleaming white tiles that seem to go for infinity. I overhear him mention a failed attempt to buy shoes at an Emporio Armani store in Rome. As I enter the massive living room, I'm first greeted with the toastiness of a fire crackling inside a two-sided fireplace. Doug nestles comfortably on their brand-new Siberian oak floor, atop a lush, cream-colored faux fur area rug. His appearance is unusually collegiate, dressed in a navy-blue cardigan over a white button-down shirt and khaki pants. The top of his hair is a river of small waves, with sides and back cut in a tight fade. Fellow members, Stephen and Reese, both dressed in similar Oxford shirts and jeans, sit on opposite ends of a beige leather sofa. Stephen waves then guzzles his wine. Reese smiles reservedly as he wipes smudges from his eyeglasses on the front tail of his shirt. Michael and Langston are a couple who found love through the group. They share a place on a matching beige chaise pushed to the center of the room from its usual position in the corner. Dressed in jeans and matching oversized turtleneck sweaters, they tip their wine glasses to me.

"Hey, guys," I say, happy to be amongst friendly faces.

"You came!" Doug replies excitedly as he rises to greet me. He tilts his wine glass like a Martini, high above both of our heads, and hugs me with his free arm.

"You smell divine," I tell him.

"Just some needlessly expensive shit Alvin bought me, but thank you."

"You're just in time to listen to Dougie tell us about his misadventures in Italy," Reese says.

"Yeah, I caught some of it from the hallway. When did you guys get back?" I ask.

"This afternoon."

"How was it?"

Doug's face goes weird. "Let's just say it was interesting."

"Here you are, sir," Alvin says, arriving with my glass of wine before anyone has the chance to press Doug for details.

My face warms after the first sip. "Yum! Is this the one I brought?"

"Of course not. Don't be ridiculous," Alvin responds, peering at me through circular wire-framed eyeglasses. He's being his usual pompous self, dressed in an expensive slim-fitting black dress shirt and tailored black slacks that probably cost more than my monthly mortgage payment. Alvin turns his back to me and says, "Stephen, that Masseto is expensive. Try not to chug it, will you?"

"Babe, Stephen's had a rough week," Doug says.

"Speaking of a rough week, Lawrence, you look as if you could get some things off your chest," Langston says.

"Oh, no, I'm fine."

"Honey, please, those worry lines on your face say otherwise. Spill it."

"But you guys were going to talk about Italy."

"It's all right. We can talk about it afterward," Doug says.

"Yeah, do tell," Alvin chimes in, feigning interest.

"Well, I think my boss is trying to fire me."

Alvin perks up. "And what makes you say that?"

"Just a hunch."

He rolls his eyes. "We have to sit here and listen to his drama all on account of a hunch?"

Doug taps Alvin's covered bicep. "Babe, don't be like that."

Alvin folds his arms and returns a dirty look to Doug. "I'm sorry, Lawrence. You were saying?"

"I don't know. Maybe it's just me being overly sensitive, but I really hate my job."

"What do you do again?" he asks.

"I manage a fast-food restaurant out at the airport."

"Well, *that's* your problem right there. If you had a respectable job, you'd be happy to show up. Unless, of course, you're already working within your limited capabilities and can't do anything else."

My face blooms hot. I want to curse Alvin out, but instead I wait for Doug to check his man. However, he avoids my glance and says nothing.

"Alvin, you ain't right for that," Stephen says, coming to my rescue.

Alvin widens his eyes and shrugs dramatically. "What did I say that was wrong?"

"Despite what you might think of me, I'm doing the best that I can," I say to him.

"Are you sure about that?"

"Well, what would you propose I do?"

"Are you hard of hearing? Go-find-a-respectable-job," Alvin enunciates as though he's speaking to someone with a learning disability.

It's funny receiving career advice from a guy who hasn't worked a day in his life. All he can do is sit in judgment while living nouveau riche inside a glass box filled with expensive shit he doesn't even need.

Stephen says, "Yo, how are you gonna dog our boy out like that? Ain't nothin' wrong with making an honest living. He could be somewhere selling his ass or out there selling drugs to our people like some lowlife. So, you shouldn't clown on a brother for doing what he can to handle his business. Hell, I don't care what anyone says, his job is respectable to me!"

"Nonsense," Alvin says, an incredulous expression taking over his face. "Don't pretend I'm being a snob. Why should I respect what Lawrence does for a living when *he* doesn't even respect what he does? Shit, I wouldn't care if he collected cans for a living. Just do it with pride."

"Even so, babe, I'm sure Lawrence works very hard," Doug says, finally coming to my defense.

"Then why are we discussing this? I get sick of people who choose to move passively through their lives, acting as if nothing is their fault or responsibility. We all have agency over ourselves. If he doesn't like what he does for a living, he should change it. But don't come here and talk our ears off about his poor life decisions!"

Am I upset because Alvin speaks of me as though I'm not in the room? Or am I upset because he's right? My chronic embarrassment is going to do me in. I'm tired of being the butt of someone else's joke. I squirm in my seat as perspiration saturates my underarms. I grip my wine glass, almost wishing it will shatter in my hand and cut a vein to put me out of my misery.

"So, Doug, tell us more about Rome," Langston says, attempting to diffuse the heaviness in the room by changing the subject.

"Yes, how was your trip?" I ask, thankful to have the attention diverted from me.

Before Doug responds, Alvin points at him and interrupts with, "So, *this* one convinces me to book a room at this quaint pensione near La Piazza di Spagna."

With all eyes on him, it's Doug's turn to shift uncomfortably on his spot on the floor.

"First of all, we had to share a bathroom with the other guests. They had the worst toilet paper. It was like scraping sandpaper in between the cracks of our asses. And don't even get me started on the staff. They were completely useless."

"Oh man," Stephen says.

Alvin continues. "No, you'll love this. So, I asked them if they had laundry to wash clothes on-site, and they said yes. I said fine, and we gave them the clothes. The next morning, around six, there was a knock on the door. I opened it to find a bag full of sopping wet clothes."

"Dude, stop playin'!" Stephen says, ready for a refill.

"Oh, there's more. I spoke to the woman at the front desk, explained about the clothes, and she said, 'You said you wanted the clothes washed. They are washed. You said nothing about drying them.'"

"She said that?" everyone asks in overlapping unison.

"Doug, tell them," Alvin commands.

Doug nods timidly, keeping his eyes averted. It breaks my heart to witness my friend's receding spirit, especially since the Doug I met years ago was outspoken and unlikely to allow himself to be disrespected. But I also remember when he used to live in subsidized housing, and he shared with me his vision boards and how he was going to snag a rich partner. Watching Alvin talk down to him, I wonder how Doug puts up with it.

"So, how did you dry the clothes?" Stephen asks.

"Would you believe they had the unmitigated gall to hang them up on a clothesline in their courtyard? Imagine us, coming back from lunch only to find our unmentionables flapping in the breeze!"

As we listen, I imagine the bag of wet clothes propped against a hotel room door. Though I wouldn't have been as rude as Alvin probably was, I would've no doubt been pissed.

"Anyway, after that, I'd had enough," Alvin continues, enjoying the sound of his own voice, "I booked us into St. Regis Rome. I should've known Doug was too ghetto to appreciate that level of luxury. He'd be content with a blow-up mattress, stick of pepperoni, and a cheap Chianti. Sometimes I forget that when I met him, he was sleeping on a beat-up, old mattress over in those low-income high-rises off the freeway. He'd probably still be there if it weren't for me."

"Anyone for cheesecake?" Doug asks, getting up from the floor.

Alvin pretends to be perplexed by Doug's sudden departure, but he doesn't try to stop him from leaving the room. "He'll be fine," he says, lowering himself to the floor to occupy the space where Doug had been.

I can't speak for anyone else, but I find Alvin's presence disconcerting. Any other time, after rattling off obligatory hellos, he'd be off hiding in the bedroom until our gathering was over. His newfound comfortability with us threatens the easy flow of our group's dynamic.

Reese cuts in. "So, how has everyone else's week been?"

Michael shares that he and Langston have found a surrogate to carry their baby but questions how involved she should be after the baby is born.

"Well, I don't doubt the two of you will make great parents but have either of you considered that having a female presence in the child's life might be beneficial?" Reese asks.

"I said the exact same thing," Langston replies. "Especially if the child is a girl. I sure as hell ain't looking forward to explaining how to stick a tampon up her hoo-ha."

Reese's face twists with revulsion. "All the more reason to invite the surrogate to be a part of the child's life."

"But what makes either of you think she wants to become that involved? She's doing it for the money," Michael says.

"Well, whatever you all decide on, put it in writing," Alvin suggests.

I listen, but my mind is on Doug, who's moving around the kitchen like a despondent zombie. I excuse myself and head over to help my friend.

"You okay?" I ask, taking a cake knife from Doug to cut the raspberry swirl cheesecake.

He smiles weakly. "I'm sorry for what Alvin said to you," he says, turning away quickly, but not before I notice his watery eyes and quivering mouth.

"I hate to say it, but your man is an asshole. Frankly, I don't know how you put up with it."

"I try not to take him seriously," Doug replies, sensing that I won't let it go.

"If you say so," I say, rolling my eyes.

"Don't start. Okay? Trust me, he doesn't mean half the crap he says. And anyway, he knows I'll dish it right back." Doug's puffy eyes tell a different story. But I know he wants as much to believe his fairytale as he wants me to.

I give him an encouraging pat on the back and decide for at least the duration of the meeting not to disturb Doug's fantasy that everything is all right in his privileged world.

We return to the living room. I'm holding a large serving tray with plated slices of cheesecake. Doug serves them to the guys. He hands me the last plate, thanks me for my help and takes the tray from me and leans it against the back of the sofa to put away later. Alvin arches a brow as he watches this.

"Well, I guess I'll leave you boys to your meeting. Have fun," Alvin says, taking his dessert in one hand and retrieving the serving tray with the other. After returning it to the kitchen he disappears down the hall.

"So, Stephen has news for us," Reese announces as Doug reclaims his spot on the floor. I sit down next to him.

Stephen becomes edgy. Although he enjoys listening to us speak about our spiritual experiences, he tends to share little about his own. "I've decided to go back to church."

Silence is passed around the room like a collection plate. It's probably not the response Stephen was looking for, and I'm aware that this is supposed to be a judgment-free zone, but his news doesn't sit well with me. All I hear is, "I'm back in bed with the enemy." I drag my fork through my cheesecake to keep myself composed. I'm not even interested in *why* he wants to go back to the very institution that kicked both Stephen and his mother out when the preacher got done fucking her. And when all of the congregants found out, they turned against them but forgave the preacher who had slept with someone who wasn't his wife. Stephen wants to go back to that? Fine. But he better not expect me to make him feel good about his decision by agreeing with it.

Later, after we wrap up. Stephen senses my disapproval and keeps his distance. Alvin reappears to say goodnight to us.

"It was great seeing you tonight," he says, nudging me towards the front door. Although he extends his hand for me to shake, something less polite lurks behind his eyes. Despite my misgivings, I shake his hand, to which his grip becomes crushing. I pull my hand away. He accurately reads the distrust on my face and slaps my back to show he was only kidding.

"Drive safely," he says before walking away to speak to Stephen.

I'm relieved when Doug joins me at the door.

Stepping outside, I ask, "Real tea, what do you think about Stephen going back to church?"

Doug shrugs. "It really isn't for any of us to say. He can do whatever he wants."

That's not the answer I want to hear. Since I'm not going to get Doug to co-sign on my opinion, I change the subject back to him and Alvin. "Listen, if you ever want to talk about whatever's going on with you two, I'm here."

"Not this again. I told you, nothing's going on."

"Come on."

He fidgets with the doorknob, turning around nervously to check that Alvin isn't within earshot. "I told you he was just playing. Why are you making a bigger deal out of this?"

"See, this is how it starts. I mean, look at you… acting like he's about to come over here and knock you upside your head."

Doug considers this, then allows his gaze to fall away. I know then that I've struck a chord. I just want him to be safe and to know he has my support. I don't need to be right. This isn't about who's right or wrong. However, Doug backs away from me, signaling that I've long overstayed my welcome.

After more consideration, he says, "He wouldn't do that."

"I'm just saying if you ever need to talk about things."

There is a flash of contempt in Doug's eyes. "What makes you think you're qualified to say anything to me about my relationship? Where's *your* man at?"

The question stuns me into silence. He's acting as though I'm trying to pick a fight with him. Before I answer, the door slams in my face. I remain on the doorstep, expecting Doug to reconsider the rudeness of his gesture, or at the very least step outside to finish talking. I don't need or expect an apology. Doug doesn't have to be alone in this. There is still time for him to get out of his toxic relationship before Alvin throws the first punch... assuming he hasn't already.

I walk back to my car with a proverbial tail between my legs. Maybe the sting of having a door slammed in my face will wear off by the time I drive away.

*****

I hate parking so far from the bar. It can mean the difference between getting there safely or possibly getting jumped by ruffians. Unfortunately, the usual parking spots are snatched up because of a sporting event going on at the Target Center.

A group of young adults congregate near the corner of Fourth and Nicollet Mall. They're dressed hip-hop stylish in glossy, bubble down coats, passing around a joint as they puff openly, almost daring someone to object. As I walk past them, they give me the once-over, gauging my easy target potential. Despite my heart pounding in my chest, I put on my fiercest mean-mug, hunch my shoulders and harden my stride.

"Look at this nigga here," one of them jeers, practically coughing on marijuana smoke as he passes the joint to someone else. "He's walking like he's dragging a dead leg across the sidewalk!"

They laugh at me. I expected as much. But I'll gladly take being the butt of a joke over being beaten, stabbed, or shot at.

"You all right, man. Go 'head on," another says.

I pick up my pace in the case any of them change their minds and decide to accost me. I can still feel the burn from their gaze, even as I scurry down the block without further hassle. However, the number of stories I've heard over the years about gay-bashings is legion. I won't relax until the burst of flashing white, pink, yellow, and plum lights on Sparkles' vertical sign comes into view.

Adam is manning the door when I finally arrive. He's an older man, tall and wide, with long grizzled hair pulled severely into a ponytail. He maintains a cantankerous disposition and always acts like he's bothered about something.

"Hello," I say, ID ready in hand. I never know whether he's in a carding mood, no matter how often I'm here.

"Hiya, hon," he says, his face softening as he gives the ID a cursory glance.

"Busy tonight?"

"Yeah, but I'd rather be home baking cookies." He hands the card back.

"What kind?"

"Peanut butter." He cracks the first smile I've ever received from him. "Have fun."

"Ahh. Well, the next time you bake some, save me a few," I reply, passing through the heavy wooden door.

The establishment was once a saloon that featured can-can girls. In recent years the current owners expanded today's incarnation into a gigantic complex split into smaller bars. The main bar (which doubles as a restaurant in the early evenings) keeps its original mahogany wood and rich burgundy motif. The stage on which can-can girls once kicked up their heels now, after renovation, houses a drag show. Off the kitchen, through a rear hallway lit with blue Christmas lights, are two additional restrooms. Through a rear door in the men's restroom is a private bar, a dark, industrial world of black walls and chain-link fences. Small white candles glow along a rectangular steel-tread bar, and vintage gay porn plays on a 42-inch flat-screen TV.

Directly across from the restrooms is a dance floor known as Dance O' Mania, which features mostly hits of the house and techno variety.

Outside the opposite entrance to Dance O' Mania, past the coat check and an elevated booth where someone sells lottery tickets and pull tabs, the hallway loops back to the main bar. On the other side of the wall, in a space that once housed a check-cashing joint, is the happy-hour lounge.

In the main bar, a drag queen emerges from behind thick, burgundy velvet curtains. "She" isn't the most convincing in the female illusion department. Her dress hangs cheaply on the performer's broad, masculine frame. The dress is a drab, black and gold beaded affair. The mangy, white feather boa slung over one shoulder has seen better days. The queen's five o'clock shadow bleeds through her makeup, and her updo wig, a mess of curly, unnaturally shiny synthetic hair, shakes as she limps across the stage, lip-syncing to Shirley Bassey's "It's My Life."

Turnout is respectable for the weekday evening. I do my usual walk-through, scanning for familiar bar acquaintances. I purchase a beer, then plop down on a spot in the corner. Bruno Mars' "24K Magic" reverberates from the jukebox in the happy-hour lounge. The sound cuts through flimsy wood-paneled walls separating the bars. I finish my beer in three giant gulps, wanting another but too lazy to get up to get it.

A cocktail server stops by the table and taps my empty bottle, his nonverbal way of asking if I want another.

"Yes, please."

The server returns almost immediately with the beer just as the drag performer Donesha hits the stage. She lip-syncs to a gospel song, dressed in a slinky wave of black and white ruffles. Beneath a black church-lady chapeau, she wears her hair pulled into an elegant, sleek chignon.

I listen to the lyrics, pondering the sacrilege of performing a gospel song in a gay nightclub. Still, Donesha's interpretation of the song moves me. In fact, I feel closer to God than I've felt in months. Even walking up to the stage to tip the performer is a quasi-religious experience. People line across the front of the stage, transfixed and waiting to bestow monetary blessings upon the performer. When it's my turn to tip, she anoints me with a kiss on the cheek for the five-dollar bill I don't realize is a five-dollar bill until it leaves my grasp.

After her performance and a costume change, Donesha works the room, mingling with her fans. She maintains a regal bearing as she coos each time someone compliments her strapless gown made from delicate white fabric that resembles translucent, crinkled paper. Blinding triangular sparkles adorn her ears, and twenty-five inches of Brazilian silky hair parted down the middle a la Naomi Campbell, swings down her back. I ask her who originally sang the song she performed.

"Yolanda Adams," she says, her false lashes aflutter. "The name of the song is 'The Battle Is the Lord's.'"

I thank her, making a mental note to download a song recognition app on my phone later.

I walk into the happy-hour lounge, a room painted rust-red and forest green with a faux stone feature wall across from a very scratched and nicked wooden bar. I alight at a booth near the old jukebox playing Destiny's Child's "Bills, Bills, Bills."

Abandoned drink glasses wrapped with damp napkins litter the table. I push them aside, along with a picked-through basket of chicken tenders and fries submerged in ketchup.

A lively trio of twenty-somethings enjoys a spirited conversation in a booth directly across from me. All three men are extensions of each other; light-skinned and more pretty than handsome, with ombre eyebrows and glossed lips. One of them eyes me disapprovingly while rolling his tongue over a red lollipop.

Despite the unfriendly, territorial reception, I nod politely. The one lapping his lollipop leans into his friends and whispers something. All three turn to me before bursting into laughter. Their malevolent howls reduce me to the sensitive young boy I once was, sitting alone in a high school cafeteria…

"Hey boy!" the girl called to me at lunchtime. She was new to the school, looking for a social in with the popular girls.

"My name is Lawrence," I responded curtly.

"Well, whatever your name is, can I ask you a question?"

My burger and fries were cooling on my tray. I was starving. I should've said no, or flat out walked away, but I allowed her to ask her question.

"Are you special?" A few of the girls snickered when she asked this.

"Well, that could mean one of two things. It could mean am I exceptionally talented or am I mentally slow."

"Yeah, *that* one," she said, pointing at me. "Because you look like a retarded monkey!"

Everyone at the table erupted into manic laughter. My mood plummeted. I went to find a seat at a table far out of the way so no one would see me cry into the food I had lost my appetite for.

"Will someone please tell me when they started letting all these ugly-ass niggas up in here?" Mister Lollipop asks, his defiantly loud voice bringing me back to the present moment.

"Chile, leave that man alone," another says. "He can't help that he was born ugly."

"You're mean. Don't say that," says the other.

Mister Lollipop raises a hand to silence the pushback. "No! Y'all gonna catch this tea! I expect to come down to the bar to enjoy myself and be around beautiful men, not stare at apes!"

His shrill, dismissive laughter cut through my forty-one-year-old spirit. After all these years, I'm still insecure. I can't even be angry with the young man. I blame his under-socialized youth and immaturity for his stupidity. But what's *my* excuse? At my age, I should be years beyond worrying about what others think of me and whether they have the poor manners to say it out loud.

Now, sitting in a dirty booth, being "read for filth" by a complete stranger has me deep in my feelings. The tears welling in my eyes don't help and aren't surprising. My mother used to tell me I'm too damn sensitive.

"Oh, waah, waah. He's gonna start crying," Mister Lollipop says.

"These tears aren't for you. They're for the shame your father must feel for wasting his nut to make you!"

Mister Lollipop shoves the candy back into his mouth, stands up, and stomps off in a huff. The two imbeciles with him follow, like the Supremes scurrying after Diana Ross.

"If you ask me, none of those fools know what the hell they're talking about," a smoky baritone voice says over my shoulder. I turn around to find a man of carob-brown perfection standing there. He's dressed entirely in black. A park ranger hat mysteriously shadows the top half of his face. An expertly trimmed mustache and soul patch accent his kissable, full lips. A Wanderer's Poncho cloaks his broad upper body, and black skinny jeans and leather boots complete the ensemble.

"I'm glad somebody thinks so," I reply sadly.

"You should never let anyone make you cry about anything," the stranger says, wiping away my tears with his index finger. "I bet you could use a proper drink."

I feel as though I've been caught red-handed in a vulnerable state. Despite my embarrassment, I force a smile and tell him I'm okay on the drink.

"I insist."

I hesitate, unsure whether to accept, but not wanting to turn off this gorgeous man by refusing his offer. Before I answer, the three men return to finish what they started with me, but pause when they see the prize specimen I'm speaking to. I feel like a fraud out of my league, as though I have no earthly business talking to a gorgeous man.

"What did you have in mind?" I ask my benefactor, unable to resist throwing in a dash of flirtation.

"How about a cocktail made for a real man?"

"Oh. Listen, I'm not big on mixed drinks."

"I understand. You're not into fruity, froo-froo drinks. I can tell that just by looking at you. You deserve something more elevated... sophisticated."

Hearing the words *elevated* and *sophisticated* make me rethink the inadequacy of my half-finished beer. The stranger raises his drink to his lips and sips with a masculine sensuality.

Mildly turned on, I ask, "What are you drinking?"

He looks into the glass, ignoring the twenty-somethings watching us. "You wanna taste it?"

"Sure." I reach to take the glass, but he scoops me in by my waist to kiss me with the lushness of a velvet tongue. It lasts mere seconds but is an explosion of organic passion. The unexpected force of his kiss weakens me at the knees. When our lips part, my eyes open with a euphoric flutter.

A brazen slyness materializes on the stranger's face. "How was it?"

"What is it?"

"It's called a Manhattan."

The bitchy queens hover close like jackals, watchful and scowling. Mister Lollipop is particularly grossed out. "Now that's just plain nasty! All that fine-ass man wasted on a nigga who looks like who-done-it-and-ran!" he complains to his friends.

"Don't y'all have anything better to do?" the stranger asks them. "Why don't y'all go in the bathroom and check each other for rashes or something!"

"Fuck you, bitch!" Mister Lollipop says before the three men take off a second time. This man, whose name I don't know (but would kill for an opportunity to scream it ecstatically in bed later) puts an arm around my shoulder, unbothered by the shenanigans of fools, and steers me towards the bar. "Now, how about that drink?"

We sit at the far end of the bar, away from the loud, grating voices of drunken queens. I take my first sip from my newly acquired Manhattan. By my third sip, warmth spreads across my face and chest. The stranger reveals his name is Hakee.

He removes his hat, and light chases the shadows from his face. His round head is shaved close to the scalp. His eyes smolder when he smiles…and halts my breath.

He tells me he's a thirty-eight-year-old Sagittarian, which is a delightfully retro factoid to offer. He explains two traits of his sign are being a "jack of all trades" and capable of getting along with people from all walks of life.

"Does your birthday fall in November or December?"

"December thirteenth."

"I'm a Scorpio. November twentieth," I tell him, waiting for the usual raised eyebrow. Instead, he grins.

"Rumor has it Scorpios are the most sexual of the zodiac."

"Wouldn't you like to know?"

"Play your cards right, I just might." He winks, and then, in an instant, he switches the topic to reveal that he's lived in many places as a child, though never in any one place long enough to create lasting friendships. The revelation makes his Wander's Poncho make sense. I get the feeling Hakee has been everyplace and yet no place at the same time.

Later, he mentions spending time in Ubud, Bali, to explore his spirituality.

"So, what did you do, meditate on hot coals?" I ask.

Hakee doesn't smile at my flimsy attempt at humor. "Meditate, yes. Hot coals, no. I did burn some strong-ass incents, though."

"Why did you pick Bali?"

"I was looking to expand my horizons spiritually. Here in the states, all I've known is Christianity. Though Indonesia is mostly Islamic, Bali is the only island that is predominately Hindu with some Buddhism. I don't follow any one religion. I just know that I love God."

"I'm trying to find my spiritual path, too. It's been a struggle detangling my faith from all of the religiosity. I think I was raised to fear God instead of love God. I went to a Christian college because it made my mom happy. I think she hoped the Holy Spirit would suck the faggotry right out of me," I reply.

"Let me guess, she didn't approve of your sexuality?"

I hesitate. It's too much of a story to lay on someone I've just met.

"I know that look," he says, taking a hint from my reluctance. "Never mind. We can talk about something else."

His understanding nature puts me at ease. "Yes, please. How about... I don't know... do you have any hobbies?"

"I love to sing. Been trying to do my music hustle. Ain't having too much luck, though."

"Can you sing something for me?"

Hakee appears unsure of himself. "I don't know."

I nudge him gently. "Aw, come on."

"What should I sing?"

"Which song makes you feel something?"

He considers for a moment, then clears his throat and places both hands on my open thighs. Hakee's strong fingers press into my denimed legs as Luther Vandross "If Only for One Night" floats melodiously from his lips.

A hush falls over the room. As everyone listens, entranced by Hakee's gift, I smile, so lucky to be near such a magical force, that when he finishes, my body buzzes from the ensuing applause.

"They like you," I yell to him over the thunderous waves of men clapping wildly.

"I guess."

*He guesses?* He has nothing else to say? I was expecting a bigger response than what he's put forth. For someone who claims to love singing, I don't feel his passion. If I had a fraction of the singing power he does and people were applauding me, I'd be eating it all up. "No, I'm serious," I reply. "The world needs to hear you."

He shrugs. "If it was meant for the world to hear from me, they would have by now."

"What's stopping you?"

"Lack of capital."

"Yeah, but you can't let that stop you."

"Being an indie artist is hard because everything falls on me. I pay for everything."

"Couldn't you cut a demo or something and go to a record label?"

"Cutting a demo means studio time, which is expensive. I already owe people a grip for unpaid studio time."

I haven't taken into consideration how much money must go into recording music. "I believe if it's meant for you, God will make a way for it to manifest. It would be a shame for you not to use the gift He gave you."

"Yeah well…"

"Don't count God out," I say, grasping how eerily like my mother I must sound. "He would never give you such a gift and not make a way for you to use it. Don't give up on your dreams because it's never too late."

"That dream is dead," he replies, having made his peace with it. "No use holding on to it."

I sit with Hakee's response. Who am I to tell him what he needs to do? I don't know what his musical journey has been until this point. Maybe he's gotten so close to success that he can blow into its face only to be disappointed. What if he's tired of only getting close?

"Thanks for letting me share that with you," he says, taking my hands into his and drawing me into his confidence. "I don't usually share my aspirations with people. I've found out the hard way that as soon as I declare it, people want to see me fail."

"No, I totally get it. I've experienced similar with certain people."

"You wanna do something?" he asks, his sly grin returning.

"I thought you'd never ask," I reply with a grin of my own.

Rising to leave, we thank the bartender. However, I can't resist one last effort to encourage Hakee to trust in his talent.

"You seem to have already made up your mind, but I think you're making a huge mistake giving up singing. Think of how your voice connected with all these people right here. Now, imagine if you were on stage, in front of hundreds of people... thousands. Think of the way you can make them feel."

Hakee squints his eyes and sexily licks his lips. "In a year from now, you probably won't even remember my singing, but I guarantee you're gonna remember the way I make *you* feel tonight."

# EIGHT

A full moon illuminates the pathway to my front door. Tipsy, I attempt to put the key into the keyhole.

Hakee takes the key from me. "Everything is about alignment." He fits the key perfectly inside the keyhole on the first try. After unlocking the door, he pushes it open. He holds out a gentlemanly arm and says, "After you."

I grab him by the hand to lead him through the darkness of the living and dining areas into the kitchen. LaSaundra's bulky purse rests on the breakfast nook table, a sign that she's home for the night.

Hakee steps into the moonlight beaming through slatted blinds on the kitchen window. Looking handsome in the pale light, he spins me around and grinds his denimed pelvis into my backside.

His soft breath tickles my neck, I'm unable to withstand my heightened desire. I usher my guest down the hallway towards the bedroom. There are ambient TV sounds emanating from beneath LaSaundra's closed bedroom door.

"Roommate?" he whispers.

"Yeah, so we have to be quiet." I go to my dresser to light a jasmine candle. Hakee closes the door.

Once the candle is lit, our eyes meet. I have no expectations for the encounter. From my past sexual experiences, exceptionally good-looking men, like Hakee, aren't all that great in bed because they don't have to be. Why be amazing when decent will suffice? They treat me as though I should be grateful to be in the presence of a beautiful man, let alone lying next to one.

Outside of Byron, most of the guys I've been intimate with have been younger. I usually find them on hook-up apps. However, there are elements of the hook-up culture I will never get used to.

I understand jump-offs aren't likely to be interested in forming deep connections, but they don't have to perform sex like it's a perfunctory task. Sure, they know the mechanics of sex (as in, where to put their penises) but a lot of these men lack passion. Nary a grunt or groan nor an interest in whether I'm experiencing pleasure. Some don't even bother to get fully undressed. Some show up, expecting to record our encounter on their phone cameras. Then they spend the entire time vamping for the camera and watching their dicks slide in and out of one sloppy orifice after the next.

The last guy I met from an app came over while LaSaundra was away, visiting family in Columbus, Ohio. He was light-skinned, thinner than I normally go for, and slovenly dressed. He looked like he threw on clothes for the sake of fulfilling a social requirement.

I knew from the man's vacuous expression and lazy stance that making a decent impression was lost upon him.

"Wuz up? You're a bottom, right?" my guest asked, pushing his way into the house without being invited. He didn't give me his name or divulge info regarding his HIV/ STI status, fetishes, or preferences. Rather, he made his way through the house, dropping articles of clothing along the corridor like Hansel and Gretel leaving breadcrumbs to find their way home. By the time we got to my bedroom, he was down to his dirty ankle socks. After a dry, closed-mouth kiss, he ordered me to lie on my stomach. When I didn't comply, my visitor became nonplussed.

"Why ain't you layin' on your stomach?" he asked.

"Aren't you forgetting something?"

"What?"

"Protection," I replied to what I thought was obvious.

"Oh, I don't use condoms," he said with a dismissive swipe of his hand.

"Why not?"

"Because it's not the same as hitting it raw. When I'm up in them guts, I wanna feel it, ya feel me? Besides, I'm on PREP."

"I hear you, but PREP doesn't protect you from syphilis, gonorrhea, or anything else for that matter."

"Yeah, but I'm clean, though."

"That may be, but I'm old school. We use condoms around these parts. You might know that had you taken the time to chat with me first, and weren't in such a hurry to get over here."

The young man stared at me as though I'd given him long division to solve in his head. "But I'm clean."

"I know, sweetie." I opened the top drawer of the dresser and pulled a foiled square from a strip of condoms. I handed it to my guest and said, "Here you go."

He looked at it, muttering, "I don't know what the big deal is." and unwrapped the condom. It wouldn't have offended me if he'd left. The only reason I went through with it was because I was still horny and it was too late in the evening to find someone else from the app to come over.

The sex was awkward and rushed. Afterward, the guy threw the used condom on the bed, said, "Aight then," and left the room to collect his clothes. I listened for the sound of the closing front door and was glad when I finally heard it.

"Hey, where did you go?" Hakee asks, tapping my shoulder and bringing my focus back to what's about to happen between us.

"Oh, I was just wondering if I had any condoms," I fib.

He digs into his jacket pocket and proudly reveals a fistful of condoms. "Don't worry. I snatched a few freebies from the bar."

I chuckle. "Hope you don't expect to use them all in one night."

Hakee tosses them onto the center of the bed. "I have no expectations, but I *would* like to make love to you."

"Don't you have to be in love to make love?"

He explains his view of sexual encounters as mini love affairs, lasting for as long or as short as both parties wish them to. In his eyes, grown men make love. Any idiot with a dick can thrash around if busting a nut is his only aim.

"But what happens if you want to end it and the other person wants to keep it going?" I ask.

He approaches closer. "I think when it's right for both people, then the situation will work itself out."

I often find myself in moments like this. Rather than enjoy the experience, I get ahead of myself, which messes things up.

"Wanna get undressed?" Hakee asks.

"Sure." I proceed with taking off my shirt, stopping midway to watch him disrobe. Never have I seen anyone take such care to fold their clothes. Seeing Hakee's sinewy nakedness leaves me mesmerized. Every cut and twist of muscle stands out in the candlelight.

He helps me out of my clothes, using the same care as when he removed his own. As we face each other in our natural state, he spoils me with deep, meaningful kisses before giving me a gentle shove onto the bed. I fall back, my arms outstretched, and my body hums with the nervous energy of a beginner.

"You're nervous?" Hakee asks, joining me on the bed.

"A little."

"You have done this before, right?"

"Yes, I have," I respond defensively.

"Then what do you have to be nervous about?" He softly tugs at the gray scruff on my chin. "Hmm?"

"I guess I can't believe I'm here with you." Not even Byron had the rare and unreachable beauty Hakee possesses.

"Believe it," he says, looking at me with glistering desire. "I wanna taste you."

He descends upon my bobbing dick, first by running his tongue teasingly along the entire length of my hardening shaft.

Receiving oral is always hit or miss for me. I must give off a certain energy that attracts few that are decent at it. Most don't bother to reciprocate (because they consider having a dick in their mouths degrading) or those that do, give head to get head. And they do just enough to justify to themselves the work they expect my mouth to put in. But my experience with Hakee is already on track to be something special. He shows genuine interest in the activity. I welcome the attention and anticipate returning the favor.

I watch each glorious inch of myself disappear into his mouth, feeling my tip hit the back of this sexy man's warm throat. His sucking and hand stroke combo method works my body into frenzied ecstasy. Despite my earlier insistence on quiet, I'm unable to resist the urge to moan loudly.

"Shh. Remember your roommate," he whispers despite being turned on by my physical response to him.

"I'm sorry, but you're gonna make me bust if you keep doing what you're doing."

"Well, we can't have that now, can we?" He grins naughtily before attacking my quivering mouth with a torrent of kisses. "I wanna taste more of you," he soon announces, lifting my legs over my head to stab his tongue into my depth. Spitting and lapping, he charges my hole like it's a source of nourishment.

With his mouth still upon me, he says, "You taste as good as I thought you would."

"Yeah, keep doing that," I moan into the sexual ether. My calf muscles contract and my toes curl so tightly they almost go numb.

"Do you want me to make love to you?"

"Ye-ye-yes," I stammer, grasping the bedsheets. I anticipate every fiber of his masculine essence as he presses his body against mine.

Hakee withdraws his sopping tongue, leaving my body aglow from a crescendo of sensitivity. He springs up from the bed. Every second away from me is like a punishment. I calm down when he rips open a condom wrapper with his teeth.

"Don't you want me to suck you off?" I ask, slightly disappointed he doesn't offer me a taste of his cock.

"Does this look like it needs any help?" he asks, giving his throbbing girth a wag. He unfurls the long rubber sheath and stretches it over his dick. "You got any lube?"

I roll to the edge of the mattress to scoop up a bottle from between the bed and a nightstand. Hakee inches onto the bed, making his way towards my open legs. I pass him the lube. He squeezes a long stream of it onto his palm before slathering it all over his manhood, causing it to gleam with readiness.

"Lift your legs for me."

I freeze with hesitation. What once seemed like an impressive endowment now overwhelms my sense of possibility.

"My dick plays well with others," he whispers, noting my concern. He delivers a spellbinding kiss, intended to melt away my apprehension. Slowly, my legs go up, providing him a perfect view of my awaiting portal. He rubs lube over it before slapping the tip of himself against it.

"You ready for me?"

I nod cautiously. Although I yearn for him, I'm all too familiar with the overly enthusiastic tops who shove themselves inside with no consideration of my comfort. Some men are sadistically turned on by the pain they cause.

"I'll be gentle," Hakee says, watching his large erection sink into my tight, warm goodness.

As he penetrates me, my body tenses, and I gasp. Reflexively, I put my hands against Hakee's pelvic bone to safeguard how deeply he slides in.

"You're gonna be okay," he says, blessing my face and neck with a smattering of kisses. "I wanna be inside you so bad. Don't push me out." His tone is almost pleading.

"I just need a sec to get used to you," I reply airily.

"I give you my word that I won't hurt you. It wouldn't be any fun if I knew I'd hurt you."

I want so badly to believe him. I'm ready for a lover whose intentions are noble and have my best interest at heart. Hakee pushes further into me. A goofy smile spreads across his face. I keep my hands up, guarding my threshold for pain in case he gets carried away.

"Are you okay?" he asks, reveling in how my walls clench around him. "Hmm? You okay?"

My panting entangles my words into knots. But as our eyes lock, I arrive at a level of trust. I answer Hakee's question by lowering my hands from his pelvic bone.

"You ready?" he asks, his eyes kind.

"Yes," I reply, my body swelling with wanting.

"Okay. Wrap your legs around my waist. I promise I'll go slow."

I follow his directive, relinquishing control to him. I brace for discomfort, but his slow, initial thrusts render no pain. After a few mild pumps, he pulls out and stares down at where he's been, sliding both his index and middle fingers inside me.

"Damn, you're moist," he says, almost marveling at this. He glides his penis back in. A bond is fast-building between us, beyond the linking of our limbs and sex organs. I can't think of anyplace else I'd rather be, or anyone else I'd rather be with. Judging by Hakee's amorous expression, he doesn't want to be anywhere, or with anyone else, either.

For a time, his shallow thrusts rock me steady until I grab him by his firm ass, beckoning him deeper. Satisfied with my comfort, he picks up momentum, shaking the bed with such ferocity that the headboard bangs against the wall. If LaSaundra isn't awake, she soon will be.

"Do you want it, baby?"

My dry tongue sticks to the roof of my mouth, rendering me speechless. For the next hour and a half, pleasure has me in its grasp. The sex I once craved from Byron now seems ridiculous and inconsequential. Often when we had sex, I felt like nothing more than his sexual vice, an outlet. I can't believe I ever interpreted Byron's one-sided sex as an expression of his love.

"Look at me," Hakee gently commands.

But I can't open my eyes. The immense pleasure he's introducing to my body is almost too much. His passion is lifting me away.

"Open your eyes for me, baby. I want you to look at me when I'm making love to you."

I open my eyes like a newborn seeing the world for the first time. Opening to the poignancy of what we're doing. "You feel so good inside me," I gush.

Hakee ogles me with a fixed, unyielding stare. "Naw, you're the one feeling good," he replies, his tongue hanging sexily from his mouth.

My mind paints a vivid picture of the future: long romantic weekends, birthdays, and anniversaries. I envision us growing old with a love of our own. However, it's a future I know will never be.

I've been down this road before… confusing lust for love… setting my expectations foolishly high and getting my hopes up. But I've grown tired of being alone. If this man isn't right for me, who is?

As I look up at his exquisite face, Hakee's patchouli-scented sweat drizzles upon me like soft rain. I stick out my tongue to catch and absorb every precious drop. He raises my arms over my head, sniffing the mild mustiness of my armpits, and grunts his approval. He slips his fingers between mine. We become one, powerfully linked in a way I could never be with Byron. Hakee gyrates his hips with a deep, cyclonic force. He's climbing a mountain towards a glorious release. I hear it in his quiet whimpers; I see it in the rising tension in his face.

I hold fast to him, digging my fingers into his stretched vines of back muscles. And then his body quakes as he erupts inside of me. I cup both sides of his sweaty, bald head with my hands to watch the blissful, involuntary contortion of his face. Then the moment passes, and Hakee's full weight drops on top of me. His face nestles inside the bend of my shoulder that becomes my neck. His breath continues to warm me, and as I remain pinned down by his heaving chest, his heart rate returns to normal. Hakee chuckles a throaty chuckle before he clears his throat.

"Thank you for that," he whispers and kisses me. "Now, how can I get you off?"

The question is a refreshing one. Byron never asked it. I reply, "I like my nipples licked while I jerk off,"

"That's a new one. Most guys jerk off while I'm up in them."

"I'm not like most guys. I'm different."

He laughs. "What is this, Michael Jackson's 'Thriller' video? Am I supposed to be the chick he was talking to in the beginning?"

"No, I'm just saying I'm probably different from most guys you've met."

A smile lights up Hakee's face. "I should hope so. Now, let me get to work. *Let me please you.*"

They are more words I've never heard come from Byron's mouth, but they sound perfect to me. His shiny head drifts lower toward my nipples. I'm soon treated with tingling flicks of his soft, wet tongue.

"How's that, baby?"

"That feels fantastic," I moan. I'm not used to someone so adept at selflessly bringing me sexual joy. I hope for as long as I remain tethered to this dream man, I'll enjoy the fantasy that is alive inside my head. And just maybe, if I wish hard enough, he'll be here in the morning light when I open my eyes.

# NINE

Hakee wants another go at me. I allow him. This makes round three. Soon, the jasmine candle has burned down to a determined flicker. After another wave of muscle-tightening orgasms, my legs and ass are sore.

"Damn, you done wore me out," Hakee says, rolling over next to me. We lay entwined in damp, crumpled bed sheets, our bodies lacquered with perspiration.

We gaze at the ceiling, delightfully worked over and comfortable in our after-sex calm. There is a sense of security having him here. Maybe it's the afterglow playing with my head, but if he sticks around past a couple of weeks, I could see myself falling for him.

Judging from the grin spread across Hakee's face, I'd say he is content, and in no rush to get dressed. Had he been a jump-off from a phone app, he would already be dressed and asking to put my digits into his phone, knowing perfectly well he has no intention of returning a single one of my calls or texts.

In contrast, I enjoy snuggling with Hakee, inhaling his scent, and kneading my fingers into his hardened pecs. If I didn't have responsibilities, I could lay here with him forever.

"What are you thinking about?" he asks me.

"Honestly?"

"Yes, honestly," he chuckles.

"I'm asking myself how the hell did we get here."

"I followed you here."

"No, I mean, I keep thinking about that dumbass at the bar, the one sucking his lollipop."

Hakee tilts his head quizzically. "Yeah, what about him?"

"I keep thinking about what he said to me."

His expression is a mix of incredulity and disappointment. "Yo, if that's what you're thinking about, then my dick action ain't what it used to be," he says, pulling his arm from me.

"Oh, no! It's nothing like that at all. You were wonderful. Sometimes random thoughts pop into my head."

Hakee pauses to contemplate whether he's comfortable with my response. A faint smile materializes onto his face, and his arm once again envelopes me. "Baby, you shouldn't let people like that take up premium space in your head. I guarantee you he ain't thinking about your ass."

"I know, it's just… I don't go to bed with a lot of men, and the ones I do, don't look like you."

"I don't believe that," he scoffs.

"No, I'm serious."

"You've never slept with a good-looking man before?"

"Good-looking, yes. But not fine."

"Can I be honest?"

"Of course."

"Your energy tells the world you're insecure… that you don't believe you're worthy of certain things. It's the reason why people like dumbass at the bar pick on you."

Hakee isn't wrong, but his opinion is about as welcomed as a slap to the face. "I blame my inner saboteur."

Hakee kisses my temple. "Tell your inner saboteur to go on somewhere."

"So, why did you come home with me?"

"I like your purity."

"I'm not pure. Trust me."

"I mean, I could tell from the way you reacted to those assholes you don't possess the spirit that would do something like that to someone else. I felt bad for you."

"Great. You're here because you took pity on me?" I hear the emotional neediness in my voice as soon as I speak, further illustrating Hakee's point. At this rate, I'm going to scare him off.

"No, babe. I'm here because you have the most mysterious eyes. Mystery is sexy. I think you're sexy. With or without the glasses."

"Anything else?"

"Okay, that and your ass. Yo, straight up, that ass of yours is kryptonite." He gets up from the bed. His feet hit the floor with a thump. "I need to drain the weasel."

I appreciate the view as he moves about my bedroom. His body is a work of art worthy of high praise. I'm a little insecure about my own body, which shows its age around my mid-section. Usually, after sex, I quickly cover myself with the sheets, but Hakee doesn't mind my imperfections. In fact, during sex, his full exploration of my body allowed me to feel desired.

He slips into his jeans and goes to the bathroom. I straighten out the bedsheets and put the fallen comforter back on the bed. Without the sounds of our sex filling the room, I hear sitcom voices and a laugh track crystal-clear from LaSaundra's room. I check my phone. Three texts from Byron. All saying the same crap... he's looking for a booty call. I scroll past in search of a reply from Kenyatta, but there isn't one. No surprise there. I bet if I had invited him to the bar he would've replied.

I lay back down, spreading myself seductively across the bed in case he wants to go another round. The clock reads 12:22 AM. I should already be in bed. Quish scheduled me to work the mid-shift later today. A mental countdown ticks away the number of hours left to sleep.

After thinking about it, I abandon the thought of sex. No need to appear hard-up or greedy. A little pillow talk will suffice, assuming Hakee is down for talking. There's something magical about the "getting to know you" phase of meeting another person. What better way to see if reality matches the fantasy playing in my head by getting to know him better?

LaSaundra slams her door, confirming that we woke her up, or kept her awake by our sexual romp.

Five minutes pass. Then ten. What is he doing in there? Is he taking a dump? I don't know whether to be offended or honored that a stranger finds it comfortable to do a number two the first night of knowing me. I'm bashful when it comes to bodily functions such as doing number twos and passing gas while entertaining a guest.

Finally, the toilet flushes, followed seconds later by the sound of a running shower. My paranoia kicks into overdrive. Is Hakee planning to wash away the evidence of having slept with me? Byron used to shower before going home to wifey. It's the modus operandi of a cheater.

Thoughts fills my head with rapid succession. Does he have a boyfriend or husband? A girlfriend or wife? Whoever it is, they're probably pacing the floor at home, wondering where lover boy is. "But he's with me, which makes me complicit in his deception," I say to no one. The longer I think about it, the more the whole thing gives me cheater vibes. If I wanted to put up with that foolishness, I could've stayed with Byron's trifling ass!

Hakee returns a short while later, refreshed and all smiles. A thick, emerald green towel hugs his waist, and a few remaining droplets of water roll down his torso.

"I met your roommate on my way to the john," he says, tossing the pants that are slung over his broad, wet shoulder onto a chair in the corner.

I chuckle, recalling LaSaundra slamming the door. "Oh? And how'd that go?"

Hakee shrugs it off, unbothered. He allows the towel to drop to the floor, revealing his jutting hard-on.

"My guess is she's jealous this ain't for her," he says, pouncing onto the bed like a large, exotic cat. He frames my face with his enormous hands and kisses me.

"You don't have a girlfriend or wife to get home to, do you?" I blurt between our locked lips. Hakee pulls away, eyeing me with a stone-cold seriousness. I immediately realize my faux pas of asking such a question.

"You're joking, right?" he answers, placing a distance between us by rolling to the farthest edge of the bed.

"Hey, I was only kidding."

"No, you weren't."

"Okay, I wasn't joking. It's just that the last guy I fooled with was one of those DL brothers. He told me he was divorcing his wife, but he has no intention of going through with it."

"Look, I'm sorry he hurt you, but I ain't him. But I guess you probably think everyone is out to hurt you."

"Not exactly," I reply, hoping my protest isn't too little, too late. "Look, I really want to get to know you better. I hope it's not off the table."

Hakee turns onto his side, facing away from me. He cocoons himself inside the sheets and comforter. Countless seconds pass before he speaks again. "I think we ought to get some sleep."

*Way to go, Lawrence. The night is going straight down the toilet thanks to your big mouth!* I've single-handedly pissed off the one decent man I've met who doesn't hump and dash. I've allowed my past with Byron Ross to scare me from appreciating my present. I can only take slight comfort from Hakee not breaking his neck to leave.

With nothing better to do, and while there's nerve to do it, I send a text to Byron, telling him to lose my number. Then, I blow out the candle, killing the last of the dying flame.

For the next hour, we both toss and turn. When I'm not staring at Hakee's back, the red numbers on the digital clock mock my inability to fall asleep.

"You awake?" he asks, sounding wide awake himself.

"Yes."

"Me too." He pulls me into his embrace, which I receive as a positive sign.

"I'm sorry I upset you," I say to him.

"Earlier you said that you wanted to get to know me better."

"I meant it."

"Okay, then. There's something you should know about me."

"What?"

"Once my moms stabbed a fork into the back of her boyfriend's hand because he called me a faggot. She's gone now, but I owe it to her to live my life openly and with pride. So no, I don't have a harem of women stashed someplace. And no, I don't have a man waiting at home. I know what it's like to be cheated on. That shit doesn't fly with me, and I wouldn't do that to someone I care about."

I'm flattered by Hakee's willingness to share a piece of his history. His openness entices me (despite feeling silly for allowing my overactive imagination to get the best of me) to learn more about him.

"I can see myself caring deeply about someone like you," he says, pulling the sheets and comforter away from our spooned bodies. His hardened dick pulses warmly against my backside. His intention is obvious… and it will give me something phenomenal to dream about. He begs to do right by my body. And later, after he's flooded yet another condom inside me, I'm faded from exhaustion, and I sleep well.

# TEN

The next morning, glorious aromas awaken me. For a moment, I almost don't realize Hakee is gone. But, when I open my bedroom door, I hear amiable conversation coming from the kitchen. LaSaundra is laughing, something I haven't seen her do in ages. As I approach the kitchen, the amazing breakfast smells intensify.

Hakee is in mid turn of an omelet. LaSaundra sits in her usual spot at the breakfast nook. Both enjoy a camaraderie that normally takes months to establish. By the flirtatious way LaSaundra runs her index finger along the lip of her juice glass, she seems mesmerized.

"Oh hey," Hakee says, grabbing a plate to slide the omelet onto.

"Hey," I reply, sounding a tad bit jealous even to me. "Why didn't you wake me? I could've helped."

"With what? You don't cook," LaSaundra says.

"You looked sexy while you were sleeping. I didn't wanna wake you," Hakee says, winking at me while presenting her with the omelet.

"That is so sweet. You got any straight male friends you can introduce me to?" she asks.

Hakee laughs and waves me over. After a kiss to my forehead, he says, "She told me you hate eggs, so I hope you'll be happy with the spicy sausage patties and home fries."

"Oh, I'll make due. Trust me."

"You got it."

I pass LaSaundra her purse to get it out of my way. "Want to do something with this?"

Hakee plates his own food and puts it on the table. "Bathroom," he announces, sprinting down the hallway.

LaSaundra fans herself with her napkin. "Okay, where did you find *him*?"

"Sparkles."

"You found him in that dump?"

"I know, right? Until last night I'd never seen him before."

"Well, I can only imagine what his stroke game is like... all that noise coming from your room."

I bow my head sheepishly. "Sorry. We tried to be quiet."

"Well, you failed, sweetie."

"Hey, it's my iron rod bed."

"Yeah, uh huh. The bed and all that moaning you were doing." She bites into her gooey omelet and smiles from its deliciousness.

I eat my first bite of the home fries, which put a peppery heat on my tongue. I never knew food could taste so delicious.

"I guess I must've lucked out. He screws *and* cooks!"

"Is he gay or is he like Byron's DL ass?"

"Gay."

"Completely?"

"Yes."

"Proof."

"He told me his mother stabbed her boyfriend in the hand with a fork for calling Hakee a faggot."

"Wow! Talk about Mama bear going in for her baby cub."

I regret indulging in this triggering conversation. It saddens me that I can't say the same about my own mother.

Hakee returns to the kitchen, plopping down to enjoy his food. Both LaSaundra and I reach to pour him a glass of juice, but I get to it first. After serving him, I polish off what's left in the pitcher between LaSaundra and myself.

"Hey, while I was in the john, I was thinking."

"About?" both LaSaundra and I ask in unison.

Hakee touches my forearm. "I was thinking about what we talked about last night. About my singing."

"You sing?" LaSaundra asks, practically swooning.

"Yes, he does, and very well," I interject, hoping he will stand tall in his greatness.

"Well, I got invited to do a paid gig at First Avenue. Until last night, I wasn't going to do it. It's not my usual venue, and I'll be out of my comfort zone, but I think you're right. I need to continue full-steam ahead in following my dream. So, if the two of you aren't busy this Saturday, I'd like it if you came to show support."

"We'd love to," LaSaundra answers, her eyes practically glowing. Having her approval affirms that I've done something right for a change.

"Cool. That's wuz up," Hakee replies, then mentions that the gig doesn't pay much but might make a dent in what he owes the studio. It's my turn to glow. I'm happy to hear he's planning to get current and continue recording.

"How much do you owe?" she asks.

"At least a couple of grand. My buddy owns the studio, but he's been more than patient."

"Any idea how you'll come up with the rest?"

"I'm always on the lookout for new opportunities," Hakee says. His eyes twinkle as a smirk bends the right corner of his mouth. "Let's just say when they come knocking, I'd be a damn fool not to open the door."

# ELEVEN

It amazes me what fantastic sex before work does for my mood. My workday has gone great. No call-outs and most of the customers are pleasant for a change.

Throughout the day, Sameer stares at me as though curious from whence my glow has cometh. Regardless of his personal opinions of me, I give him credit for his professionalism. Whatever those opinions, he never allows them to impede the overall running of the restaurant. But today he's different. He's cracking a few smiles and lame jokes, all of which soften his usually intense aura.

Quish shows up unexpectedly as the lunch rush dies down to prepare for her two o'clock closing shift. I didn't realize she was closing. Besides doing month-end inventory, it's rare that she works evening shifts, but being the head boss, she enjoys knowing what goes on at all times in the restaurant. She's surprised to see me, and motions to me with her index finger to come into the office.

"I thought I told you to take some time off," she says.

"I know, but I really think keeping busy will help me get through this. If I take time off, all I'll do is sit around the house drinking."

"Fine," she replies, her stare as cool as her tone. "But if I have to call you back in here to talk about your performance, no ifs and or buts, you're taking the time off. Do I make myself clear?"

"Yes."

"All right. Don't let me down," Quish says, leaving me alone to notice Dan's name crossed off the closing schedule and her name scribbled in above it. Upon further examination, she'd already reworked the schedule to cover me not being here.

Later, after Sameer stocks for the dinner rush, he offers to assist me with the lunch deposit. I accept, figuring four hands is better than two and will get us out much faster.

"So, why were you all smiles today?" he asks me.

"I'm not sure it's anything you'd be interested in hearing about."

"Why, did you get laid or something?"

That gets a double-take from me. Sameer is always so serious; I want to be sure I heard him correctly. "What did you just say?"

"You heard me," he replies with a conspiratorial grin.

"What do you think?"

"Must've been one helluva time. I've never seen you smile for an entire shift."

"Well, when it's good, it's good."

Sameer is about to say something else but pauses to poke his head outside the office to ensure no one hears us. Returning to the counter, he's now pensive. In a low voice, he asks, "So, uh, you've had sex with a man, yeah?"

His bluntness surprises me. I glance down at Sameer's wedding band. Upon my scrutiny, he fidgets with the ring, spinning it on his finger.

"Uh, I don't think this is really anything you want to hear about."

"I've told no one this, but for years I've been having these feelings…" Sameer shrugs as his words drift off. "I don't really have anyone to talk to about it."

"Oh. Uh, sure. I understand." It's strange to hear him speak so candidly. He's never given off a gay vibe.

"Could we grab a drink after we're finished here?" Sameer asks, his eyes wide and hopeful.

"Sure," I reply without thinking, nor knowing what I'm getting myself involved in.

"Thank you." He relaxes his hunched shoulders. "I'm going to the bathroom. Once we finish up and drop the deposit, we can go get that drink."

"Sure thing."

"Thanks again," he says, walking buoyantly out of the office.

Now it makes sense why Sameer always seems tense. I can relate because I remember how it felt to hide my sexuality. Before I came out, it was both difficult and exhausting to play down who I really am to pacify other people's discomfort with homosexuality. These are the same people who are quick to accept the notion that gays are same-gender attracted because of a perverse need to rebel against God and society. Many of them believe the archaic idea that we are the result of domineering mothers and distant fathers. Junior's father used to torment Ma about my sexuality by convincing her that she failed as a mother and that my being gay was her fault. That was especially hard for her to "accept" considering her gay best friend, Clayton, had also experienced hardship for being who he was. Clayton's family disowned him, and after subsequently receiving an AIDS diagnosis, he killed himself.

My phone chirps. I read the text message from LaSaundra. *Call me!!!* the text appears to shout. I dial her number. She picks up after the first ring.

"Have you seen my debit card?" she asks in a panic.

"No, why?"

"Because it's missing!"

"Calm down. Have you retraced your steps?"

"I know exactly where it was. It was in my purse. Now it's not. Why do you think that is?"

"I don't know, but don't you…"

"I knew he was too good to be true," she interrupts.

"Wait… what? You think Hakee took it?"

"Hell yeah, I think he took it! Who else could've taken it?"

I don't like the inference that I brought home the very big bad wolf she warned me about. "Hold on just a minute! You don't get to fire off an accusation like that without proof."

"Yesterday I had my debit card. Today I don't. I don't know how many times I've told you about bringing strange men home with you!"

"I still don't understand what Hakee has to do with anything."

LaSaundra scoffs. "Were you not listening when he said he was having difficulty paying off his studio debt? Were you not listening when he said he'd be a fool not to take advantage of an opportunity? Yeah, the son of a bitch took the opportunity to rip me off!"

I recall how long it took Hakee to return from the bathroom after sex. "Look, before you go crazy, let me call and ask him."

"I can't live like this. You don't respect me enough to keep either of us safe. What if he had wanted more than my debit? What if he was some psycho looking to slit a throat or two?"

"I said, I'm going to call him!" I hang up and scroll through my list of contacts until Hakee's name and number appear. I dial it.

"*We're sorry. You have reached a number that has been disconnected or is no longer in service. If you feel you have reached this recording in error, please check the number and try your call again.*"

The recording puts a sinking feeling into my stomach. I replay the last twenty-four hours in my mind, pausing around the time I met Hakee at the bar. Paranoid thoughts ensue… How convenient was it that he swept in like a knight in shining armor when those idiots were giving me a hard time? Had he been watching from the shadows? Had I given off a vibe that made me an easy target? I don't need anyone to tell me I moved too fast with him. I already know that I was following a fantasy that doesn't exist. Why am I always chasing someone who makes me throw away my common sense?

Sameer returns from the restroom, his eyes shining in a way I've never seen before. Yes, he needs me, and I don't want to be the bad guy by reneging on my word, but I have to.

"Listen, something's come up."

In an instant the light fades from his eyes, replaced with something heavier; a disbelief similar to the moment I told him Grandma passed away.

"What's wrong?"

"Someone stole my roommate's debit card. She's pretty upset right now, and I told her I would help her figure out what to do."

"Fine," Sameer says flatly.

"I'm sorry. How about we get together tomorrow?" I ask, trying to be conciliatory.

"No. It's all right. Forget I asked."

We finish counting the lunch deposit in silence. I try to think of something to say to allay Sameer's suspicion that I'm blowing him off, but nothing comes to mind.

On the way home I feel like a complete asshole. I listen to Diana Ross and the Supremes' greatest hits from my phone. Traffic is beastly, and I resign myself to the fact that I'm not going to make it home any time soon. I pass the time replaying the previous night's events, but instead of assurance that what LaSaundra alleges is a grave mistake, it validates what Ma used to say when going through her own man-trouble: *Men are dogs.... they all start biting sooner or later!*

# TWELVE

Someone flashes their high beams as I pull into my driveway. The driver's side door opens, and my sister-in-law, Nadine, staggers out of the car, struggling to get onto her feet. She holds her right side and winces with pain. I dart over to assist her.

"I didn't know where else to go," she says, unable to hold back tears.

"No, no. You're okay. Let me help you."

"I'm all right. Can you take LaTavia out of her car seat, please?"

I open the rear passenger door to unbuckle my niece. The child stares up at me with large, inquisitive eyes. I'm not a lover of children, but I love holding babies. They're innocent, clean slates before the world screws them up with parental indoctrination and social conditioning. However, my enjoyment of babies is contingent upon knowing I eventually pass them back to their parents. Kids LaTavia's age cry the moment they lay eyes on me. I'm relieved she reaches out her tiny arms to be picked up.

"I should warn you now, my house isn't the most kid-friendly."

"Don't worry. I won't let her out of my sight," Nadine replies.

After unlocking the front door, we step inside the house. I instruct Nadine to take LaTavia into the living room and make themselves comfortable. I return with an open bottle of red and two glasses, Nadine sits on the couch with LaTavia playing with a stuffed bear on the floor.

"I thought you could use a glass of wine."

Nadine shifts slowly in her seat, trying for a level of comfort that doesn't come. "Glass my foot. With the way I'm feeling, I can kill that entire bottle by myself."

"I guess I don't have to ask how you got injured," I reply, pouring into the glasses.

"Your brother is crazy."

I nod politely and hand her a glass. She isn't saying anything I don't already know. In fact, I'm well aware of the monster my brother is. He's a bully, just like his father. I'm glad Nadine finally abandoned the flimsy excuse she gave us earlier that LaTavia kicked her in the eye.

"The thing is, he didn't use to be like that."

"No, he's always been crazy," I correct.

"I mean, he used to be really sweet."

"Of course, he was. You think you would've got with him if he came out swinging at you from the outset?"

Nadine laughs, grabbing her aching side. "You can't make me laugh. It hurts."

"What did he use? Fist or foot?"

"Oh, he's gotten smart. After you asked about my eye at your mom's place, he only hits me below the neck now." She partially lifts her shirt to reveal a large, bluish-purple amoeba-shaped bruise along the side of her ribcage. "I got this beauty after he kicked me for smiling at the drive-thru cashier at McDonald's."

"How did he manage that in the car?"

"He waited until we got home. I knew he was angry, but that seemed to come out of nowhere. The next thing I knew, I was on the floor. Food went everywhere."

"When did he start acting like this?"

"He was always jealous, but he used to do it in a cute puppy dog kinda way. It wasn't stifling. But things became physical when he slapped me for telling my mother about our personal business. I left him for about a week, and he promised he wouldn't do it again. And he didn't for a while. Instead, whenever he got angry with me, he either hit the wall with his fist or blew off steam somewhere else."

"When did he start up again?"

"After our daughter was born. The first time he really beat me up was because LaTavia wouldn't stop crying when he was taking a nap, and he complained about the noise. All I said was if anyone should complain it should be me because I'm the one who's with her all day. I put up with her crying all the time. But he didn't give a shit about any of that. He said since he's paying the bills, the least I could do is keep her quiet."

"And he beat you for saying that?"

A fixed, distant look comes over Nadine, as though the memory itself is directly across the room. "He beat me so bad; he almost ruptured my eardrum."

Her story awakens a hatred I haven't felt towards my brother since we were kids. Back then, Junior vigorously went along with the cruel things his father said and did to me.

"I hope to God that one day Plez tries to punk the wrong person and they kick his ass around!"

"I hate to say it, but sometimes I wish I'd never married him."

"Divorce his ass!"

She shakes her head angrily. "And do what? Where am I gonna go? Do you have any idea how hard it is to be a single parent? My mother was a single parent! I swore to myself that I would raise my child in a two-parent home. I mean to keep that promise."

"What's the point of a promise like that if you're dead?"

"No, he wouldn't do that."

"You said yourself the man is crazy!"

"I just need a day or two away from him. If we're not around, he'll start missing us. He's always on his best behavior when he thinks he'll lose us."

"That might work for now, but what about next time?"

"Do you think we can stay here a couple of days?" Nadine asks, ignoring the question.

"I don't know. I mean, I'm not the only person living here. I need to talk it over with LaSaundra."

"Sure," she says, her face growing despondent.

"You know what? Let me go change out of this uniform and I'll see what I can do." I place my glass on the coffee table and head to the bedroom. A piece of legal pad paper is on my bed. On closer inspection, it's a letter from LaSaundra.

*Lawrence,*

*Enough is enough. I can't live like this anymore. I don't feel safe, and your need to bring men home every night trumps any respect you may have for me. Maybe you don't respect me. If you did, you would care that your "piece of trade" went into my purse and stole my debit card. I'm glad I finally know where your priorities lie. I'm going to stay with a friend until I can figure out what to do next. I'll text you when I'm ready to get my things. Hope the sex was worth it…it cost you a best friend.*

The thought of my friend casting me aside brings on light-headedness. I lower myself onto the bed to better process the letter. After a moment of sitting in my new reality, and unsure of what to do next, I return to my guests.

"Looks like my roommate's going to be away for a while. You can stay over."

Nadine's face turns jubilant. With everything she's been through, I'm happy to see her happy about something. No need for both of us to be miserable.

"I'm going to go out and get our bags," she announces.

I chuckle to hide my hurt over just being abandoned. "I guess you came prepared, huh?"

She smiles and goes to retrieve some items from her car. I hope having Nadine and LaTavia around will help take my mind off LaSaundra and my alleged thieving one-night stand. And then again, maybe it won't.

*****

I cook a kid-friendly dinner of fish sticks and mac and cheese. During the meal, Nadine mentions that she thinks Junior impregnated her on purpose.

"We were at the park one day, watching the kids playing, and he started talking about how he thought we would have beautiful children. If I'm honest, I didn't want to get pregnant right away. But he kept pushing me about it. I finally leveled with him and told him as much, and I thought that was the end of it."

"Famous last words?"

"You're telling me. Suddenly, I couldn't find my birth control pills. I kept them in a particular spot that the only way you got to them was to dig around for them. He acted all offended when I asked him if he'd seen them. Now, remember, I didn't accuse him of taking them, I just asked if he'd seen them."

"What did he say when you asked?"

"He said, 'What do I look like using birth control pills? Men don't take them.'"

I roll my eyes. That sounds like something Junior would say.

"So later he wanted sex. I told him I wanted to wait until I could get a replacement on my pills. He said not to worry, he would wear a condom."

"And he didn't, did he?"

"Oh, he wore one, all right. I think he cut a hole in the tip."

"Wow! Talk about extreme."

"I know. But I can't shake the feeling that he planned to knock me up to trap me. And here I am... trapped."

Later, while relaxing on the couch, my niece dozes off and slouches over my lap. I get up to change the sheets on LaSaundra's bed for my two guests to sleep there.

"We would've been fine on the couch, but I appreciate it," Nadine says, lovingly scooping up her daughter to bring her into the bedroom. "I'll be right back."

Once Nadine is around the hall, a loud banging interrupts my intention to open another bottle of wine. The sound comes from the front door. I open it to find Junior standing there. His face is stern and menacing, the same way his father would look whenever it was ass-whipping time.

"Where's my wife?" he asks, his angry gaze traveling beyond me, blazing towards the interior of the house.

I position myself to obstruct Junior's view. "She's safe. If you're in a fighting mood, why don't you go down to the bar and pick on one of those men and see what happens!"

He pushes past me. "Nadine! Get your high-yellow ass out here now!"

"Look! Don't bring that shit in here!" I yell, stepping closer to pull his focus.

Eyes hardened, he says, "Fine. When Nadine comes out with my child, we can leave."

I inch closer, almost touching his chest with my own. Fear bubbles in my stomach. "She's not going anywhere with you!"

He smirks, hardly taking me seriously. "Wanna bet?"

Nadine appears suddenly. Though a safe distance away in the hallway, she's visibly shaken. "How did you find me?"

"It's called a tracker, bitch! I put one on your phone!"

"Great, I have a stalker for a brother," I say, surprised by the lengths Junior has gone to find his wife.

"Can't stalk what's already mine, nigga! Nadine, get LaTavia, and let's go!"

"I told you she's not going anywhere with you!"

Junior thumps my chest with his open palms. "What's your faggot-ass gonna do?"

It's a fair question, minus the use of the word *faggot* and the heat from his stale cigarette breath. Am I prepared to do whatever is necessary to keep my niece and Nadine safe? Or am I just perversely voyeuristic, coming between the chaos of consenting adults?

"Next time you see a faggot, beat his ass," I reply, affixing a sneer to my words. But it's as if I had never spoken. Junior returns his attention to his wife, freezing out my silly proclamation with blustery intimidation.

"Get LaTavia so we can go!"

"I don't want to go anywhere with you. Besides, LaTavia is already asleep."

"Then wake her little ass up!"

"No!"

"You heard her," I interject. "She doesn't want to go with you. Now leave!"

"No? Bitch, did you forget who the hell you're talking to?"

"She's talking to you! Now leave or I'm calling the cops!"

"You call the police and I swear by the time I'm through kicking your ass, they won't be able to recognize you," Junior says, his eyes blazing diabolical. "Nadine, don't make me come over there and drag you out of this house!"

Without thinking, I elbow him in the ribs. He grimaces, appearing momentarily startled by the audacity of my actions. For a second, I'm proud of myself for having inflicted pain upon him. But it's a short-lived victory. In retaliation, he lands a solid punch to my clavicle. The brute force knocks me to the floor. The next thing I know, he unleashes a squall of kicks upon me. I guard my head with my arms, leaving the rest of my body vulnerable to his typhoon of stomps.

"Stop it! You're hurting him!" Nadine screams.

LaTavia's frightened cries sound from the other room.

"Okay! Okay! I'll come with you!" Nadine yells, moving cautiously towards Junior. "Just stop beating him, please!"

I remain on the floor, my body in unnatural twists. Every inch of my stinging flesh balloons beneath my clothes. As I sense my brother approaching, I hold my breath for fear of risking more of his wrath.

"See what you made me do?" Junior shouts, pacing back and forth like a provoked bull.

I'm unsure which of us he's talking to. With my face covered, I can still see the living room between the slats of my swelling fingers. I make out LaTavia's toy bear, and Junior's legs and feet as they move about. Nadine positions herself by the front door, her legs and feet turned in my direction. She teeters, as though wanting to make her way over to me to help me up, but I pray for both our sakes she doesn't.

"Bitch, take your ass outside," Junior says to her. He's no longer yelling, though his directive is tinged with danger.

Once they leave, the door closes behind them, separating their world from mine. I painfully rise to my feet, middle-age doing me no favors. I limp to the bay window. I almost hear the spewing of Junior's verbal ferocity and the thwapping sound of the back of his hand connecting to the side of Nadine's head. I watch helplessly as he forces her into the front seat of his car. Neither bother to get the car seat from Nadine's vehicle, leaving her with no choice but to hold the child in her lap.

The engine starts, and the troubled couple takes off into the night. I crane my neck for as long as they stay within view. Eventually, I search for my cell phone to call the police. As I dial, my body throbs mercilessly and an awful thought strikes me ... what if Junior is waiting until he gets his wife home to give her his very worst? I can't imagine what the cops will find once they show up there.

Despite blistering pain, I attempt to get some rest. But a nightmare insinuates itself into my sleep, making it anything but restful.

I wake up in a fetal position, sweat rolling down my face and neck. My arms are up, protecting my head as though what I experienced earlier is a present danger, but thankfully that threat is no more.

I struggle to get back to sleep. I blame Junior for manifesting his viciousness into my dreams. I wish Hakee was here. Nothing left to do except process what happened, and whether I should've involved myself in Nadine's drama in the first place. I don't understand what made me think Junior, a man capable of kicking his wife in the ribs would think twice about striking his own flesh and blood.

He's a blight on my past and entwined so closely to his father, Plez Sr., that I often regard them as a single entity. Especially since Junior appropriated his father's knack for beating up women.

It surprises me that I'm as worried about Nadine as I am. We aren't especially close. Cordial at best. But I remember a time when Plez Sr. beat Ma horribly because she dared speak truthfully on how dark her life was behind closed doors. I can't get over how eerily similar the expression that monster made on his face then was with the one Junior wore when he barged into my home. While I have no choice over the familial bond I share with my brother, Nadine chose him as a husband and father to her daughter.

Unable to sleep, I roll out of bed to make a bowl of butter pecan ice cream, my go-to vice for flaring anxiety. After that, I swallow another dose of Ibuprofen and cross my fingers that my high blood pressure doesn't spike.

# THIRTEEN

The Ibuprofen stops working by mid-morning. Searing pain makes getting out of bed laborious. I limp towards a commotion coming from LaSaundra's room. I watch from the doorway, in partial disbelief that she's going through with it... she's actually moving out. She chucks her clothes and a few other items into a large garbage bag. It takes her a few minutes to notice me standing here. Once she does, she practically jumps out of her skin.

"Damn it, boy, can't you announce yourself?" she snaps.

"I could say the same thing to you. I thought you were going to let me know when you were coming over."

"I sent you a text."

I lean my weight against the doorframe to rub the pain in my leg. "Haven't checked my phone yet."

"What happened to you?"

"Don't ask."

"Bad date?" LaSaundra scoffs.

"You'd like that, wouldn't you? That way you can justify moving out."

"Look, kiddo, I didn't come over here to argue. I just need to get a few things. I'll get the bigger stuff the next go-round."

"Who are you staying with?"

"What difference does it make?"

"Must make a big difference if you won't tell me."

LaSaundra resumes tossing items into the bag. I'm tempted to help her pack just so she can't use packing as an excuse not to talk to me.

"Can't we have an adult conversation?" I ask.

"I've been trying to get you to have an adult conversation all along, Lawrence."

"Okay, now's your chance."

She drops the bag at her feet. Her mouth opens to speak, but she thinks better of it. I snatch the bag away from her, intending to hold it hostage if only to make her speak to me.

"Gimme my stuff," she says.

"Not until you talk to me,"

"Boy, I'm not playing with you!"

"I'm not playing with you either. I think I deserve better than some note you scribbled."

"Oh, so this ain't about what you've done to get us to this point; this is about you feeling disrespected because I left a note?" she asks, arms crossed and eyebrow arched.

"Look, I'm sorry, okay? You're my best friend. I don't want you to move out."

"I can't deal with all the men coming through here. It's like after whatever you called yourself having with Byron ended, you've gone into this slut mode."

"I really wish you'd stop saying that. You know good and well there hasn't been that many guys, LaSaundra."

"In all the time we've lived together, how many men have you seen me bring home?" she asks with a hand on her hip. "I'll wait."

"None. But isn't that your choice?"

"I never said I haven't brought anyone home. I asked how many have you *seen* me bring home."

I chuckle. "Girl, please. Who have you been sleeping with? You're so tied to your Bible that your bed would burst into flames if you put a man on it."

"I'm a progressive Christian, so don't project all that sanctimonious bull crap onto me just because you get it from your family. I don't care who you sleep with. Just be discreet. The reason you never see who I sleep with is that I'm discreet."

"Yeah, right. You mean to tell me you've been in here getting it in?"

"I'm still a grown woman with needs like everybody else. Trust me, kiddo, I know my idea of Christianity makes more than a few church ladies lose their Sunday wigs."

We both laugh. Speaking for myself, it feels wonderful to do so. Our friendship is built on twenty-five years of laughter. And I appreciate LaSaundra's "brand" of Christianity. Yes, she believes homosexuality is a sin, but she doesn't fixate on it nor does she position herself as morally superior to me. I hold dear the values we agree on, and accept there will also be things we won't.

I grab an unused garbage bag to help her remove smaller traces that she's ever been here. But I want her to see the dejection in my face. Maybe it will be enough to get her to rethink things and settle back into our normal routine.

Instead, she tells me to bag whatever items I see. It's a shame that after all these years, I have no clue what she's thinking. Moving forward, I predict there will be less laughter between us and only memories and hard feelings to hold on to.

I haven't figured out why being alone bothers me so much. Maybe I have unresolved abandonment issues; maybe the prospect of spending time by myself, ruminating over the choices I wish I made, terrifies me. Having a roommate helps me quiet the pesky inner voice that convinces me that I'm unworthy of a happily-ever-after.

At least when I thought Nadine and my niece were staying for a few days, it was rewarding to feel needed. Having them around would've filled, albeit momentarily, a void in the center of my soul. But now, this void reduces me to outright begging, and it's pathetic.

I hand LaSaundra a filled bag of her belongings. "Seriously, you don't have to go," I say, more determined than ever to change her mind.

"No, I have to move out," she says, committed to what she's come to do.

"So, you're willing to throw away a quarter of a century's worth of friendship?"

"Don't you get it? I'm leaving to save our friendship. I have no right to change who you are. You'll have the entire house to yourself now. You can bring as much trade home as your tight ass can handle. Go crazy."

"Until now, I didn't realize how much it bothered you. I thought maybe you were jealous. But today, if I have to pick between my best friend or bringing home guys, then I say forget the guys." A deep, ugly cry is building, and I'm unable to keep it at bay. I hate compromising myself emotionally. However, if it will help my best friend see how much our friendship means to me, I'll allow her to witness me at my worst.

LaSaundra sighs, trying her damnedest to hold back her own tears. I believe I'm breaking through.

"I know you mean it now," she says. "And I thank you for that. But it's going to take me some time to get over everything."

"I'm sorry your debit card was taken. I guess I wanted to believe Hakee was different."

"For what it's worth, he fooled me too. With a damn omelet and a smile."

"Full disclosure, I have every intention of going to his little show at First Avenue tomorrow night. I'll be waiting for his punk ass after his set."

"If you're going, then I'm going."

"No, I know how you are. I think it's better if I handle it my way."

"Yeah, I know all about how *you* handle things. Leave it to you and he'll be right back in your bed by the end of the night. No, you need me there to keep your horny-all-the-time-ass focused."

Given my track record with letting Byron's trifling ass back into my life, I let her little dig slide. Yes, the possibility of what LaSaundra suggests is definitely there. She's seen for herself how good-looking Hakee is, but he stooped to an unheard of low. How would it look if I hopped back into bed with the very guy who stole from my best friend?

"Okay, fine. But let me do the talking. The last thing I need is you creating a scene, no matter how much he deserves one."

It's a lot to ask. Truth be told, I can't imagine how I would react if it was my money Hakee snatched up.

"Fine," LaSaundra said after giving it some thought. "Are we riding together or am I meeting you there?"

"Whatever's clever."

"I suppose you'll want a cocktail... or two."

"Don't start!"

"I'm trying to look out for you. No need for you to catch a DUI. I'll pick you up."

"Fair enough."

"Just promise me one thing."

"What?"

"Promise me you'll read him for filth."

I wink. "Promise."

I leave her to finish getting what she needs, happy that there's still a friendship worth saving. I'm also looking forward to challenging Hakee at First Avenue.

He doesn't know how lucky he is that I'll be the one confronting him and not LaSaundra. Because leaving it up to her, she'll mess around and make a fool out of all of us.

# FOURTEEN

I stand in the middle of my bedroom, wearing only black briefs and dress socks. Clothes are strewn about. After changing my outfit five times, nothing looks or fits right. LaSaundra is outside, earlier than expected, beeping her horn impatiently. I hope she stays in the car. I don't want her breathing down my neck, accusing me of dressing to impress, even though that is precisely what I'm doing. I want to show Hakee what he's missing out on... assuming he cares enough to notice.

I decide on a pair of black slacks and a cranberry-red V-neck sweater. After a final satisfactory look at my reflection, I take a deep breath and will myself the courage to complete the task awaiting me at First Avenue.

I step out of the house and lock up. Inwardly, I hope to mask my nervousness before getting into LaSaundra's white Toyota Corolla. But it's no use. I crawl into the passenger seat, groaning as my knee joints pop, an unwelcome sign of aging.

"You're getting old there, kiddo," LaSaundra says.

I close the passenger door and buckle in. "Don't remind me."

"You look spiffy, though."

"Thank you."

"You remember what we're going to do, right?"

"You mean what *I'm* going there to do, and yes, I do."

"What's the matter with you?" she asks, her demeanor changing. Distrust enters her eyes as it did when she first brought the missing card allegation to my attention.

"What are you talking about? Are you okay?" I ask.

She takes one of her usual long pauses and adjusts her rearview mirror. "I'm fine."

"You don't sound fine."

"I said I'm fine," she replies sharply.

I retreat into my thoughts. What am I going to say once I'm alone with Hakee? Do I have the strength to resist his charm? Not that I'm worried about being seduced, I just don't want him getting off too easy.

*****

Hakee is a spectacular performer. His impromptu singing at Sparkles is nothing compared to the vocal stylings he brings to the stage. From acoustic to jazz and throwback R&B arrangements, he presents himself as a dynamic, versatile singer. I marvel at his command of the stage, and the ease in which his sex appeal translates across the racial and gender-mixed audience. He possesses mature confidence that transcends overt sexiness.

It's easy to get caught up in the show, almost to the point of forgetting my primary objective. I dislike being placed in the middle of LaSaundra's issue with Hakee. And I resent the very real possibility that if he's done what she alleges, I will end up hating him for it.

He changes the colors of the performance by speaking to the audience. He talks about his life as an indie artist, sharing with us how unglamorous his journey is. It's all about the grind, a phase in his career in which he still finds himself.

"And the love y'all are showing me is making all this hard work worth it! I wanna thank y'all for—"

"Yeah, you're working hard, all right... working hard stealing from people!" someone shouted, interrupting the smattering of applause to Hakee's sentiment.

A wave of murmurs rippled throughout the audience. Hakee appears bemused under the soft blue stage lighting. He shades his eyes with his hand, turning in the direction he believes the snarky comment came from.

I turn to get LaSaundra's reaction, but she's gone. In my awe of watching the show, I never noticed her leave my side. Now, she's no longer within my view. I look around with the urgency of a parent having become separated from their child in a mall. Only after the voice screams out again, "Did you think you would get away with it?" does it dawn on me that the voice belongs to LaSaundra.

The musicians exchange confused glances among themselves as though unsure whether to resume playing.

I push my way through the crowd to get to my best friend. When she's within reach, I dig my fingers into her arm. "Girl, what are you doing?"

LaSaundra pulls away from me, never taking her eyes off of the star of the show. "Why don't you tell all these people how you seduced my best friend and took my debit card!"

"Folks, I have no idea what this woman is talking about," Hakee says faintly.

"Come on! Weren't you just in my kitchen making me and my best friend breakfast the morning after you fucked him? Probably fucked his ass so good he fell right to sleep afterward. That way, he wouldn't be awake while you dug through my purse, you thief!"

Audience murmuring intensifies. LaSaundra has betrayed me by proclaiming my sexual proclivities for all the world to hear. And everyone will realize that I'm the one who brought Hakee into my home and gave him the opportunity to thieve.

Clenching my teeth, I ask again, "LaSaundra, what in the hell are you doing?"

"Tell them, Lawrence! Tell them how he came into our home and stole my bank card!"

A follow-spotlight holds us in its hot glare. My embarrassment rises along with my body temperature. Sweat soaks my armpits. I feel like a little boy in school squirming with discomfort when the teacher calls on me. I'm stuck for a response. I can't bring myself to commit to her character assassination of Hakee.

LaSaundra scoffs. "I knew you would do this!"

Feeling the gawking eyes of those around us, I reply, "I thought we agreed that I would talk to him after the show."

"Yeah, right. I can tell by the way you're freezing up that you won't handle things like you're supposed to!"

"I'm embarrassed! How did you expect me to react?"

"No, it's okay. I get it. You'd rather suck his dick than do right by your best friend. Fine! Hope you choke on it!" LaSaundra storms off, leaving me to share public humiliation with Hakee, who stares at me. Genuine hurt cuts through his gaze.

The audience, once united to have a great time, now doesn't know what to do with itself. Some people walk out in dismay. Most stick around, probably licking their proverbial chops in anticipation for whatever drama unfolds next. Aggravated, I retreat to the bar area, keeping my eyes averted to avoid the leering of those in my path. As I watch Hakee's last two numbers, the back of my neck is hot and sweaty. I try to enjoy the rest of the show, but the performance is depleted of the superstar energy he began with. I blame LaSaundra for killing his vibe.

After the show, following the audience's mass exodus, I go on the lookout for Hakee. However, after what happened, I doubt there's a confrontation left to be had. All I want now, more than anything, is to let him know LaSaundra's outburst was her own.

He emerges from the backstage area, changed from his neo-soul, bohemian outfit into an all-black ensemble of jeans and a wool pullover. His duffle bag hangs from his shoulder. Despite everything that transpired, he appears in high spirits, even fist bumping some of his musicians.

With my heart racing, I move in close from behind. It's the closest I've been to him since our night together. I'm nervous as all hell. As I wait for a break in Hakee's conversation, I want to reach out and touch the width of his back. The gesture isn't much compared to being in his embrace, but I'll gladly take it. Before I extend my hand, one of his band members glances at me from over Hakee's shoulder, piquing his interest as to who they're looking at, Hakee turns around. There's a hint of a smile intended for a groupie or pimply-faced fan, but it fades when our eyes connect. His are hard like jagged stone. I'm the last person he wants to see. Saying nothing, he rushes past, leaving me in the band's detestation. But I follow nonetheless, needing to know whether this man, who gave me the most enchanting night of my life, is nothing more than a conman, capable of something as lowdown as what LaSaundra accuses him of. My legs carry me within inches of him, close enough to grab his shirt. He spins around furiously, and I prepare to have my jaw dislocated.

When it's apparent Hakee won't strike me, I ask, "Can I talk to you for a minute?"

"After the shit you pulled, I have nothing to say to you!"

"No! We need to talk," I say, half begging and half commanding.

"Did I stutter? I said I ain't got shit to say to you!"

"You owe me an explanation."

He scoffs. "You brought that bitch down here to embarrass me. She ruined my set and you think I owe *you* an explanation?"

"I didn't know she was going to do that."

"Bullshit!"

"No, I mean, she… we had an agreement. She knew I was going to wait until you finished the show to talk to you privately."

"And what's this nonsense about me stealing her bank card?"

I shrug, trying to act as though I'm just as surprised by the accusation as he is. "That's what she said."

"And you believe it?"

My problem is, I don't know what to believe. My hesitation to answer him probably conveys it.

"Wow," Hakee mutters in disbelief.

"Yes…no… I mean, I don't know."

"What kind of answer is that?"

"Look, the night we were together, you took an awfully long time coming back to my room."

"Yeah, I took a shower. I always take a shower after I have sex."

"Then you were up early cooking breakfast. You had at least two opportunities to go in her purse."

"She was already up when I went in the kitchen. I told her I was going to run to the store to grab some items to cook everyone breakfast. And anyway, what motive would I have?"

"You owe your friend money for studio time."

"So, let me get this straight. You think I laid some dick on you so I could scrounge through your roommate's purse for money to pay for my studio time?"

"I mean, I don't know. Maybe—."

"And not only that, you came down here to accuse me of this shit. Did it ever occur to you to call and ask me?"

I've been waiting for this moment. I whip out my phone to produce evidence. "You put a bum number into my phone."

Hakee grabs it from me. His fingertips briefly graze mine. Though it's unintentional and brief, I'm secretly grateful he's touched me. He reads the number. "I hit the wrong digit. That last number is supposed to be seven, not four. See for yourself. Dial the number I gave you but hit seven."

I dial the number and Hakee's phone comes alive with a vibrating buzz in his hand.

He holds up the illuminated screen. "See?" he says with self-vindication.

I expected him to be smug, but Hakee's forlorn expression reveals no satisfaction from proving me wrong.

"Did you take her card?" I ask, putting my phone away.

"Oh, you're just gonna keep going with that, huh? Do you know how insulting that question is?"

"I have to ask."

"I didn't take her fucking card, bro. That shit ain't my style."

There is a stuffiness in the way he calls me "bro." Like he's speaking to a stranger and not the person he once made passionate love to. As Hakee walks away to rejoin his band members, leaving me with the mental picture of his lips curled downward from disappointment. But it's the hurt in his eyes that stings the most. Still, I wait, hoping he will turn back, but he never does.

After our conversation, I'm just as confused as ever. Sure, he seemed sincere in his denial as LaSaundra was in her accusation, and yet, I still don't know who to believe. I only know who I want to believe, but am afraid to make the wrong choice.

It's gotten much colder when I exit First Avenue. I fasten my coat and trek down to Sparkles. With my phone still in hand, I call LaSaundra. I have some things to get off my chest, and she's not going to like what I have to say.

# FIFTEEN

"Voicemail. Damn it!" I mutter to myself as I cut through an alley. The frigid November wind sends empty aluminum cans rattling down the pavement. A homeless man squats inside the brick alcove of a building. His pants are rumpled around his ankles, his bare ass exposed to the cold. He holds a large wad of newspaper smeared with shit. He examines it before tossing it aside. There isn't an ounce of shame on the man's face, and I continue on my way with the disgusting imagery burned into my memory forever.

I arrive at Sparkles soon after. A group of smokers huddle together out front. Their cigarette smoke whirls seductively into the air, then kisses my face, igniting my cravings. I resist the urge to bum one from the group. I go inside. Just beyond the door, an attractive, stocky-built Latino bouncer skulks in the foyer.

"ID, please," he says in a cranky voice.

"Busy tonight?" I ask, motioning past him towards the main bar.

He snatches the ID, annoyed with my attempt at small talk. He barely looks at me. He's one of those types who knows how good-looking he is and doesn't waste his kindness on anyone he isn't attracted to. He reeks of self-entitlement, as though he gets off on denying people entry to the club or roughing them up before tossing them out onto the street.

He hands back my ID. "Have a good time," he replies curtly and turns his attention back to his phone.

There's a decent number of patrons milling about inside. Few of them pay attention to the gangly, sandy-haired go-go dancer shifting dispiritedly from side to side. Pink and neon green spandex shorts hang loosely on his bony, malnourished frame. He mistakes my passing eye contact for interest and tries to ramp up his enthusiasm. I don't have the heart to leave him empty-handed, so I stuff two bucks into the twink's kneepad and walk away before his pleading glance begs for more money.

I wander into the happy-hour lounge. Most of the men present are dressed in black. Phyllis Hyman's song "Old Friend" plays hauntingly on the jukebox. Somber energy vibrates throughout the room. I pass a trio of men discussing the death of and funeral services for a barfly I know superficially named Oliver. Police found him behind the wheel of his car with his throat slashed. His death makes the seventh one since the beginning of summer. A fourth man within earshot turns to them and says he learned it was the work of a serial killer.

Just beyond the men, Doug is alone at the far side of the bar, two seats down from where I sat with Hakee the night we met. Considering our last encounter, I'm dubious about approaching him. Our eyes connect before I have the chance to walk away. I smile and offer a cautious wave.

"Boy, bring your tail over here," Doug says, rolling his eyes playfully.

"Are you alone?" I ask, half-expecting Alvin to materialize suddenly.

Doug nods and notices my hands are drink-free. "Can I buy you a cocktail?"

"That depends. Are you going to throw it in my face?"

"And waste good booze? Are you crazy?"

I chuckle. "In that case, I'll take a Manhattan."

"Since when?" he asks with a raised eyebrow.

"Since now."

"Well, all right, Mr. Sophisticated. Bartender, get my friend a Manhattan."

When the drink arrives, we clink our glasses in the spirit of being on speaking terms again.

"Consider that drink as my way of saying sorry for slamming my front door in your face," he says.

"Actually, I should be the one apologizing to you. I had no right meddling in your relationship. It's none of my business."

Doug runs his finger over the condensation rolling down the side of his glass. "No, you were right to be concerned."

I bite my tongue, allowing my friend's observation to hang there. I don't want to piss him off again by asking the wrong questions. But saying nothing might read as me being indifferent. I want him to sense my apprehension and throw me a bone. Eventually, he does.

"The night you came over, Alvin and I had a fight,"

"Before or after group?"

"Before. He was pissed because I wanted to get everyone together the same day we got back from Rome."

"Has he ever hit you?"

"No. Alvin's power is in his words. He knows just the thing to say to make me feel like shit. And I tell myself I don't have it so bad because there are women out there who get it worse than me. They get beaten."

I've never understood why people rationalize that. These jokers know what they're doing. First, they dismantle their victim's self-esteem. Make them feel worthless. Once they know they can say anything they want to their victim and nothing will happen, they commence with the ass whippings. That's how it was with Ma. For years I watched her lose her self-worth. She tolerated Plez Sr. abuse for twelve years. Got so bad that he busted a beer bottle over her head. Yet, it wasn't until she caught him in bed with another woman that she finally left him. When will Doug realize that Alvin isn't going to wake up one morning and stop disrespecting him solely because it's the right thing to do? It's going to get worse unless he puts his foot down and says enough is enough.

"Sometimes I lay awake at night and think of ways to kill him," Doug says, spinning his glass between both hands.

"Leaving him before it comes to that is probably a smarter choice. Besides, I don't want to visit you in prison."

He shakes his head bitterly. "Thanks to him, I no longer have any relationship with my family. I've got nowhere to go."

"You can stay with me for as long as you need. Hell, you can come over tonight if you want to."

The proposition goes unanswered as both our phones chirp simultaneously. I receive a text: a pic of Byron's dick with the caption: *Miss Me?* I delete it as Doug stares with concern at the text on his phone.

"What does it say?"

"He wants to know when I'm coming home."

"Tell him never."

"I can't tell him that."

"You aren't seriously considering going back there tonight, are you?"

Doug runs his hands over his head, resting them at the nape of his neck as though the weight of his world rests there. He sighs a long, cheek inflating sigh, conveying the difficulty in making such a decision… one not taken lightly.

"Yeah, I'm gonna head on out," he announces.

"You don't have to do this, you know."

"I know. As soon as I get home, I'm gonna tell him he needs to change. Like you said, enough is enough."

"Do you really think he's going to change?"

Doug gets up from his bar stool. "If he expects me to stick around, he better."

For my worries, I receive a hug, and kiss on my left temple. He says, "Thanks for the talk."

"Anytime." I watch him walk away. I wish I felt better about the way we left things, but I don't. And there's nothing I can do that won't place me back in horrible standing with him except be here when he needs me. Looking into my empty glass, I wave to the bartender. "May I have another?"

*****

The moment I put my key into the door lock, someone calls out, "Hey." The voice is semi-familiar and cuts through the rustling tall pine shrubs that hedge the front of my house. When the voice speaks again, I spin around.

Byron steps from the shadows into the brightness of porch light, brushing pine needles from his arms.

"What are you doing here?" I ask.

"You got my text, yeah?" he slurs while trying to appear suave.

"I deleted it," I reply, pushing open the front door. I want no part of his foolishness.

"Can I come in?"

"No."

"Aww c'mon. You know you want some of this dick." Byron dry-humps the air, expecting to both flatter and turn me on. He pauses mid-hump, stands up straight, and shoves his hands into his pockets, affecting a boyish innocence.

"I miss you," he says. There's an uncertainty in his expression, as if he's suddenly aware of the emotional risk to say such a thing. And despite his sincerity, I know he abhors himself for saying it. And as much as I want to believe him, I doubt he will remember having said it by morning.

"That sounds like a personal problem," I reply, hoping my tone conveys that his declaration means nothing.

"You don't miss me?"

"No, I don't."

Byron approaches. His eyes blink incessantly. "I'm so fucked up!"

I don't hide my satisfaction. Finally, this alleged straight man, cocooned in self-loathing and pity, is famished for *my* affections. It's gratifying to be the one sought after for a change. However, I'm almost moved by the long, rolling tears on Byron's miserable face. And as much as I don't want to make him my problem, it would be irresponsible to let him drive in his condition. It's a miracle he got here in one piece, and an even bigger miracle if no one died along the way.

"Come inside and watch TV in the living room," I tell him, reneging my answer the first time he asked to come in.

Byron lowers his head like a puppy caught being naughty. "You mean, you don't wanna make love?"

Asshole! It took him long enough to say it, didn't it? And yes, I went to sleep many nights wishing upon the day Byron would utter those words to me. But now they are sweeter when Hakee says them. But thanks to LaSaundra's shenanigans, I'll never hear him say them again.

"No. I don't," I answer coldly.

Byron stumbles back on an uneven footing. Even pissy-drunk, he's disturbingly handsome, flashing a charming yet drunken smile coupled with his gyrating hips. "C'mon, you know you want some of this."

"If you knew how you looked, you wouldn't do it."

The gyrating stops and the drunk smile vanishes. Waving his car keys, he says, "I shouldn't have come. I'm sorry. I'll go."

I grab the keys, which he hands over with little resistance. "Seriously, I can't let you drive like this. You're going to come in and have a seat or I'm calling the cops."

My former lover obediently follows me into the house. He drops onto the sofa in a sloshy heap. After a brief struggle to take off his shoes, he gives up and lays across the sofa, passing out within seconds. I dutifully remove his shoes and reposition him properly. I bring him a blanket from the closet and place it over him, covering him from his chin to his dark socked feet.

I turn to leave the room, but something holds me here. I should feel sorrier for him than I do. But to do that, I'd have to forget the wife Byron has no intention of leaving or the hurtful and dismissive ways in which he tosses me aside after having his sexual fill. Suddenly, what once nurtured my compassion now fuels a much darker emotion. I stare at him lying there… blissfully unaware that I can do anything I want to him, thereby saving someone else from the agony of a broken heart. Thankfully, that wave of malevolence passes. I turn out the living room light and retire to my bedroom to re-read my favorite biography, *Call Her Miss Ross*.

Once cozy beneath the covers, with my open book resting upon my quilted chest, I assure myself that my good deed of keeping Byron off the streets will be the last good deed I do for him ever. Then, I say a prayer that he won't wander off, and by morning, will be exactly where I left him.

# SIXTEEN

In the middle of the night, I open my eyes to Byron jerking off in the doorway of my bedroom.

"Will you please go back to sleep?" I say, summoning the patience of an exhausted parent.

"No. I want what I came here for," Byron replies, his voice lustfully petulant.

"Well, you're not going to get it, so I advise you to go on back in the—" but he lunges at me before I finish the sentence. His speed turns him into a menacing blur. The last thing I see is 4:44 AM on the clock before everything goes black. I will remember this as the precise moment Byron tries to rape me.

"What are you doing?" I croak in a small, muffled voice.

"Stop acting like you don't want this dick!" Byron yells at me, pinning his forearm against the back of my neck and forcing my head deeper into the suffocating pillow. Despite how drunk he is, his strength is that of a sober man fully aware of his actions. "I came here for some pussy!"

He yanks my jogging pants down to the middle of my thighs and rips from the waistband of my underwear briefs down to the center in one clean tear. After massaging my ass with rough, circular strokes, he gives it a sadistic, heavy-handed slap.

"That's right, make that ass bounce for me," he commands of my stinging flesh. "Yeah, you thought I was playing when I said I wanted some pussy, but you're gonna give it to me today!"

The same vulnerability I wished upon him a few hours ago now befall me. With impaired sight, I listen for clues as to what is happening, all the while praying he will come to his senses.

I brace for the inevitable as 4:44 AM flashes repeatedly behind my closed eyelids. How much time has transpired since? Are the seconds ticking away slowly, like ceaseless drops of water? Amidst my fear, I see faces... first Doug's, then Ma's, followed by Nadine's. How sanctimonious I've been, judging their abusive predicaments. And here I am, struggling beneath the weight of my former lover, a man LaSaundra warned me countless times to get rid of. Now that man is here, weaponizing the very thing I once craved about him.

Byron spits into my exposed hole and stabs his fingers inside to stretch me open. The coarseness of Byron's jean denim scrapes the back of my thighs. The bed creaks as he loops his forearm around my neck in a chokehold. With his other hand, he scrambles to get his pants down. However, unable to unbuckle his belt, he removes his forearm from my throat. The shift in movement allows me the chance to raise my head. My watery eyes can see once again.

Byron's floundering gives me a split-second to act before he impales me with his dick. I use every ounce of strength I have left to thrust my weight backwards, head butting him, and knocking him off the bed.

"Ahh, shit! My nose!" he cries, leaping about in pain.

I roll from his grasp despite being entangled in my disintegrated underwear, and jogging pants. I get up from the bed to pull up my clothes. Byron crumbles to the floor, his hands cupped over his nose.

"You fucking broke my nose!" he screams in a voice gone unexpectedly shrill.

The longer I stare, the more enraged I become. I snatch Byron's belt from the bed and clobber him with it, allowing the metal buckle to do most of the damage. He's too tipsy to fight me off, and the sound of his yelping as he pleads to me to stop hitting him amuses me.

"Get the fuck out of my house!" I yell.

He staggers to make himself upright, all the while holding one hand to his nose. Blood trickles between his fingers.

"I'm gonna get yo' punk ass for this," he warns once he's a safe distance down the hallway.

"You come back over here and I'll have you arrested."

In the living room, Byron shoves his feet into his shoes, then tucks in his blood-stained shirt. I'm glad I caused him bodily harm. After the beating I received from my brother, it's good to know I'm not a complete wuss.

Byron searches between the sofa cushions and beneath the sofa itself.

"What are you looking for?"

"My fucking keys!"

"On the credenza," I tell him.

He snatches the keys from the credenza and opens the front door, straightening his gait before leaving the house. For an additional asshole move, he leaves without bothering to close the door which I slam and quickly lock. As far as I'm concerned, Byron Ross not only walked out my front door but out of my life.

I limp to the bathroom, cursing Byron every step of the way for re-injuring the previously administered aches by Junior. Pushing through the pain, I lift my T-shirt. Purple and black bruises mar both sides of my torso. It's the same thing on my thighs and calves.

I'm too amped up on adrenaline to go back to sleep. I have a hankering for a toasted cinnamon and raisin bagel and head to the kitchen. However, after digging out a bag of moldy bagels from the rear of the refrigerator, I settle for a bowl of cereal and a cup of coffee.

Back in the living room, I watch a few episodes from the *Noah's Arc* DVD before sleep finally takes me out on the sofa.

Later, I awaken to an unusually loud ring from my cell phone. I don't feel like limping back to the bedroom to answer it. From the intensity of the sun coming through the bay window, it's late enough to be my job calling. I answer by the last ring, not bothering to check the caller ID.

"Hello?"

"Hi," Ma says brightly.

"Yeah?" I reply, now wishing I had checked the damn caller ID.

"I had a bad dream about you last night and I wanted to make sure you're okay."

*Did I drag myself back here for this?* After what I've been through with Byron, the last thing I'm interested in is Ma stirring up my anxiety and casting a pall over the day. Still, I take the bait. "What happened in your dream?"

"You were in the hospital. Sickly and lying in a bed, with patches of white hair growing on your back."

"Let me guess, I had AIDS?" I ask, exasperated.

"I sang you your favorite lullaby. Remember which one that is?"

"Cheryl..."

"Why are you calling me by my first name all of a sudden? I'm your mother, boy!"

"You've lost that privilege," I reply, matching her tone of annoyance. She's lucky the only thing I address her as is by her first name. She can't really believe she has the right to call me up and act like we just spoke a couple of days ago, especially when she knows I don't mess with her like that. I refuse to engage in the phoniness,

"Listen here, I gave birth to your smug ass! Show some respect!"

"Why should I respect someone who constantly chooses their men over her kids? When are you going to realize those choices affect other people besides you?"

"You need to stop blaming me for the things not going right in your life."

Her dismissiveness bugs the hell out of me. How does she expect us to move forward if at the very least she isn't willing to admit her part in this?

"You're a grown man, Lawrence. My choices ain't got a damn thing to do with how you choose to live your life."

"You don't think so? Okay, tell me this… did your good son tell you what happened when he stopped by my house the other day?"

"No, what happened?"

"Why don't you go check in. Tell him we spoke." I hang up the phone before I curse her out. If my guess is correct, her curiosity will wear her down, and she's going to call Junior.

There's also a text from Kenyatta sent after midnight: *Hey Boo! Sorry I've been missing in action. I got evicted from my spot because they found out I had some trade staying with me. I'm more than happy to tell you all about the drama over drinks. Whatever you spend, I'll give it back to you when my check comes through.* He's the only person I know capable of getting himself kicked out of Section 8, where he only pays forty dollars a month in rent. I delete the text, casting it as much out of sight as out of mind.

The texts I sent LaSaundra begging her to hear me out are unanswered. Just when I thought we worked everything out, she went and pulled that stunt at First Avenue. In her pursuit of vengeance, she behaved like a reckless, mad-woman. Nothing I said to her previously in her bedroom had gotten through. She had no intention of taking in what I said to her. As usual, she expects me to run behind her like a puppy to salvage our friendship. Why do I always have to be the one to make things right?

I hobble past her room and peek inside. The room is in disarray, her unmade bed as messy as our friendship.

My fingers spring into action on my cell phone keypad, tapping out an angry text that says: *This ain't no storage unit! If you want to end this, then come get your shit and let's end it!* Satisfied, I press send. Knowing her, she will most likely cuss me out for rushing her to come for her stuff, but I'm ready for the verbal sparring.

Almost immediately she replies with a disappointingly succinct: *Fine!* I leave it at that.

I head to the linen closet to fetch a clean towel and washcloth, only to discover that Byron, in his drunken stupor, mistook the linen closet for the bathroom. I remove everything on the lower shelves and dump them into the laundry hamper. Now I have an excuse to throw a couple of loads into the wash.

After I finish laundry, the doorbell rings.

"Who is it?"

"It's your mother."

I roll my eyes. "What do you want, Cheryl?"

"I've already told you about calling me by my first name," she replies with a maternal sternness I remember from my childhood.

Against my better judgment, I open the door a few inches to look her in the eye. "Fine. What do you want, Ma?"

"Eeew! What happened to you?" she asks, noting my haggard appearance.

"Nothing. I just woke up," I lie. I'm not explaining my mouth cuts or the bruising around my neck being the results from almost being suffocated.

"I got another question for you. Since when do you hang up on people? You know good and well I didn't raise you that way."

"True. You just raised us around a bully who taught his son to be a bully." I open the door wide enough to allow her entry. As Ma enters the house, a fleet of birds chirp and fly overhead. My neighbor across the street puts his briefcase and a duffle bag into the trunk of his car. He smiles and waves. I reciprocate, giving the false impression all is well in my world.

"I didn't come over here to argue," Ma says, returning my focus to the goings-on inside the house.

"Then what did you come here for?"

"We need to talk. I think an adult conversation is in order, don't you?"

# SEVENTEEN

"Do you know why I named you Lawrence?" Ma asks, making herself comfortable on the sofa.

I don't answer right away. She thinks she's slick; thinks if she waxes a little nostalgia, it will take me out of my funk with her. The other thing that has me miffed is the way she enters my house, looking around with rigid judgment, like it's her first time being here and she disapproves of everything in sight. She's been to my home twice: once for my housewarming party and the second time to drop off some fried chicken wings I paid her to fry up for another party I threw.

I clear my throat before I answer that no, I don't know why she named me Lawrence. My head is partially in the clouds anyway, still deciding whether to offer my guest something to drink. If things go the way I think they will, she won't be here that long.

"I named you Lawrence because I thought it was the perfect name for a future gentleman. You've always conducted yourself with integrity. All of this fighting between us needs to stop today. Life is too short for the foolishness." Her voice is soft and maternal, like when she used to read stories to me that began with once upon a time. Her tone captures a time before I had to compete for her love and before I ultimately lost it.

"Let it go, son," she says, her voice falling to an emphatic whisper. "Don't let anger mess things up. It's a waste of time, and it'll destroy you."

If she were talking about anyone else, I would agree with her. I'm giddy that she assumes it's going to be easy chiseling through years of hardened resentment. I can't wait to see her disappointment when she realizes how wrong she is.

"I'm sorry, I can't," I respond, pretending to give her request some consideration.

"What is your problem?" she asks, her face darkening as her voice returns to its usual no-nonsense cadence. "Why do you have such a chip on your shoulder?"

My eyes widen with disbelief. "You're seriously asking me that?"

"Yes, I am," she snaps, annoyed that I'm countering her question with such a silly response.

"Hold that thought." I go to my bedroom and open the closet. It's as if I've known this day would come. Between the pages of a journal that I write in intermittently, is an aged, ripped piece of paper I Scotched taped back together long ago. The expectation being if Ma and I ever came to this moment, I want her to read it. Over the years, whenever the masochist inside me needs a reminder of the genesis of my hurt, I read this letter. In fact, I read it often enough that I can recite its content...

*Dear Martin,*

*You were right. I know a guy where I work who's been telling me it's all right to be the way we are. I'm glad I have him to talk to because I know my ma and stepdad would flip the fuck out. You're lucky, though. You told both of your parents a long time ago and they accept you. But my ma keeps bringing me to church, and I know that just by what the minister talks about there, that she'd never accept me. Plez would probably kill me if he knew.*

*I can't wait until I move out of the house so I can find a nice guy to fall in love with. I'm happy for you and Rick, that you two can go on about your lives and not give two shits about what anyone at that school thinks of you. But while I'm happy for you,*

*I fear for you, too. I know that some of those thuggish dudes and those jocks hate our kind and want to not just kick our asses but put us into the ground.*

*But you two are lucky because you're going away to college soon. I'll be stuck in that school with people who don't understand me. I don't know what I'll do then. I'm glad that you both aren't afraid to be seen with a lowly underclassman, like me. (Smile.)*

*I guess I'll just go back to reading my GQ magazines and wishing I could be as gorgeous as some of those male models. Martin, you know you have it made because you're light-skinned. That's why your ass can pull a white guy as cute as Rick. Do me a favor, though. When you're done reading this, throw this into the garbage. I don't want the wrong people seeing this. I can't imagine the embarrassment.*

*Lawrence*

The letter is a revelation as to where my head was at the time. Surely a more naïve, hopeful, younger version of myself wrote it. Today, this decades-old paper serves as evidence of an infraction I'm unwilling to forgive. Armed with it, I rejoin my mother in the living room, the crinkling page flapping in my hand.

I wait for her to look in my direction, but she ignores me, pretending to distract herself with the random knick-knacks filling the built-in-shelves. Suddenly, a New York City snow globe fascinates her. She moves on to check out a bronze Eiffel Tower figurine I bought in Paris and a crystal elephant a Jamaican friend gave me for good luck. Next, she'll have me believe she is genuinely interested in an empty decorative Chambord liqueur bottle.

Ma continues on, looking through my things with the same nosy eye she entered my house with. At the bookcase, she pauses in front of my cherished collection of signed E. Lynn Harris novels, selecting *Just As I Am* from the lineup. It would serve her well to read it.

"Is this any good?" she asks, holding the book over her shoulder.

"It's very good. I cried at the end of it."

"May I borrow it?"

"Please do," I reply. There's no actual harm in playing along with her feigned interest. She could learn a lesson from it on how parents ought to treat their gay children, though I doubt she will even take the book once we finish our conversation.

Ma holds up a second book. "What in the world is *B-Boy Blues* about?"

She knows perfectly well she doesn't care about a James Earl Hardy novel any more than the E. Lynn Harris novel. Ma slides the book back in its place and picks up a framed photo of LaSaundra and me wearing hideous Christmas sweaters. She smiles.

"Look how happy the two of you are. She could've been my daughter-in-law."

I ignore the comment, having no interest in her version of what could've been. I extend the letter to her. "I want you to look at this."

She snatches it from me, and I sit down on the sofa. Her eyes scroll across the first lines on the page. It isn't her first time reading the letter. She read it years ago. And back then, there was a fury in her eyes when she did.

When Ma finishes, she calmly folds it in half. "I thought I threw this away," she mutters.

"You did, but I fished it out of the trash. Thought it only appropriate to keep this as a memento from the night you threw me out of the house."

She sighs her exasperation. "Do we have to go through this again?"

"Yes!" I scream, losing my patience as I pound my fist on the coffee table. Ma flinches, startled by my visceral burst of emotion. "Because evidently you seem to think since you've moved past it, I should too."

"Well, yeah. I mean, it's been almost thirty years," Ma says, letting rip the sarcasm.

*Doesn't she see my hurt?* Revisiting that night is no walk in the park for me, either. We both have had the same number of years to work through this, but neither of us have. While I've settled into bitterness, Ma chooses to forget. But what she hasn't counted on is that I remember every detail of what happened that night.

It started when she invaded my bedroom. Ma yanked my earphone cord from the tape deck. Miche'le's "Something in My Heart" blasted through the stereo speakers. I sprang awake to face the wrath on her face and the singular vein pulsing on her forehead.

"What? *What?*" I shouted, jumping out of bed to shut off the music.

"You need to explain this shit to me," she demanded, squeezing my words from the twisted crumple of paper in her hands.

One look at that paper and I knew two things: one, she'd read the letter. Two, if I didn't calm her down, she would do to me what she'd done to the letter.

"Okay, okay. If we talk about this, we need to talk like rational human beings."

But she was beyond any semblance of reason. She was uninterested in being pacified; she wanted answers. "You mean to tell me you like *boys* now?"

It felt like one of Ma's ambushes; striking when I least expected it, and my defenses were down. It was as if she'd taken something personal that I'd spent years secretly trying to grow into and thrust it in my face half-baked. Her catching me off guard left me at a loss for what to say. Half-asleep, my otherwise reasonable vocabulary became cluttered inside my throat like a clogged pipe.

"Ain't nothin' you can say that's gonna make me accept this!" she hollered. Had the windows been open, she would've alerted the homeowners on either side of us of our family business.

"But…" I began.

"Boy, I'm gonna give you a choice," she said, eyeing me with disgust. "I'll either give you the razorblade to slit your own wrist, or I'll kill you myself, because I didn't raise you to be like that!"

Having my life threatened by my mother was worse than the multitude of times complete strangers had called me a faggot. Equally hurtful was the ease with which she did it. There was no compassion or understanding forthcoming. I sat upright in my bed, and for the next hour carefully chose words to dissuade Ma from physically harming me and to convince her that everything written in that letter was a reaction to what everyone thought of me. I told her I'd been getting called "fag" ever since grade school, and by high school, was conditioned to accept how others viewed me. But my efforts were in vain. Plez Sr. had been listening at my door and demanded that she kick me out because he couldn't have his son, Junior, exposed to my faggotry.

I hoped she would fight for me in a way that I couldn't fight for myself. She never did. The next day I was sent to live with my grandparents.

That evening haunted me for years, and while now as an adult I no longer care what she thinks, it would still be nice if she displayed a modicum of regret for the way she treated me. But from the way she plops down on the sofa and flips through *Just As I Am*, that isn't going to happen.

"I don't know why you're bringing up all this crap now. I mean, what's the point?" she says, emotion straining her voice.

"Because ever since Grandma passed, you've acted like we're supposed to just pick up like there's no bad blood between us. If you want to know why our relationship is the way it is, then you need to be honest."

Ma continues to flip pages; a sign of discomfort from being confronted.

"It's not going away just because you say so."

"It ain't gonna go away with you bringing it up!"

"You know, sometimes I really…"

"What?"

"Nothing."

"No, say what you were about to say."

"Sometimes I really hate you." There it is. Too big of a truth to take back. I've thought about it numerous times over the years, but kept it buried deep enough as to not make an unpleasant situation between us worse. Never once did I think I would be forced to say it out loud.

For a second, Ma looks at me as though she couldn't possibly have given birth to me. Her fingers draw inward, grasping at the fabric of her blouse. "You hate me?"

Despite her reaction, yes, I hate her. And sometimes, I wish my grandmother had been my mother.

Baffled, Ma continues to stare at me, her eyes bearing revelations. In them, I see her processing what I've said to her. The heat from my words incinerates her feelings. However, she isn't about to give me the satisfaction of seeing her cry. And though she resists her natural inclination to do so, her tears betray her and come anyway.

"And now?" she asks, wiping the tears from her face.

"And now what?"

"You still wish my mama was yours?"

I allow my silence to speak for me.

"Ah, okay. Well, while you're enjoying that fantasy, I'm sure you know it was my mama's idea to send your black ass to that Christian school to have you fixed."

She's playing dirty. Slinging my mud right back at me. It's a desperate move from a desperate woman, pissed that I hurt her feelings. Except, she's grinning at me. She's found the chink in my armor.

"Why do you think she insisted on paying your tuition?"

"You're lying."

"I ain't gotta lie to you, boy! Hell, you lived with my parents! You know how they are!"

"So, once again, you let someone else decide what was best for your child?"

"What do you want me to say, huh? I was fighting for my own survival. If that sounds selfish, tough shit! I did the best I could at the time!"

"Did you ever stop to think that maybe your best wasn't good enough?"

"What would you have had me do?" Ma asks, hurling years of inner conflict at me.

"*Fight for me!* You were always screaming at me to fight for my place in the family, but when you had the chance to save me, you gave up. And it wasn't the only time." And with that, an emotional weight lifts from my shoulders, followed by the reward of telling her she sucked as a parent.

"Save you? How was I supposed to save you when Plez was over there kicking my butt and playing his head games? And as for my mama, she knew I didn't have the money to pay your tuition. I accepted her conditions because after years of barely talking, we were finally in a good place. I didn't want to go back to not getting along."

"I'm glad you were able to do what was right for you."

"And on top of that, I had an abusive husband to contend with. You were right about him, you know?"

"This ought to be good. How so?"

"Remember when you used to say you thought Plez hated your guts? Well, he did. He hated everything about you."

"And why should he have felt any different? You cosigned some of the shit he would say!"

Ma looks at me like I'm talking crazy. "What are you talking about?"

"Do you remember when I was having trouble in school, and you were receiving a bunch of calls from my teachers?"

"Yeah?"

"Well, around that time, I overheard you and Plez talking about me. You thought I was asleep but I had gotten up to use the bathroom. You were upset because you didn't think I was applying myself to my schoolwork. Plez told you to accept the fact that I was stupid. I waited in the hallway, hoping you'd defend me. But no, you know what you said instead? You said, 'I know he is.'"

"How was I supposed to know you heard that?"

"Because you heard me go into the bathroom and start crying. When I went in, your bedroom door was open. By the time I finished my business it was closed. You knew how he felt about me and yet, you stayed married to him!"

"As I said, I did the best I could in the moment. Believe me, sometimes I wish I never met Plez Darnell Jackson, but if I hadn't, I wouldn't have Junior."

The mention of those two bullies makes me want to throw up. She has no idea how often I've tried imagining a world without them. However, Ma must've read my mind because she adds that it's a damn shame I don't get along with my brother, blaming Plez for it.

"Which one?" I ask.

"Senior. He's the one who came between you and me and put nasty thoughts into your brother's head to make him hate you, too. If you want to be mad at someone, be mad at Plez Sr. But stop punishing me for things that happened a long time ago."

*A long time ago?* How about everything since she married her fake-ass pastor? Like the time she tricked me into coming to see him preach, only to have me sit through an entire sermon about the so-called "Gay Agenda." Or the countless looks of disgust he tossed in my direction whenever he was around?

"And don't go putting all that shit on Tyrell," Ma says, correctly guessing my reaction. "I've wanted to accept you being gay, but I still struggle with it. It isn't the life I would've chosen for you."

"I didn't choose it for myself, either."

"*I know,*" she says with a lilt of exhaustion.

"Then, if you know, why are we arguing?"

"Unlike Tyrell, I don't have any moral objection to it."

"But what good is that when I can count the times you've watched him call me an abomination, and you didn't do or say shit to stop him!"

"I only go along with his nonsense so I don't have to hear his mouth. Hell, every damn thing I do is just to avoid getting into it with him."

Bad sign. She's already done the domineering husband routine. Living under Plez was like living in a house of terror. He trained her (and to some extent me) to kowtow to his whims and moods. If Tyrell is anything like Plez, he'll eventually graduate to beating her.

"Does he hit you?" I ask, doubting she'll tell me if it were true.

"No. He ain't crazy," she scoffs. "He's just old school in his thinking. He thinks the man is the head of the household and the wife must go along with everything the husband says."

I stare for a moment, waiting for her unconcerned facade to crack, but she's much too smart to allow her story to crumble under my scrutiny. "He thinks he's got you wrapped around his finger."

Ma gets up in a huff to put the book back in its place on the shelf. "I don't want to talk about him anymore."

"But he…"

"My issues with your sexuality have nothing to do with him."

"You're going to have to do better than that. You don't get to shut down the conversation because it's uncomfortable. It's a disgrace the way you let that man treat me."

"Do you know in all these years you've never brought a significant other to meet me?"

*Wait, what? She's deflecting now?* I say to myself.

"It's true."

"My love life isn't up for discussion."

"I'm trying to make a point here. When's the last time you introduced me to someone you were seeing?"

"I haven't."

"You're damn right you haven't."

"And why do you think that is? You've given no indication you would be receptive to me finding someone special. You can't even accept me being gay."

"I accept it. But I'm scared for you."

"Why, because of what happened to your friend?" I asked, rolling my eyes.

"Boy, I will slap them eyes off of your head! Who are you to shrug off my dearest friend? Clayton is the reason I became a nurse. He was such a wonderful example of what a nurse ought to be. And he sure as hell didn't deserve to get AIDS! Sure, times were different back then, but his parents still didn't have the right to toss him away. Maybe if they came around, he wouldn't have taken his own life. As a mother, I know I'm not perfect, but in my own way I've always tried to be supportive."

"Yeah, right."

"Look, I'm gonna be honest, I don't understand what makes you attracted to other men. But you're still my son, and I don't want anything bad to happen to you."

"What do you think is going to happen to me?"

"Aren't you listening? You could catch AIDS!"

"You act like I'm out here having all kinds of unprotected sex. I know the risks, and I protect myself. And a lot has changed since the early years. People aren't dropping like flies like they used to. As a nurse, you should know that."

She isn't reassured. "Maybe if you found a good, steady man, I wouldn't worry so much."

I laugh. "You, the queen of lousy judgment, are going to school me about the importance of finding a good man?"

"You know what? Forget it! I'm leaving." She walks to the door. Her hand grips the doorknob, but she whirls around. "First you tell me you hate me. Then you say you wish you had a different mother. If you want to spend the rest of your life angry with me, feel free!"

"Wait a sec," I call out, scrambling to get up from the sofa.

"The reason I hoped you'd find a good man is because…" her words trail off.

"What?"

When she hesitates, it crosses my mind that her running for the door is a ploy to get me to feel sorry for her.

"Seriously, Ma, what's wrong?"

"I'm not happy," she says, her eyes distant. "Not with Tyrell or with my life."

I knew it. He's probably figured out a way to beat her without leaving bruises. "What's really going on over there? Tell me the truth, is he putting his hands on you?"

"I said no!"

"Okay, then what's going on?"

"You know what? Never mind. I've probably said too much as it is."

"Ma, listen…"

"No, you listen!" Again, she hesitates. "It was a mistake to come here." She opens the door to the outside chill. "I hope one day you'll see that I never meant to hurt you. Maybe then you won't hate me anymore." She buttons her camel-colored overcoat before passing through the screen door. I catch it before it slams in my face. I'm disappointed with the way things have turned out, though not surprised. Still, I give her an A for effort even if I'm not ready to give her my forgiveness.

Ma backs out of my driveway, her car's tailpipe coughing out a departing breath of exhaust. A brisk fall wind blows the fumes into my house. I close my front door, but not before my moment of confusion turns into grave worry.

# EIGHTEEN

There's always construction… never-ending patches of disruption and inconvenience going on throughout the city. It's the same thing on I-35 W. Cranes and crushed concrete for miles. Past Diamond Lake Road, four lanes narrow down to two. And, as always, whenever there's any traffic impediment, people behave like first-time drivers, piddling along until the lanes open again on the 62 Crosstown.

Besides traffic woes, I divide my thoughts between Ma's parting words and how many callouts I can expect at work.

The moment I walk into the restaurant, there's no visible managerial presence. I stop by the office to hang my jacket, but the door is closed. I peek through the office window. Quish is talking to Sameer. Neither one of them looks happy. I lay my jacket on a prep table across from the hand sink. Someone has placed my shift setup on a nearby counter and crossed off seven employee names on it. Most of the seven are pains-in-the-ass who no doubt would've spent the entire shift trying to get sent home early anyway.

Seconds later, Sameer emerges from the office, red-faced. He breezes past me without speaking. I follow him to the fry station. "What's wrong?"

"I'm being transferred," he says, angrily lowering a basket of fries into the oil vat and sets the timer.

I step out of the way of flying speckles of grease. "When and where?"

"Tomorrow. Hiawatha."

"Yikes. Do you want to grab a beer after work?"

Sameer offers a weak smile. "You read my mind."

\*\*\*\*\*

After our hectic shift, Sameer suggests Champps Sports Bar on West Seventh Street because it's close by. The place is packed. The Minnesota Vikings game is on every flat screen across the room, which explains why most of the patrons are wearing yellow and purple-colored jerseys and filled with an uproarious competitive spirit. Sameer and I follow the scent of fried bar food to a high table tucked away in a corner. There is a large flat-screen TV suspended above us, garnering much attention from those within our vicinity. Some people are staring at us. Looks vary from casual glances to typical drunk, tough-guy attempts to intimidate.

The server working our section is busy with a table of blonde twenty-something women, coquettishly twirling their hair. I glance at my watch. The ladies are cutting into my drinking time. Finally, my eyes connect with the server and I wave him over. Up close he's a cutie. Light-skin and light eyes. Possibly bi-racial. Lenny Kravitz-inspired Afro. He introduces himself as EJ and informs us of a two-for-one special going on until midnight. He advises us to order any food quickly because the kitchen is closing soon. We order two Jager shots and a couple of draft beers. Sameer adds an order of chicken nachos to split.

It's odd sitting in a bar with Sameer. He's hardly my first choice for a drinking buddy. The only other time we've interacted socially was at a holiday party held at Quish's house. Sameer brought his wife, Anaya, who, after five very potent eggnogs, told anyone who would listen that she couldn't wait to get pregnant. Later, she threw up all over the kitchen's linoleum floor.

EJ returns with beers and shots on a black drink tray. A lingering glance passes between him and Sameer. After EJ walks away, I clink shot glasses with Sameer.

"Do you find him attractive?" he asks after shooting back his Jager.

"He's reasonably attractive, sure. You?"

Sameer shrugs, dragging his hand through his thick, wavy, black hair.

I sip my beer. "So, what's on your mind?"

Sameer's face sours. "My life is a mess."

"In what way?"

"My wife left me."

"Oh, man," I reply, feeling a sudden kindred-spiritedness towards him. Sure, LaSaundra moving out isn't the same as a spouse calling it quits, but I relate to the loneliness of returning to an empty house.

Sameer gulps his beer. "She found a gay porn site in my search history on our computer. I guess I forgot to delete it."

"What did she say?"

"She asked me if there was something we needed to discuss. I told her yes and that I'm gay. She said she wanted to remain married, that we could work out an arrangement because she wanted children."

"Very progressive of her." I try to sound as though there's a silver lining in an otherwise dismal situation.

"They frown on homosexuality in my home country, but what she proposes, I'm not sure I can live with that."

When I ask if he's the least bit attracted to her, he explains that whenever she initiates sex, he comes up with an excuse. The times they have intercourse, he rushes to have an orgasm. I listen to him, wondering how either gets any fulfillment from the sex. It can't be enjoyable for her if it's barely tolerable for him.

"So how do you get it up?" I ask.

Sameer looks down bashfully. "There's someone I think about during sex. Anyway, I told her I wanted out of the marriage."

"Good. You were being honest. What did she say to that?"

"She reminded me of our arranged marriage and threatened to tell everyone we know back in India. Next thing I know, she's on a flight back to New Delhi. Now everyone is going to know what I am." His eyes hold an expectancy that I'll reassure him everything will work itself out.

Before I muster an attempt to give him that, I'm startled by cheers erupting throughout the bar.

"Well, the good news is you don't have to hide who you are anymore," I say once the noise level returns to normal.

"But my family will disown me."

"Are you sure she told them?"

"No, but I suspect any day now I'm going to get a call from my parents telling me I've disgraced my entire family."

"They could come around. You never know."

"My parents are religious conservatives. They would rather have a murderer for a son than a practicing homosexual."

"You've been cheating on your wife?"

He puts a hand to God and says, "Never. Sometimes I thought I could compartmentalize it. Maybe find a special friend with whom I could explore this side of myself."

Sameer's frankness is a refreshing contrast to his usual aloofness that I'm better acquainted with. I'm flattered that he's chosen me as his confidant, and my heart goes out to him. Sure, it is rough having family members disapprove of my sexuality, but I would never go so far in search of their approval as to marry a woman. It's a lot of pressure to put on one's self, not to mention unfair to the woman because she'll never receive the love she deserves. Hearing Sameer speak of his inner turmoil, I'm thankful that I own the courage to live my life truthfully.

We drain our beer mugs. He flags down our server to order another round.

"You know, one time I went down to that bar on Hennepin Avenue," he says once the server leaves our table.

"Sparkles?"

He tells me he's made it all the way to the door, but can't bring himself to go inside. Another time he thought about driving over to the cruising area around Loring Park, but knew the temptation to cheat would be too great, and didn't believe Anaya deserved to be two-timed like that. That was admirable. A lot of guys in Sameer's situation say to hell with it and cheat.

The second round of drinks arrives right on time, followed shortly by nachos. Sameer picks up a tortilla chip stretched with melted cheese. He chuckles. "You know, I almost wish I had done it. Maybe then all of this would be worth it."

"I know it seems that way, but you did the right thing."

He doesn't seem convinced. After guzzling his beer down to the midway point, he says, "I'm not looking forward to starting at Hiawatha tomorrow."

"Not to freak you out, but it's rough over there. I heard they can't keep staff, plus they've been robbed seven times."

"Great. Who needs to worry about being outed? I'll probably get shot first."

"I don't enjoy working at street locations for that very reason."

Sameer excuses himself and heads to the bathroom. On his way, he speaks to EJ and orders another round of shots.

When Sameer returns, he asks, "How many street stores have you worked at?"

"Just Richfield. Then I transferred to the airport. Been there ever since. Knock on wood I'm there until I decide to do something else.

"Lucky you." He raises his shot. Again, we clink glasses and toss back the liquor.

"You know, it's crazy that we're here together like this. I always thought you hated my guts."

Sameer finishes the rest of his beer and watches the TV monitor across the way, leaving me on the line with my observation. More game cheering erupts throughout the bar.

I switch gears to talk about reality TV. To my surprise, Sameer is a fan of *The Real Housewives* series on BRAVO TV. It's hard to believe he actually knows who Nene Leakes is.

After we finish the nachos, we have one more round of beer before I signal to our server to bring the check. "I think it's time to head out."

"Was it something I said?" Sameer jokes.

"Not at all. I figure we both need to still get home in one piece. You're starting at a new restaurant tomorrow. I don't think you want to show up good and smashed."

"I guess not."

After I pay the tab, we head out to the parking lot. Our cars are parked side by side beneath a flickering streetlamp.

"You'll be okay to get home, right?"

Sameer stands there, glassy-eyed with hands in pockets.

"Hey, man, are you okay?" I ask, giving his shoulder a friendly nudge.

"I hate going home to an empty house," he replies.

"Me too. Story of my life. But you're okay to drive, right?"

Sameer doesn't answer.

I wave my hand in front of his face. "You know, I'd feel a lot better if I knew you're going to be okay to drive."

He nods and slowly approaches me. He stops in his tracks the moment a couple of drunks come outside. One of them yells to the other that he needs some pussy. The other laughs, and steps away from his friend as though he's been given an indecent proposition, and says, "Man, that sounds like a personal problem!"

Sameer waits until they drive off to continue inching into my personal space. His eyes are dark and romantic. He sensuously glides his tongue across his sepia-colored lips.

He caresses my face with large, soft hands. I had no idea he could be this tender. I watch his supple mouth open, then draw closer, making his intention known.

A surge of longing enters my body as Sameer pushes his tongue into my mouth, his kiss forceful and desperate.

Momentarily dazed, and despite enjoying our lip lock, I push him away. "We shouldn't be doing this,"

Sameer looks as though he's awakened from a deep trance. "I'm sorry. I shouldn't have done that. You said earlier that you thought I hated you. The truth is, I'm very much attracted to you."

I chuckle. "You could've fooled me. You're so serious most of the time. I never would've guessed."

"It's true. I've never hated you. If anything, I'm jealous of your freedom. You get to live a life unencumbered."

"Looks can be deceiving. My life is far from unencumbered."

We're silent. It's the perfect moment for us to say goodnight and go to our cars, but neither of us moves. I remain where I am, swimming in Sameer's gaze, all the while undressing him with my mind. His body is composed of solid, lean muscle; his dick is probably long and slender, curving downward. I would love to claw through his thick head of shiny, black hair, and feel the soft tickle of his silky chest hair against my bare skin as he stares at me with stern intensity. The prospect of giving myself to him causes my body to shudder with anticipatory delight.

But how do I know Sameer isn't just another Byron, a good-for-nothing who wants his cake and to eat it too? Maybe his wife is really at home, unaware of her husband's predilections.

"I want you to come home with me," he says finally.

"I'm sorry, but as much as I want to, I can't." Sameer has no idea how much it pains me to say it, especially with a cold, empty bed waiting for me at home. To justify my answer, I point to the gold band on his left hand. "Besides, you're a married man."

"This means nothing to me!" Sameer yells, like a wolf calling to the moon. He pulls the ring from his finger and flings it across the parking lot. "Now will you please come home with me?"

I don't know what else to say beyond "no," but I can't walk away. Sameer senses my hesitation and approaches me again, grabbing me firmly.

"I want you in my bed," he moans, bringing me in for another kiss. His tongue is greedier than before. We're so involved in our connection, neither of us hears the car pull up beside us.

"Hey, this ain't San Francisco!" the driver shouts from his open window. "Take that faggot-shit somewhere else!" He screeches off laughing.

"I'm sorry, I have to go. It's better this way," I say, escaping to the driver's side of my car and ignoring the arousal happening in the crotch of my pants. After buckling the seatbelt, I put the key in and turn the ignition. After putting the car into drive, I'm off, leaving Sameer standing alone and equally aroused.

On the freeway, Diana Ross and the Supremes sing "Forever Came Today" on the oldies station. It's difficult to shake the memory of Sameer's warm, thick lips and the prickle of his stubble against my chin.

I think fondly of those fleeting drunken times I picked Sameer from my mental Rolodex of sexual fantasies to jerk off to. I would imagine the close nakedness of our glistening bodies; the air scented by his soft, exotic musk. Would it have been so wrong to offer myself to Sameer for his first time? What harm would it have done, when it's unlikely we'll see each other again, or at least not regularly? Hakee isn't in the picture. Maybe a night with Sameer would satisfy my own lonely heart. What would it have hurt to find passing companionship with each other?

I wish I had Sameer's number. I want to tell him I've reconsidered. The strummed chords of the song, "Love Is Here and Now You're Gone" begins. I exhale, resigning myself to the fact Sameer will just have to be an opportunity for dick that got away.

On the way home, I stop by my neighborhood SuperAmerica to get some gas. I'm about to pay at the pump, but an attendant both LaSaundra and I know is working inside.

"Hey, DeAndre! When did you start working the late shift?"

"When I realized the rent was due and I wouldn't have money left after paying it."

"Ain't nothing wrong with doing what you gotta do, right?"

"Exactly. You're coming from the bar?"

"Sports bar."

" A sports bar? Well, aren't you just full of surprises?"

"I want to put forty on pump four, and I'm going to grab a few things. Do you mind?"

"Mind what? It's your money. Besides, it's been pretty quiet the last couple of hours. You'll be giving me something to do."

I walk away from the counter to begin my jaunt down the snack aisle. My impulse shopping kicks in. I select a bag of chips and a box of miniature powdered donuts from the dry food shelf and grab two tuna sandwiches from the cooler.

"By the way, I have a bone to pick with that roommate of yours," DeAndre says.

Why is he bringing up that bitch? I roll my eyes. "I think you mean my ex-roommate."

"Uh-oh. Spill the tea. Whatcha'll goin' through?"

I hadn't intended to tell LaSaundra's business, but it's late and I'm a little tipsy and a tad petty. While adding a two-liter of soda to my finds, I reply, "She accused someone I'm interested in of stealing her bank card."

"Now, she knows she needs to stop all that," DeAndre says, waving his hand dismissively.

"Stop what?" I ask, returning to the counter.

"Tellin' stories."

"What are you talking about? What stories?"

"Ain't nobody stole her damn bank card. She left it in the ATM, but she got it back."

There's no way my best friend *lied* to me. "What do you mean?"

"It was my second to last day shift before I started taking overnight shifts. Usually, she pays at the pump, but that day she came in to use the cash machine. We spoke for a little bit, and then she went to use the machine. I heard the machine dispense her money and saw her pick it up. But then a panhandler got into a fight with another customer over something said about him being a bum. They started fighting and ended up where LaSaundra was standing. I literally saw her jump to get out of the way. I figure in all the excitement she must've forgotten her card after making her withdrawal."

My eyes squint with confusion. "I thought you're supposed to dip your card and take it out."

"Yeah, with newer machines. But we got one of those old models. The machine keeps your card until the transaction is complete."

"How do you know she got it back?"

"Because, after the two guys left the store, I heard the beeping alert coming from the machine. I guess it's supposed to warn the user to take their card, but since she was scared away by the two fools fighting, she took the money but forgot her card."

"That still doesn't tell me how you know she got it back."

DeAndre puts his hand on his hip, annoyed with my slow comprehension skills this time of night. "Because I gave the thang to her!"

"How soon after she lost it?"

He pauses to scan the items. I tell him to put sixty bucks on pump four instead of forty. Then, I give him my debit card to swipe. We wait for the card authorization. My tired eyes ache from the unusually bright fluorescent lighting.

Finally, DeAndre finishes his thought. "The very next day. When I told her she'd left it in the machine, she got a funny look on her face, like she knew the jig was up. Then she snatched the card from me when I handed it to her. I should've just let the machine eat it up, or let somebody take it."

"I can't believe it. So that means when she was raising all that hell, she had the damn card the entire time?" I feel like the victim of a cruel prank everyone else is in on except me.

"Boo, that's your friend!"

"No, LaSaundra's many things, but she's not a grimy person. She wouldn't do that to me." I reply, hoping if I say it out loud it will make it true.

DeAndre gives me back my card, accompanied by a look that says I should know better. "You sure about that?"

I want to say that yes, I am sure. But what I *actually* say is nothing at all.

# NINETEEN

The next day the house is chilly. The cold makes me prone to sleeping late. I don't roll out of bed until the afternoon. After adjusting the thermostat, I make myself a bowl of cereal.

My phone chirps, alerting me to several text messages and missed calls. The first text is from Ma. She hates the way we left things and suggests getting together for lunch next week. She asks me to text her back right away because there's something else she wants to discuss. But I'm in no hurry to reply. I erase the text. Yes, I'm also unhappy with how we left things, but unless she plans to come correctly and admit her fault in this, there isn't anything else to talk about.

The next series of calls are from Sameer. I had no idea he knew my phone number. The first voicemail left was at two in the morning. Between the street noise and Sameer's sobbing, I barely understand him. In a follow-up text, he says succinctly, "I'm sorry."

If I'd known how much of a mess Sameer was, I wouldn't have been so quick to dash off. I understand all too well the emotional upheaval that happens when a person deviates from societal expectation to embrace their authentic self. Been there, done that, bought the T-shirt, and screwed around in it. Knowing what I've been through with my family, the church, and the usual bigots, I should've been more sympathetic towards Sameer than I was.

Another voicemail marked at eleven this morning. It's from Quish, informing me that Sameer didn't show up at the Hiawatha location. No one has heard from him. I get the sinking feeling one gets when someone they know goes missing. Two dark scenarios come to mind... what if they find him chopped up behind an abandoned building in some desolate part of town or naked with a slit wrist in a bathtub of overflowing bloody water?

Quish requests me to come into work because she's already promised the management over at Hiawatha another employee since they're already down three people. It's her way of "gathering nuts for the winter" as she calls it, which means sending our employees to other restaurant sites to help so when our restaurant needs help with staffing during the Holiday seasons, she can call in favors to get help. In the voicemail, she sounds more annoyed than concerned, and upon hearing it I don't call her back immediately. Instead, I dial the number attached to Sameer's text. But the call goes directly to voicemail, worsening the sinking feeling in my gut. *Hey you,* I tap quickly on the texting keyboard. *Hope you're doing okay. Worried about you. Call me.* I hit send.

The last text is from Kenyatta: *Hey, Boo! Moved into my new place. Thought we'd go out and celebrate. You won't even have to buy my booze. Surprised?*

I'm no longer interested in exposing myself to his selfishness. And there's no way I can respond to Kenyatta's text without cursing him out. Instead, I delete the message and resume eating my cereal before it becomes too soggy.

The more I think about it, Kenyatta isn't worth the time or effort to curse him out. After DeAndre's late-night revelation, that energy will be better used to confront LaSaundra. I call her. The phone rings continuously until I hang up to dial again. Another series of rings. I try one last time. This time the phone rings twice before cutting off. I send a quick text telling her to call me, then slurp down sugary cereal milk.

An hour passes, and still nothing from Sameer. I call the restaurant to ask the manager on duty for Sameer's address. I'm flustered when Quish answers the phone.

"You're just now getting back to me? I called you hours ago!" Her tone rattles me, forcing me to cough up an excuse.

"I just now got your message."

"Yeah, right. We got our asses handed to us today. I wish I hadn't promised Hiawatha an extra person, and Sameer never bothered to show up."

"About that. Can you look at his file and give me his address? I'm worried about him."

"The only person who needs to be worried is Sameer. He can kiss his job goodbye."

"No, Quish, there's something going on with him. We went out for drinks after the close last night and he told me some personal things going on in his life right now. I think something may have happened to him. That, or he did something desperate to himself."

"What's his problem?"

I paused. "I'd rather not say."

"Are you sure this isn't just him being pissed about being transferred?"

"No, it's something else. Anyway, I'd like to check up on him."

"Why don't you get the cops to do a wellness check? I mean, you don't know what you might walk into."

She has a point. Still, I'm partially responsible. Quish clears her throat when I don't offer an immediate response. After a dramatically long sigh, she says, "Gimme a sec."

She gives me the address, though not without informing me that I'm being foolish. To smooth things over with her, I offer to work, not because I expect her to accept the offer, but so I can appear conscientious.

"By the time you get here, the worst will be over with. So, no. Let me know the story with Sameer."

I agree to keep her informed and hang up. I jump into the shower, hoping Sameer calls or texts while I wash up. I'm not looking forward to driving all the way out to South St. Paul, but I'd want someone to check up on me if the shoe were on the other foot.

After my shower, Kenyatta calls as I'm drying off. I'm tempted to let the phone ring, but it's been ages since we last spoke, not to mention a rare occurrence that Kenyatta would call first.

"Yeah?" I answer as nastily as I can.

"Eeew. What's wrong with you?"

"I just got out of the shower."

"Oh. Well, do you want me to call you back?"

If I respond yes, I won't hear from him again. Then, if I bitch about it, he'll remind me I had my chance to talk when he called the first time.

"No, you're good."

"Uh, do you have some allergy to returning texts that I don't know about?"

"Things have been crazy."

"Give me the tea."

"Nothing in particular. There's just been a lot going on."

"Oh." Kenyatta already sounds bored. "Anyway, I thought I would call your ass to see if you want to go out tonight. I can't remember the last time I saw you."

"Oooh! Oooh! Oooh! I know!" I reply, feigning excitement. "It was the night you ditched me for a random stranger."

"Travelle isn't random. Chile, I've had my eye on him for months."

"Oh, excuse me. My mistake. I could've sworn you had volunteered to be my ride home that night."

"Boy, you're still salty about that? You got Uber on your phone, don't you?"

Usually, the crap he says doesn't surprise me. But this time he gets me to say, "Wow, Kenyatta. Just wow."

"Don't act like you wouldn't have done the same thing if there was a guy you'd been trying to get with forever and a day."

"I ain't like you. I just hope he was worth it."

"Chile, he was *beyond* worth it. That man beat the brakes off my pussy!"

*Okay, he's got me with that one*, I think to myself, bursting into laughter. "You're nasty."

"No, I'm not. You're just jealous."

"That's funny. Tell another one." My voice is still elevated from laughter.

"I'm dead serious. When's the last time somebody's been up in your stuff?"

My body shudders in memory of the night Hakee and I spent together. I'm about to speak his name when Kenyatta lapses into an explanation of how being kicked out of his last apartment is a blessing in disguise. He's settling well into his new place, a room in his cousin's restored Victorian home she shares with her husband.

"They agreed to let me stay there for fifty dollars a month! Can you believe that shit? It's highway robbery, I tell you!"

"Fifty bucks isn't a lot considering what most people pay in rent."

"Yeah, but it's more than what I really want to pay. They ain't hurtin' for money. They could help a brother out."

It astounds me how self-entitled Kenyatta is. How quickly he forgets his responsibility for why he no longer pays what he once did in rent. He continues to blather on about how no one understands his plight. I put the phone on speaker and get dressed, listening for pauses in Kenyatta's soliloquy to interject a "yep" and "mmm, hmm."

"But, chile, you'll never guess the real tea!"

"Let me have it."

"I've been trying to figure out where I recognize my cousin's husband from. Then I realized it was from back in the day when he was trolling the adult bookstores."

"How sure are you?" I ask, admittedly intrigued by this morsel of gossip.

"Seventy-five percent."

"You aren't going to say anything, are you?"

Long pause. He's just grimy enough to enjoy wielding the power to destroy a marriage. "I don't know, yet. Depends how I feel."

The doorbell rings. "Listen, I might see you later at the bar. I gotta go." I end the call before Kenyatta responds. I peek through the blinds to see Nadine and LaTavia standing on the front steps. A flashback of Junior pushing his way into the house comes to mind, but thankfully he's not with them.

"I'm leaving your brother," Nadine announces upon the door opening.

I give her the once over, searching for fresh bruises or broken limbs. From the looks of it, she seems physically fine, and the bruising beneath her eye is virtually gone.

"Great. Does he know?"

"No. I waited until he went to work."

I'm cautiously relieved, though, after the last time, I don't look forward to telling her she can't stay here.

"Where were you planning on moving to?"

"Oh, don't worry," she says, reading my mind. "I'm not staying. I've got a friend out-of-state I'm going to live with until I can get on my feet."

"Awesome! Where does your friend live?"

"I'd rather not say. If you don't know, you're one less person Junior will have to force to tell him."

"I appreciate that, but you're taking his daughter across state lines. You don't want to mess around and get charged with kidnapping, do you?"

Nadine looks down at LaTavia, who stares at me with curious wonderment, as if seeing me for the first time.

"I'm doing this for my daughter. I don't want her growing into womanhood thinking a beating is normal. And I don't want to continue living in fear. I don't want to wonder if the next time he beats me, it's gonna leave my daughter without a mother."

"I hear you, and I completely understand, but I don't think you want the cops on your tail. Junior will make you out to be an unfit mother."

"But you can attest to what I've been through. Hell, you can tell them what your brother did to you!"

Just like that, anxiety floods my system like a virus. It's as though Junior is right here, ready to smash my door in. "With all due respect, I'm not sure I want to get involved in any of this. I mean, couldn't you file for an order of protection?"

"There's no time for that. As soon as we get into that car, we're out. What Plez feels or thinks about it makes me no never mind. I've been saving and have a decent little nest egg. It isn't much, but it'll get me through until I can get stable."

I have to give her credit; she's thought this through. No wishy-washy back and forth. Her mind is definitively made up.

"I guess I'm not sure why you've come here."

"Because I won't forget the way you stood up to your brother on my behalf. No one has ever done that for me before. I felt bad that he hurt you. I just wanted you to know that I really appreciate what you tried to do for me."

"You won't believe how terrified I was. Not for me, but it worried me that he was going to kill you."

"That night, he was acting really crazy. It was different from the other times. He went out for about an hour, and I went to sleep. I figured he couldn't argue with the sleeping. I also put LaTavia in bed with me because I knew he wouldn't try to hurt me if our daughter was close by."

"But he did, didn't he?" I ask, taken by the suspense of her story.

"When he came home, he came into the bedroom and said, 'Wake up, bitch! You ain't sleep!' But I just laid there as still as I could, praying he would leave me alone. He went out of the room for what seemed like forever, and I still didn't move. Then, he came back and stood at the foot of the bed, watching me. I heard what I thought was someone cocking a gun. I couldn't open my eyes because I didn't want him to know I was awake. But, when I heard him say, 'I should just kill the bitch,' I was so scared, I peed on myself!"

"Oh, my goodness. I'm so sorry he did that to you." I don't know whether I'd have the balls to withstand the unspeakable terror Nadine must've experienced that night.

"So, you see why I can't wait around for him to make good on that?"

"Of course."

"I prayed to God that night, if He allowed me to see daylight, I would walk away. Since then, I've been doing things to prepare for this, not knowing when exactly, just that it had to be done. Today is the day."

"Will you do me a favor? Can you please make sure when you get to where you're going that you let my mother know where you are?"

After some hesitation, she agrees.

"Aren't you worried he'll track you down like he did last time?"

"No. I bought a pay-as-you-go phone. It's charged and ready to go. And I traded my car in for a clunker he won't recognize."

"Sounds like you've thought of everything."

"I really hope you'll change your mind about telling the cops what you know…if it comes to that."

"I will."

Nadine puts a hand to her chest, relieved to have my support. I count one hundred dollars from my wallet and hand it to her. "Use this however you see fit. Good luck to you."

"Thank you so much. You're a good man, Lawrence."

"Thanks. Glad someone thinks so," I reply with a smile.

"Wave bye-bye to Uncle Lawrence, LaTavia," Nadine instructs her daughter. The child smiles shyly and hides behind her mother's leg.

"I'm on my way out. I'll walk you two to your car." I escort them out to a nondescript midnight-blue vehicle. Nadine belts LaTavia into her car seat and closes the rear passenger door.

"Thanks for everything," she says and hugs me. Had we made the effort, we could've been great friends. It's too bad my abusive brother had to be the common denominator between us. As I watch them drive away, my neighbor from across the street pulls into his driveway. The slim, middle-aged man gets out of the car and makes his way to the trunk to unload groceries. He halts as if realizing he's being watched. He waves at me. I wave back, then turn my focus back to Nadine's car, now a moving dot in the distance, driving towards freedom.

# TWENTY

The sun sinks behind the clouds as I drive to Sameer's place. Traffic is hellish. When I finally get there, I find his car parked outside a modest yellow bungalow. A faint light glows inside the house. I park across the street and call Sameer's phone. No answer. I send a text announcing that I'm outside. Minutes pass as I wait for a reply that never comes.

A man walking his boxer puppy pauses to allow the dog to squat in front of Sameer's yard and do its business. He inverts a poop baggie and bends down to pick up the dog's feces, all the while keeping a suspicious eye on me. I get out of my car. Both the boxer and man are on alert. The dog growls as I approach. The man tightens his grip on the leash.

"Hey there," I say, using my professional-sounding voice to allay the man's suspicion.

The man slowly loosens the leash around his wrist, lessening his grip. He eyes me warily. "Good evening," he says in an unfriendly tone. He gives me the impression he's going to stand there and watch me until I leave.

"I'm a colleague of Sameer's. Do you know him?"

He considers my question for a moment, deciding whether I'm worthy of a reply. His face relaxes. Sensing its owner relax, the dog stops snarling. The man says, "I don't *know* him, know him. We're friendly."

The boxer approaches my legs and feet and sniffs merrily. Only seconds before it behaved as though it wanted to taste my blood.

"We missed him at work today," I lie, extending my hand for the dog to sniff. "Thought I'd check on him." I resent explaining myself. Yes, I'm a stranger to this man, but I doubt he would be this concerned if my skin were shades lighter. But I better stay cool, otherwise, this guy could turn into another George Zimmerman on me.

The dog soon loses interest and returns to its owner's side.

"Frankly, I see his wife more than I see him," he says, his tone becoming less antagonistic. "Is there something wrong?"

"I honestly don't know. I hope not."

"Well, I suppose I should be on my way," he said, imparting a smile. "C'mon, Bailey." He gives the boxer's leash a slight tug, and the dog follows obediently.

From my peripheral view, a shadow passes through Sameer's living room window. I sprint up the pebbled walkway onto crumbling steps leading up to a white iron screen door. I ring the doorbell and listen closely, but hear neither a bell nor chime. I open the screen door, which swings out and back, slapping against the back of my shoulder with a padded snap. I knock on the front door. White Chantilly-like lace hangs on the door's interior window. I ring the doorbell again. My casual knocks turn into urgent pounding. Still nothing. I give up, letting the screen slam shut.

The cold annoys me. But my curiosity burns hot, guiding me to the rear of the house. I peek through every sheer-curtained window along the way until I spy Sameer in a bedroom, slumped on the floor, his back against the wall. He looks dazed and disheveled like he's been drinking all day. I knock on the window.

"Fuck off!" Sameer screams, staring straight ahead without flinching.

I back away from the window. One of his neighbors watches through her kitchen window. I stare directly into her eyes and say loud enough for her to hear, "Just here to check on my friend."

Alarmed, the woman pulls her blinds closed. Seconds later, the room goes dark. I hightail it back to my car before I hear the blare of a police siren.

*****

Disappointment and anger hang like a storm cloud the entire drive home. On the one hand, I'm glad Sameer is alive, but it pisses me off that I wasted a drive all the way out there for him not to answer his damn door. Then again, he's going through something life-changing and is dealing with it the only way he knows how. Lord knows I've done more than my fair share of sorrow drowning with booze. I figure I'll text him later to let him know I'm available if he wants to talk. After that, the ball is in his court whether he wants to take me up on the offer.

I arrive home to find an enormous, black truck parked in the driveway. Inside the house, lights are on that weren't when I left. Someone propped open both the screen and front doors. I enter the house. The backside of a tall, stocky man with a nice ass comes towards me, dragging LaSaundra's mattress. I move out of the way to allow the man to pass.

"Damn, baby, I can't wait to get this back to my crib. Think of all the damage we can do on it," he says.

"Yeah. It'll give you an excuse to throw away that raggedy thing you sleep on," LaSaundra replies, noticing me standing behind him.

"I like how you showed up unannounced, yet again," I tell her.

She waits until the man secures the mattress in the cargo bed of the truck to answer.

"What do you mean, 'yet again'? I texted you. Not my fault you don't read your messages. As for today, this was last minute. He had some time while on his work break and said he could help me move."

"So, this is who you've been staying with?"

"Yeah…my man. I'm allowed to do that. Lawrence meet Wesley. Wesley meet Lawrence."

Neither of us says hello. Wesley steps protectively in front of LaSaundra like some hired gun. He's a hulking mass of muscle with crazed eyes that disrupts an otherwise handsome face. Eyes that communicate that all he needs is one word from her to pummel me, a job he'll gladly do.

"You good, baby?" he asks, posturing to do battle.

She hesitates long enough to put doubt in his mind. "Yeah, I'm good."

"Aiight. I'm gonna go in for the box spring." Wesley walks past, deliberately bumping me along the way. I breathe easier the moment he reenters the house.

"Now that your bodyguard is gone, do you mind explaining why you haven't returned my calls or texts?"

"To be perfectly honest, it was the lowest thing on my to-do list."

"What's with the attitude?" I snap.

"I don't have an attitude. I simply need to move in a different direction."

"Let me guess, that doesn't include me."

She folds her arms, staring at me with the coldest of indifference.

"I'll take that as a yes."

"You can't fault me for wanting something more out of life than to be your fag-hag. You probably thought we were gonna grow old together like a couple of spinsters."

"I never asked you to be my fag-hag, and I would never expect you to forego your own happiness."

"I'm glad you said that, because I don't want my life to go down the drain like yours."

"Damn, why don't you tell me how you really feel?" I scoff.

"I'm telling you. Not my fault you can't handle it."

"I'm grown. Of course, I can handle it!"

"Fine, then I'll tell you. You're a loser. And the sad thing about it is everyone knows it except you, Lawrence."

How long has she been holding on to this? Is she hitting below the belt out of anger or has she always felt this way? Either way, the insult stuns my mouth open to the point cold air floods it.

"You're comfortable enough with where your life is. Sure, you say you aren't, but you have no real ambition. All you do is work your dead-end job, sleep around, and drink yourself to death. Frankly, I can't believe I've hung around this long to watch."

Suddenly, it's like being in sixth grade all over again, when Jenny Cryer told me no one wanted to play with me anymore. That day's humiliation broke my young spirit. Now I'm getting the same rejection from LaSaundra, which causes my middle-aged lips to tremble. But unlike my younger self with Jenny then, I'll be damned if LaSaundra is going to see me cry this time.

"Who are you to judge me? Last I checked, you weren't setting the world ablaze your damn self!"

"You're absolutely right! And as long as I'm associated with you, I never will. I'm not gonna allow you to take me down with you. It's time we go our separate ways."

Responding to LaSaundra's raised voice, Wesley appears at the door on high alert. "Eh, you aiight, baby?"

"Yes, I'm fine. we're just talking."

He grimaces like someone wiping dog shit from his shoe. Only after LaSaundra nods does he retreat slowly from the door.

"Why do I get the feeling your boyfriend doesn't like gay people?"

"No, he just doesn't like you."

"I've done nothing to him to dislike."

"My happiness is his happiness. He understands my friendship with you doesn't make me happy."

"Or he's just whipped."

"Yeah, well, my man actually sticks around after screwing me. Where's yours? Oh, I forgot, you don't have one!"

LaSaundra's recent machinations come to mind. "Yeah, thanks to you!"

"Don't blame me because you can't hold a relationship together!"

"I'm not talking generally. I mean because of that little stunt you pulled."

"What stunt?"

Now, the bitch is playing dumb? She knows good and well what I'm talking about. It pisses me off to have to explain it to her.

"I'm talking about accusing Hakee of stealing your bank card when you had it the entire time! I'm talking about publicly humiliating the one decent person I've met in a long time!"

"What, so you and your starving artist can be losers together? My bad!"

"So, you admit you lied?"

LaSaundra sighs hard and throws her arms up. "Fine, I lied! Big deal! I did what I had to do to get out of a suffocating situation."

"Did it ever dawn on you that you could've just told me the truth?"

"I'm telling you the truth now. And I bet it hurts, doesn't it?" she says, pushing past me to rejoin Wesley in the house.

Dejected, I get into my car before LaSaundra and her goon come back outside. The word *loser* sits in my head like a song lyric that won't go away. I start up the car and take off down the street, unsure of where I'm going next, and leaving what is left of my self-respect blowing in the autumn wind.

# TWENTY-ONE

Diego is working the door at Sparkles. I approach, holding my ID up to deflect the bouncer's unfriendliness. He looks up from his phone only for a second and brusquely waves me through, never bothering to check the ID. I say thank you. Diego says nothing.

A beautiful trans woman asks whether I'm interested in having dinner. I nod. She seats me at a table in the main bar. Her gold, dolman-sleeved gown shimmers with her every step.

"Carlo will be your server," she says, placing an oversized, laminated menu in front of me. She walks away, leaving a powdery, musk scent to keep me company.

Elderly men pack the room, looking as though they've arrived from an assisted living facility. They are probably here to enjoy the prime rib Early Bird special.

A handsome, bearded black man walks by, dressed all in black, reminding me of Shaft. His leather coat looks as though it's cold and hard to the touch. He's wearing Aramis, a cologne Junior's father used to bathe in. I'm surprised they still make it. He grins, showing a multitude of gold fillings. The stretch of his skin ages him by at least five years. I return his smile until he's out of my view, and then my face goes flat.

Carlo presents separate checks to a table of six. As I wait, a spiky-haired, bleached-blonde lesbian in an ill-fitting satin tuxedo tickles the ivories with "The Girl from Ipanema."

Someone from a neighboring table of senior citizens complains about autumn, blaming the ensuing cold for worsening his gout. Another man worries the potatoes from his meal have spiked his blood sugar. It will be only a matter of time before I'm sitting at a table with my peers, rattling off a litany of aches and pains.

Carlo arrives at my table, carrying a pitcher of water and a scowl on his face. He smiles obligatorily as he pours water into a red, textured, plastic cup. He's cute, sloe-eyed with sexy full lips and wet, just out of the shower black hair. A large spit curl swoops across the middle of his creased forehead.

"Rough night?" I ask.

Carlo rolls his eyes. "Honey, don't get me started," he replies, taking his pen from the chest pocket of his uniform. He uses it to point to the list of dinner specials.

"I should tell you we're out of the prime rib. Sold my last piece just now."

"No problem. I was more interested in the pan-fried walleye pike. Can I also have steak fries instead of rice pilaf?"

"Certainly," he says, sliding the addendum back inside the menu and places it beneath his underarm. "Can I interest you in anything to drink besides water?"

"A Manhattan, please."

"You got it, sweetie," Carlo says with a wink.

A man requests the song, "And I Am Telling You" from *Dreamgirls*. He puts money into the pianist's glass bowl. From her face, I can tell she doesn't know the song. She gets up, lifts the top of her bench, and rummages through scores of sheet music, no doubt hoping she doesn't find it. Eventually, she does. She lets down the bench seat, takes a deep breath, and awkwardly plunks away to the song.

Before my dinner arrives, I go to the restroom. Two guys are at the urinals, staring at each other's dicks. Startled by my presence, one man quickly flushes and leaves without washing his hands. The other smiles goofily. I smile back and wash my hands.

Passing an alternate entrance to the happy-hour lounge, I hear Kenyatta's distinctive cackle from inside. I follow it to his booth where he holds court, surrounded by the likes of the three imbeciles who gave me a hard time the night I met Hakee.

"Hey, boo!" he says, waving me over. I foolishly step into his lion's den.

Surprised, Mr. Lollipop says, "Y'all know each other?"

"Hell to the yes, we know each other. This is my best friend in the whole wide world," Kenyatta oozes as though he means it.

Mr. Lollipop eyes me seemingly through a fresh perspective. His followers remain silent, awaiting their leader's next move. Mr. Lollipop smiles. I take it to mean all is forgiven, and he is willing to water his disdain for me down to cautious neutrality. Now that I'm in his good graces, he offers me a seat in their booth.

"Actually, I have dinner waiting on the other side, but thank you," I reply coolly. After the way he and his fools treated me, they deserve an attitude much ruder than the one I've just served. "Kenyatta, why don't you stop by my table a little later?"

"Yeah, all right," he says, looking almost relieved that I'm not staying.

I return to my table as Carlo places my drink down. "Can I trouble you for another?" I ask as he's about to step away.

"Sounds like you've had a rough night of your own."

"You could say that."

Dinner arrives shortly after. Carlo places a plate of grilled walleye in front of me. I stare at it.

"Something wrong, sweetie?" Carlo asks in a charged tone as if expecting me to complain about bullshit.

"I'm sorry, but I thought I ordered the walleye pan-fried."

Carlo's eyes frost over. "This is pan-fried, sweetie."

I stare at the food. I've ordered the walleye enough times to know this isn't close to pan-fried. Carlo puts a hand on his hip and taps his foot, almost daring me to proceed with my protestation. If I send it back, I imagine the horrible things some cranky, woefully underpaid cook will do to my food in retaliation.

"Tell you what, I'll eat it as it is."

Carlo's face and tone lighten. "Are you sure?"

"Yep," I say, spearing the fish with my fork. Carlo scurries away.

Nearby, a table of old-school gays wearing Hawaiian shirts over turtlenecks and Party City tiaras (and probably still use Mary and Sister as terms of endearment) reminisce about the Minneapolis gay scene before AIDS. Someone complains that the current generation doesn't appreciate how good they have it; that they owe their sexual freedom to those who marched for gay rights, AIDS research, and for those who died waiting for a cure. I listen intently, agreeing with him as I pick bones out of my fish.

The piano tune changes to a campy, saloon-style rendition of "Everything's Coming Up Roses," which the pianist plays with gusto. Diego comes inside from the cold and warms himself beneath the large circle-faced clock. Our eyes connect and he smiles with playful flirtation. I'm silly for having misjudged him, and I smile back, averting my eyes shyly. When I look up for a second helping of Diego's attention, I realize he isn't smiling at me but rather the trans hostess walking past me on her way towards him. He embraces her and gives her ass an ample squeeze.

After dinner, Carlo asks if I want dessert. He recommends the apple crumble. I order it.

Kenyatta zig-zags between tables, executing a model turn that shows off his maxi-length leather coat. I pretend to be in awe. I saw this style coat in the latest issue of *GQ*. It's too expensive for Kenyatta to afford on his own. I wonder which man of many gave it to him.

Up close, the coat is musty and stinks of stale cigarette smoke, proving he's incapable of appreciating something so luxurious. He opens his arms to hug me. I don't bother getting up.

"Do I detect a little shade?" Kenyatta purrs, his beady eyes shimmering with their usual mischief. He leans down to hug me in my seated position and anoints both sides of my face with air kisses.

After the hug, Kenyatta sits down across from me. "How was dinner?"

"Good, considering Carlo brought me the wrong thing."

"Did you send it back?"

I shake my head, sipping from my drink. I'm suddenly self-conscious that Kenyatta can tell it's my third cocktail.

"I never eat the food here. No way," he says, smiling wryly. "Management only hires ex-cons."

"Nothing wrong with giving ex-cons opportunities."

"Boo, trust me, the owners ain't doing it out of the kindness of their hearts. They hire ex-cons because aside from undocumented folks, they're the only ones who'll accept shitty pay without complaining about it. But those prison boys ain't innocent. I hear they drop food all on the floor before they cook it and don't believe in washing their hands after using the bathroom."

"Okay, are you trying to make me throw up?"

"Just telling you what I know. Anyway, you look well."

"Thanks. So do you."

The compliment means little to him. He's heard it before. He sits devilishly toothsome, primping soft, chemically texturized curls with his hand. The manner in which he crosses his legs is demure yet masculine. "I do what I can," he says.

LaSaundra has expressed on more than one occasion that she's never liked Kenyatta. She calls him a trifling albatross who thinks the world owes him something just because he lucked out in the looks department.

Carlo brings the apple crumble. In light of what Kenyatta told me, I stare at it, expecting it to crawl across the table. Kenyatta clears his throat and twirls his watered-down drink.

"Would you like another?" Carlo asks.

"Can I have a Tanqueray and tonic?"

Carlo nods and leaves us to talk. I push the dessert away. "So, how are you settling into your new spot?"

"Yeah, about that. So, why did my cousin's husband come home from work this afternoon and stand in my doorway butt-ass-naked, stroking his meat?"

"And what did you say?"

Kenyatta unrolls the unused silverware and daintily wipes his mouth with the napkin. "We didn't do much talking if you know what I mean."

"You're unbelievable," I scoff.

Kenyatta giggles, reveling in his messiness. "I knew I recognized him from the dirty bookstores."

"No, I mean, I can't believe you actually slept with your cousin's husband!"

"I didn't sleep with him. I just slobbed on his knob."

I shake my head. His revelation would be funny if it wasn't so ill-intentioned.

"Oh, come on, you mean to tell me you'd let a good dick go to waste?"

"If it belonged to my cousin's husband, yes."

"Yeah, that's why you're over there letting your kitty cat dry up."

My dried-up kitty cat notwithstanding, this isn't about me. It's about Kenyatta's lack of common decency. That woman was gracious enough to allow him into her home, and he repaid her good deed by fooling around with her husband.

"Hey, ain't nobody told her to marry a down low brother," Kenyatta replies, noting the judgment on my face.

"Fine. When she throws your ass out, don't say anything."

"She's not gonna throw me out. And even if she does, oh well. I'll be aiight."

"I'd re-think that if I were you. You don't have a lot of options for places to stay right now."

"So, if I just so happen to find myself on the street, you wouldn't let me crash at your place?"

"No, I would not."

"You would do me like that?" he asks, his eyes widening.

"Please don't make me say something I'll regret."

"What's that supposed to mean?"

"Never mind. Let's just hope the day never comes when you're kicked out of yet another place."

"Hold on, I'm still trippin' off you saying you wouldn't help me. I would never do you like that."

"Yeah, right."

"You clearly don't agree. Is there something you'd like to get off your chest?"

"Fine, since you asked, it would terrify me to rely on you for anything. You can't even help yourself."

"Since when do you get to be so high and mighty?" Kenyatta leans in, hissing at me. "Not that long ago you were lettin' a married man all up in your pussy, lest we forget."

"That was different. He told me he and his wife were separated."

"Bitch, please! That's what you told yourself whenever he came over to fuck so you wouldn't feel guilty. So don't sit here judging people because truth be told, you ain't no better than me. Maybe it's time you accept the fact we're cut from the same cloth."

I'm beginning to realize how much time I've wasted with him. He's too self-important to understand what it means to be a genuine friend. Real friends don't choose dick over people they claim to care about, then shrug off the hurt feelings they've caused. They don't use everyone they come in contact with as a means to an end.

Kenyatta lives in a perpetual mess. Things can be going well for him, and he'll engineer a way to throw a wrench into his circumstances. This, like most predicaments he finds himself in, is a drama of his own making. Thankfully, unlike him, I have a stable job and place to live, no matter how beneath LaSaundra's standards they are.

"You and I are *nothing* alike," I say finally. "The difference between us is that I'm trying to fix the shit that's wrong with me. You celebrate the foolishness you do!"

Kenyatta blinks, as though taken aback by my words. "That's not fair. I'm trying to get my act together, but it's hard," Kenyatta says.

"Maybe it is, maybe it isn't. You just have to decide to do what you have to do. Frankly, I don't believe you will because you're always pulling stunts and getting over on people. And then, when it all blows up in your face, your ungrateful ass expects someone to save you. But I'm telling you now, you better hope that lady doesn't find out what you're doing with her husband because if you get kicked out of this place, don't even think about calling me!"

I rise from the table to find Carlo, who's fast approaching us with Kenyatta's drink. As a parting gift, I ask him to add the drink to my bill. Kenyatta sits there, pretending to process what I've said, but I know it's gone through one ear and out the other. Despite Carlo's insistence that he bring the check back to the table, I follow him to his side station to pay the check. As I hand him my credit card, I look back to see if Kenyatta has vacated the table, but he's still sitting there, stupidly expecting my return, but I don't return.

Later, during the drive home, my phone rings repeatedly. I figure it's Kenyatta, revved up and ready to curse me out for abandoning him. But I'm not going to argue with a person who never thinks he's does anything wrong. Our friendship no longer matters to him. And, for the first time, it doesn't matter to me, either.

My intention is to go home, change into my pjs and curl up on the sofa with my favorite soft maroon blanket with frayed edges. Since leaving dinner without eating the apple crumble, a brand-new pint of butter pecan ice cream awaits me in the freezer.

A text notification chirps. I ignore it. Both LaSaundra and Kenyatta are garbage excuses for friends, and for that, they're going into the trashcan of my memory. With friends like them, who needs enemies?

# TWENTY-TWO

Lasaundra and her things are gone by the time I return home, but the effect of her earlier insult remains ever present. I need a shower to wash the loser off my skin. However, no matter how hard I scrub, my sense of inadequacy is baked into my flesh like the markings of a curse. After my shower, I change into my navy and white striped pjs, and settle comfortably on the sofa. My first scoop of ice cream is spooned and ready to go into my mouth. The TV is on, and Diana Ross thrashes about in a padded cell in *Lady Sings the Blues*.

Another damn chirp from my phone. Probably an even angrier message from Kenyatta because I ignored his first. It was my intention to ignore this one too, but my masochistic curiosity prevails. I pause the movie at the precise moment a correction officer enters the cell to place Diana in a straightjacket. I pick up my phone, annoyed by Kenyatta's foolishness, and ready to delete not only his flurry of texts but him from my contact list.

*I should be pissed as hell with you, but I can't get you off my mind*, the first text reads.

*Can I come over so we can talk?* continues the second.

I recognize Hakee's words upon seeing them. The longer I stare at them, the faster my heart races. After being duped by LaSaundra, shame hindered my reaching out to him. Beyond an apology, I'm lost for what to say. If it were me being accused, I wouldn't have been able to rid my accuser from my mind either, but for very different reasons.

*I owe you a huge apology!* I type, adding three sad face emojis to emphasize how pitiful I am. Then I hit send.

Hakee's reply is immediate: *You can make it up to me when I come over.*

The thought of seeing Hakee again sets my groin ablaze. I'm suddenly proud of myself for turning Sameer down. Even though we're not officially a couple, it would be inappropriate to reconnect with him after receiving a hot pounding from Sameer.

*How soon can you get here?* I answer.

Hakee doesn't respond. Fifteen minutes go by. Then a half-hour. After an hour, my exhilaration turns into deflation. I've made a fool of myself twice in one day. Hakee has no intention of forgiving me. He's simply testing his appeal to see if I'll come running when he calls. Same shit I tolerated from Byron, and now, I've foolishly given Hakee's ego the stroking it craves.

As another half hour passes, I lose interest in the movie. I stare at my phone, willing it to ring, but it doesn't ring. Hakee's rejection cuts deeply and serves as confirmation of how much I've screwed things up. There's no way he's going to give me a second chance, nor do I deserve one. Predictably, tears roll down my cheeks, and my ice cream melts down to a sea of floating pecans.

*Yep, LaSaundra's right. I am a loser!*

The sound of the doorbell ringing doesn't immediately drive those words from my brain. I push up from the sofa to bring the ice cream bowl to the kitchen. I yank a sheet of paper towel from the spool and wipe my face. I chuckle for being stupid enough to believe Hakee left me hanging. The tides have turned in my favor. I'm once again flying on renewed hope. I'll be sure to reward him with a playful pinch for pranking me, followed by something steamier to welcome him back into my life.

The ringing starts again. This time incessant. Delirious make-up sex beckons. I predict any small talk will be short-lived. Unable to take our hands off each other, Hakee is going to love me down the way he did the first night we met. But when I open the door, Junior is standing on the other side. My face drops.

"What do you want?" I ask.

He looks a shade of pitiful. I almost feel bad that his wife left him.

"Get dressed. We've gotta go," Junior says mournfully.

"Go where?"

"Ma's been in an accident. They brought her down to Hennepin County Medical."

Ma's flurry of text messages comes to mind, and my headstrong refusal to reply to them. My adrenaline kicks in, soaring from zero to ten. "Is she going to be okay?"

Junior shakes his head. Tears spritz from his eyes. "It's bad, Lawrence. Really bad."

*****

I damn myself for not insisting upon driving my car to the hospital. And because of that choice, I'm stuck listening to Junior lament over Nadine taking off with their daughter and how irresponsible she is. I don't care, nor do I pretend to. The only thing on my mind is whether our mother will be alive by the time we get to the hospital.

"She'll be back," Junior says, still carrying on about his self-made disaster. "She always comes back."

Mercifully, the conversation ends, and Junior scrolls the radio dial to KMOJ. Some hip-hop artist I'm unfamiliar with brags about the trappings of prosperity. Junior nervously taps his knuckles rhythmically against the steering wheel in keeping with the beat of the song. I look at my phone. I find a message from Hakee: *I'm outside. Why aren't you answering your door?*

I respond that I'm on my way to the hospital.

*Are you okay? Which hospital?*

I explain everything, adding the name of the hospital, and promise to make it up to him.

*For sure.*

I put my phone away. Hakee's forgiveness is a pleasant relief.

Junior cuts off the music. "I mean, what kind of mother does that, huh?" he asks, back on his Nadine tirade. "And she picked the worst time to pull this shit. Ma could be at death's door, and that bitch goes and does this!"

"Okay, you're going to need to calm down."

"Don't tell me to fuckin' calm down! I have no idea where my wife and child are. That ain't nothin' to remain calm about!"

I don't say another word, once again allowing myself to be punked by my younger brother. Junior is lucky I'm not much of a fighter, because if I was a different person, and we ever came to blows again, I'd probably have to kill him.

# TWENTY-THREE

My brother and I enter the hospital on a mission. We proceed to the information desk. I ask the pleasant (almost saintly) elderly woman sitting there where Cheryl Greene's room is. Junior corrects me, changing Greene to Murphy. That does the trick. The nice information lady tells us where to go. Approaching the elevators, Junior says, "Really, Lawrence? You're never gonna acknowledge the man gave Ma his name?"

I'm not going to answer because Junior isn't interested in one, only to shame me for being petty. He'd much rather I go along to get along; to pretend that I'm looking forward to seeing our stepfather. As far as me acknowledging Pastor giving Ma his last name, the day he stops being an asshole, I'll think about it.

Pastor is at the far end of the waiting room, distressed and running his palms back and forth against the back of his bowed head. If there was ever a time for me to act like an adult, this is it. But our shared reason for being here doesn't inspire me to rise to the occasion.

"Any news?" Junior asks.

Pastor raises his head. His eyes are bleary and sorrowful. "They said the X-rays revealed some internal bleeding. They have to do exploratory surgery to find out where the bleeding is coming from." He sinks into a nearby chair, too emotional to offer us reassurance. If I'm not careful his infectious melancholy will spread between us like a virus. I need to escape its path. For this, I search the room for something else to hold my attention. Most of the people surrounding us are quietly transfixed by cell phones and tablets, their faces aglow and eyes collectively glazed over. They are casualties of a technological malaise... technology often passed off as necessary to human evolution. It steals their souls. But they're unaware that their souls are already partially gone. And yet, I want to become infected as well. It will serve as a welcomed distraction from the uncertainty of Ma's predicament.

"Tell me she's gonna be all right!" Junior screams. People look up from their digital gods to witness him making a scene.

"Hey, why don't we say a prayer for Ma, huh?" I suggest, steering Junior away from tugging at Pastor's jacket sleeve.

He steps back in retreat, his palms cast out. "Fine, I'm down with that."

Swallowing my disdain for Pastor, I say, "Why don't you lead us in a prayer?"

He clasps his hands together. Without looking at me he bitterly tells me no.

"I thought you were a man of God," I reply, happy to point this out.

"I am. But God can't fix this."

"Ain't preachers the ones who are supposed to lead their flock? Where are you leading them to if even you don't believe the bullshit you're telling them?" Junior asks.

Without saying another word, Pastor takes off down the corridor. Junior attempts to follow, but I stop him.

"Let him go," I say. "People process things in their own way." I spot a chair on the other side of the room. "I'm going over there."

Pastor returns much calmer than before, bearing vending machine loot which he allows to fall onto a table like slot machine winnings. "Help yourselves," he says, opening a bag of chips. I help myself to a chocolate bar. Junior stares at us both as though eating something during this uncertain time is traitorous. Taking his self-appointed position as watchman seriously, he stays where he is in case someone comes to update us.

An hour passes. Hakee texts me that he's downstairs. I reply that I'll meet him upstairs at the elevator. I wait by the doors to usher in my second chance with him. My anticipation of seeing Hakee again is akin to a child's anticipation of Christmas morning.

When he arrives, the first words out of my mouth are "I'm sorry." He deserves that much and more.

Hakee smiles and puts his index finger to my lips. "Let's just concentrate on your moms." He holds out his arms, his eyes inviting me into his embrace.

Our affection is to the chagrin of Pastor and my brother. They say nothing, but their glares speak volumes.

"Any word on how she's doing?" Hakee asks as we part.

"She's in surgery. The doctors are trying to find the origin of some internal bleeding."

His eyes widened, looking as alarmed as I was when I found out myself.

"Anyway, thanks for being here. I can definitely use a friendly face right now."

"For sure."

Another hour passes. Junior paces the floor, pausing in front of the nurses' station to ask if Ma is out of surgery. He's incensed to learn she's still being operated on. Junior pounds the desk, demanding to know why the procedure is taking so long, and to speak to someone who will tell him something different. The nurse patiently reminds him that the doctor will be out when the surgery is completed.

I question my brother's sincerity, even marvel at the difference between his present concern over our mother's well-being and the complete indifference he exhibited back when his father was beating her. Where was his outrage then?

My aunt Marva shows up and sits next to Pastor. Hakee and I watch and listen to her read scriptures aloud from her Bible. Her presence comforts Pastor. I wish I could say the same.

Hakee taps my leg. "Do you pray?" he asks.

"Honestly, sometimes I don't think God is interested in anything I have to say."

"You don't really believe that, do you?"

"I don't know what to believe. All I know is what I've been taught, which is, God won't bless those of us who have turned our back on Him."

"And have you?"

"I don't think so. But it's been pounded into my head that God is displeased with me being gay. On a conscious level I know it's not true, but subconsciously, I'm scared that it is. And since I've supposedly "chosen" to live this way, God has stopped taking my calls sort to speak."

"The church maintains control over people's lives by instilling fear and guilt. You get rid of the fear and guilt, people will begin to think for themselves and there won't be any reason for organized religion."

"So where does that leave God?"

Hakee shrugs. "Depends on which version of God you believe in. Would you like me to pray with you?"

I consider his offer. A conversation with God is long overdue, but prayer and I don't have the best relationship. When I was in high school, I used to go to bed at night, crying as I begged God to make me straight. The teasing had gotten so bad that I once found a hand-drawn picture of two male stick figures, one bent over with the words *No Fags Allowed* stuffed inside my locker. I was so angry, I demanded to speak to Principal Gloria Wayans, an African-American woman who wore her hair in a neatly kept Afro. She always wore the same silk rose pinned to her outfit, whether or not it made fashion sense. There was a rumor that she locked herself in her office at lunch periods to read her Bible and pray. When I pushed the crumpled picture across her desk, all she said was, "Perhaps if you didn't give off homosexual energy people wouldn't bother you." She then suggested I ask my then stepfather, Plez, to show me how to do "manly" things around the house.

There were also the times I prayed for God to stop Plez from beating my mom. I suppose He finally came through on that one when Ma caught Plez in bed with some skanky female, and she left him.

However, when Grandma was sick, I prayed that He would heal her. He didn't. And it affirmed my belief that God no longer heard the prayers of the sinner, especially one like me who settled comfortably into a "sin" like being gay. Whether or not I believe it works, at least prayer is familiar.

"I don't mind," Hakee says, pulling me back from my thoughts.

I nod and accept his extended hand. Even though my head bows and my eyes close, I don't have the slightest idea what I want to say, nor do I want to sound like an idiot.

"You don't have to say it out loud," Hakee says, giving my hand a soft squeeze. "Your relationship with God is your own. It should be special. Private. You don't have to impress me."

His words of encouragement bring my nervousness down from a ten to a four. The words finally come to me: *Dear God, if You can hear me... if You want to hear me, I ask that You guide the hands of the surgeons and technicians performing not just Ma's surgery, but those of others. I ask You to heal all those afflicted, and those in recovery. And if it is Your will, I ask for another chance to make things right with Ma. However long it takes for us to arrive at a place of healing, I'm willing to do it. In Christ's name I pray, amen.*

I open my eyes. Hakee is still praying. When he finishes, he announces he's going to McDonald's and asks if anyone wants anything. I request a Big Mac and a large fry. Both Pastor and Marva respond curtly, "No, thank you." Junior's answer is yet another menacing glare.

"Right. I'll take that as a no," Hakee says.

I offer to walk him out.

"Listen, I was thinking, maybe I can spend the night at your crib tonight. Unless you want to stay with your family," he says before getting into his red Volkswagen Beetle.

This is music to my ears. There's no one else with whom I want to spend the rest of my evening. The idea gets the ole rusty crank on my imagination turning. I envision us on Friday nights, snuggled on the sofa, a bowl of buttered popcorn between us, and our hands touching whenever we each reach in for popcorn. Lovelight radiates from our eyes.

"No, I wasn't planning on it. But let's wait and see what the doctor says after she's out of surgery," I say, coming out of my daydream.

"Good call."

I turn to leave, but Hakee pulls me in for a kiss. After which, he strokes my cheek, then winks before disappearing inside his car and driving off.

I run back inside the hospital. When the elevator doors open on the correct floor, Pastor is waiting for me.

"You just couldn't help yourself, could you? Your mama is in there fighting for her life and you disrespect her by bringing *him* here!"

"If you don't like it, you don't have to look at us."

Pastor is about to reply but stops suddenly, as though the desire to argue has left him. Over his shoulder, Junior and Marva talk to the surgeon. We join them.

"Cheryl had some internal bleeding in her abdomen. There were some complications…" the doctor tells us.

"What kinds of complications?" Junior interrupts.

"Extensive abdominal bleeding. So much so that it was difficult to find its origin. The good news is that we found it and applied sutures to stop the bleeding."

Junior eyes the doctor skeptically. "What the hell are sutures?"

"A kind of stitch," the doctor says, as though speaking patiently to a young child.

"Can we see her?" I ask.

"She's heavily sedated and won't comprehend who you are. Why don't you let her sleep tonight and then come back tomorrow morning when she'll be in a room and you can see her then?"

"Thank you, Doctor," Marva says before dropping to her knees, hands clasped in rejoicing. "Praise God!"

Pastor walks away, offering no comment. I follow him back to the elevators. From his stony expression, he is unmoved by the good news.

"Looks like prayer works," I say, happy to know that maybe God still listens to me.

Pastor's eyes are bereft of the relief one might expect to see in someone who only a few hours earlier could've lost their spouse. "Listen, I'm glad your mama pulled through, but I meant what I said before. God can't fix this."

"What does that even mean?"

"She wasn't alone when she got hit." Pastor presses the down button on the elevator.

"How do you know that?"

The down arrow lights up red, followed by a dinging sound. Elevator doors open. He steps inside, wiping his eyes with a white handkerchief. "The cops told me."

"Who was she with?"

"I'll let your mama tell you," Pastor says, another of his creepy grins slinking across his face.

I don't know whether he's playing me, but before I ask anything else, he's gone. Only after the doors close do I recognize the hatred in Pastor's eyes. And for the first time, I can honestly say it wasn't meant for me.

# TWENTY-FOUR

Hakee returns with food. He hands me a greasy bag and says everything is there. Force of habit, I check the bag anyway, careful of where I place my fingers.

I hand the bag back to him. "You don't mind if we eat this at the house, do you?"

"Whatever's clever."

Junior announces he's leaving. He splits a dirty look between Hakee and myself and says, "Thanks for bringing that fag shit along."

"Thanks for being your usual asshole self. I see why Nadine left you."

Junior's eyes morph into the evil I've seen in his father's. They share a boiling rage that flicks on with the ease of a light switch. Junior wants to charge at me, but luckily for me is cognizant of where he is. Instead, he wags his index finger at me, then turns to leave. I pass a relieved look to Hakee.

"So glad you got to meet my brother. Isn't he a charmer?"

"I got one in my family just like him."

"A brother?"

"No, an uncle. Just as angry as can be, too."

"Oh yeah? How do you handle it?"

"I let him be. I mean, he is who he is."

"So, in other words, he gets a pass," I scoff.

"Not at all. My uncle is hypocritical scum. He's got four baby mamas and can't tell you when's the last time he's seen any of his seven kids. But mention homosexuality, and he'll talk all day long about how against God or disgusting it is. Never mind the seven kids he doesn't take care of, or their mothers he never married. People like that have to find a scapegoat, something they deem lower than themselves. I said fine. I don't argue with fools, anyway. And it's not giving him or people like him a pass. It's realizing that we're not in the business of changing the minds of those who don't wanna be changed."

I'm learning life lessons from a man younger than me. Not a lot younger, but enough for me to realize I was never as self-aware or in tune with my emotions as Hakee is. "You're a better man than I am."

"No, I'm not better than any man. I've just grown to learn what's important and when not to waste my time."

I glance over at Marva, sitting with her honker of a Bible open on her lap, holding vigil. For someone who proclaims to have found joy through the Lord, she comes across as one of the unhappiest people I know. At least today she has reason to be unhappy that extends beyond her perception that heathens are taking over the world.

"I don't know what kind of company I'll be, but I don't want to be alone tonight."

"I got you. Are you ready to go now?" Hakee asks, rubbing my back.

"Yes."

"Anything you wanna talk about?"

"Not right now."

"When you're ready, I'm all ears."

During the ride home, Hakee doesn't push me to share my feelings. However, something he said back in the waiting room begs further discussion.

"Hey, earlier before we prayed, what did you mean by it depends which version of God I believe in?"

"Some people believe in a loving, fair and just God. Others believe in a God that is as petty and vindictive as they are. They get happy knowing someone is going to spend eternity in torment. People make this shit more complicated than it has to be. I mean, life in and of itself is complicated. Why can't we just be good to one another? Love one another? Hmm? Why is that so fucking hard?"

I'm unsure whether the question is rhetorical, but the thought of the wrathful God I was raised with frightens me even now. To think, there is a superior being up there, watching us scurry around like lab rats in a maze, doing messed up stuff to each other, while He sits back and keeps score of it all.

Hakee continues, "Know what I think? I think we're all one big sociological experiment. God put different ethnic groups, sexual orientations and socio/economic classes together to see how we treat each other. Can we love each other in the same way we claim to love God?" he says.

Good insight. And if that is truly God's intention, we're doing a piss-poor job living up to that objective.

"So, when did you come to this realization that we're all part of this greater movement?" I ask.

"It started a couple of years ago when I was in Thailand. I spent most of my time in Bangkok, but took a side trip to Pattaya. I was meditating in a temple. The monks burned these incense that were the strongest I've ever smelled. But after I sat in silence for an hour, the idea came to me. But it wasn't until I went to Bali, Indonesia that the idea stuck."

"Must've been one hell of an experience."

"It was one of the greatest experiences of my life. It's the reason why today I strive to live my life as a good person for goodness's sake and not out of fear of being punished."

I sit with what Hakee has said. An excitement passes through me. It's the excitement of being privy to a new way of thinking that many refuse to understand. I want to roll around in the newness of it before sharing it with the other guys in group. I wonder how many of them have come to similar conclusions? How many former members discovered this on their own?

Conversation dies down again. Hakee gives my leg a squeeze, just so that I know we're still connected. He isn't one of those people who needs to fill a sound void with idle chatter. I like how secure he is in those conversation lulls. But I feel like I owe him something. An apology might be a good start.

"LaSaundra had the bank card the entire time," I announce.

He chuckles. "I could've told you that."

"She left it in an ATM, but one of the gas station attendants saw to it that she got it back. She used it as an excuse to move in with her boyfriend."

"She couldn't just leave? She had to do all of that?"

I shrug. "What can I say? She has a flare for the dramatic."

"I guess," he says with a shake of his head.

"Anyway, I'm really sorry, Hakee."

"Look, I've tried to take a step back and see things from your perspective. I don't appreciate her ruining my show, but I can't fault you for believing your friend. You had no reason to think she'd dog you out like that."

More reason to fall for a guy like him. Hakee is level-headed and mature. I don't think most people would take the high road after having their integrity called into question. He kisses my hand before enveloping it with his.

"I like you, Lawrence."

"I like you, too."

"It's crazy, but ever since the night we spent together, I've been wanting to see where this goes. Am I moving too fast?"

"Probably. But I feel the same."

And that's all it takes for Mr. Hakee to put a smile on my face.

*****

I was in such a hurry to leave for the hospital that I forgot to turn off the TV and DVD player. Hakee kicks off his shoes and stares at Diana Ross' less than glamorous visage freeze-framed on TV.

"What were you watching?" he asks, making himself comfortable on the sofa.

"You've never seen *Lady Sings the Blues*?"

He shakes his head.

I gaze at him with disbelief. "You do know who Diana Ross is, don't you?"

"Of course."

"And Billie Holiday?"

"Of course."

"Well, this is sort of a biopic."

"What do you mean 'sort of'?"

"It's been said the film is honest, if not entirely true."

"Gotcha." Hakee nods.

"Wine?" I ask.

"Only if you're having some."

I grab two plates and two wine glasses from the cupboard. After putting them on the portable island, I open a chilled bottle of blush. Hakee sneaks up behind me and tickles the back of my neck with feather-like kisses.

"That feels nice," I encourage, leaning back into blissful sensations.

"Thought you could use some help," he says between kisses and a slow grind against my ass.

"What kind of help did you have in mind?"

Hakee pats me on the butt. "How about I bring the bottle and glasses into the living room?" he replies with a chuckle. He takes the items into the living room without waiting for an answer. I bring the plates, all the while willing away the beginnings of an erection.

I divvy up the burgers and fries as Hakee pours brimming glasses of wine; the kind I pour when I'm home alone.

"Not bad," Hakee says, taking a sip before leaning back comfortably into the corner of the sofa.

"Glad you approve," I reply, slurping from the other full glass.

It's nice to have him here, in part to fill the emptiness of losing a roommate, but also because I think I've found the right puzzle piece that fits without being forced. But there is a looming danger whenever connecting so quickly with a person. We have to question whether things are moving too fast. Can things move quickly and still hold promise, or is this the calm before an inevitable disaster?

He rubs my thigh like the perfect lover. "So, do you want me to watch this movie with you?"

"If you want to."

"Restart it to the beginning."

We watch the movie from the beginning, a movie I've seen enough times to quote every line of dialogue verbatim. It's a habit LaSaundra loathes. However, my recitations delight Hakee. And like that, we've slipped into something that feels as though it's always been. I enjoy sharing the experience of watching my favorite movie, and Hakee doesn't mind my enthusiasm to get him to love the film as much as I do.

"I know one thing, Billy Dee Williams is a suave son of a bitch, isn't he?" he says as Billy Dee's character, Louis McKay, descends the stairs inside a nightclub.

Later, I wake up with my head burrowed in Hakee's lap. My eyes open to the last scene in the film when Diana's "Billie Holiday" raises her arms triumphantly at Carnegie Hall.

"I didn't mean to fall asleep. You should've woken me," I say, sitting up.

"You were tired."

"Still, I didn't mean for you to watch the film by yourself."

"Don't worry about it. It was a good flick. Did you know you purr when you sleep?"

"Do I?" I ask, wiping drool from the corner of my mouth.

"Yeah. Kinda cute, actually."

I look down at the empty wine bottle and crumpled fast food bags and wrappers surrounding it. "I should start cleaning this up." As I pick up the items, an image of Ma lying in a hospital bed, flatlining, forces me into a panic. My body shudders from the false thought.

"Do you want some help?" Hakee asks.

"No. I'm good."

Hakee's eyes warm with concern. "Hey, you okay? You're sad all of a sudden."

I throw on a phony smile to shake off whatever he sees on my face. I change the setting on the remote to access TV channels and hand it to him. "Here, amuse yourself while I'm gone." I exit the room, but I can sense Hakee's eyes following me.

I go into the kitchen, carrying plates with the empty bottle laying on top. As soon as I turn on the light, the bottle rolls off the plates and shatters on the floor. Startled, I drop the plates, which also break. The magnitude of my mother's condition, coupled with my night of hell with Byron, cuts me at the knees. Slumped over, staring at broken fragments on the kitchen floor, I sob.

Hakee appears in the doorway. Concerned, he kneels at my side and pulls me into his arms.

"Let it out, babe. It's all right."

I cry until I no longer feel the floor beneath me. "My head's all over the place. On the one hand, I've got this guilt about the way things are between my mother and I, but on the other, I'm still super pissed at her."

"Emotions are confusing sometimes," Hakee says, gently stroking the back of my head. "You don't have to understand them right now. You have every right to feel how you do."

I limp to the breakfast nook, taking Hakee's words with me to process. He gets busy removing shards of broken glass and plates from the floor. I want to share with him what Byron attempted to do to me. It's fast-growing into an emotional boil that desperately needs lancing. But the courage to do so is nowhere near me, and instead, I beg Hakee not to bother with the mess. I'll clean it up later. Even that much is a struggle to articulate. The rest is blathering... random, floating thoughts circling my brain, waiting to land. I'm sure I look like a certifiable nut... until Hakee's smile shines in my direction.

Once he throws the larger pieces into the trash, he sweeps the remaining pieces into a dustpan. Soon the floor looks as it did before my breakdown.

"All done," Hakee says, joining me at the nook. He reaches over and gives my hands a comforting squeeze. "You all right?"

Not really, but I nod anyway and welcome the strength of his hands cupping mine. I had hoped make-up sex would help cancel out the nightmarish memory of Byron, but it isn't Hakee's responsibility to heal that wound, nor is my head in the right place.

"Wanna talk about it?"

I hesitate. He deserves something more than the word no.

"This is a judgment-free zone. Believe me, I have my share of problems and demons too," he says.

"I thought I was past this."

"Past what?"

"Anger. Hatred."

"You hate your mother?"

No, I hate Byron, but instead, I say, "Yes. I don't want to, but I do."

"Why?"

I wasn't expecting a therapy session. I'm not comfortable unloading my problems onto Hakee, even with his promise of non-judgment. Everyone judges a little. Judgment is baked into our humanity. And although Hakee's empathy is genuine, I'm conflicted over putting such darkness out there. I don't want him to see me as fragile. Talking about my mother is an easier option.

"Let's just say my mother didn't always have my back. But part of me doesn't want anything bad to happen to her."

"You can be angry with someone and still care about them."

I smile. "You should be a therapist."

"Naw, I don't think so," he replies, his eyes lighting up at the sight of me smiling again. He gently taps my chin. "I'm not sure I'd be strong enough to leave my clients' problems at the office."

"I hope I don't send you home with my trials and tribulations on the brain."

Hakee winks then kisses my forehead. "Yours I can handle."

"I'm better now. Thank you."

"Do you want me to stick around tomorrow?"

"Yes," I reply, more eagerly than I intended to. "That is if you don't mind."

"I don't mind at all. Sometime tomorrow I can swing by my place and get another change of clothes."

"Okay. Um, behind the mailbox, there is a wooden plank. You'll find a spare key to let yourself back in."

Hakee grins. "I get my own key?"

"Uh, no. You can put it back when you're done with it."

He chuckles. "I was just playin' with you, man. I'll be sure to put it back where I found it."

I smile. "Sounds good. Okay, I guess I'm going to jump in the shower."

"Would you like me to join you?"

The prospect is enough to ignite my imagination. I envision our wet, lathered bodies gliding against one another. It's another fantasy that under better circumstances I wouldn't mind making real.

"No, I'm good."

"I guess I'll be right here watching the news," he says, his tone sounding slightly disappointed.

"I won't be long."

I finish my shower; dry off and put on a sweatsuit. After, I return to the living room. Hakee is on the sofa, riveted as a cable news anchor asks a panel what effect Hillary Clinton's emails are going to have on the outcome of the election Tuesday.

"This is some bullshit," he says, though unclear whether he's speaking to me or at the TV.

A Gallup poll reveals Trump closing the gap between himself and Clinton. I join Hakee on the sofa.

"Polls say one thing one day and something entirely different the next," I say.

"Yeah, but you don't find it funny that this email shit is coming up so close to the election?" he replies.

"I try not to give those conspiracy theories any attention."

"Yeah, okay. Think that if you want to. When Trump wins, you'll pay more attention."

"He won't win."

"How do you know?"

"Because I believe in God, and God doesn't like ugly."

"Last I checked, God's let plenty of ugly slide in this world," Hakee snaps. He pushes onto his feet with a huff and storms into the kitchen.

I hang back, worried that I've angered him again. His concern about the election isn't so off-the-wall. Maybe I shouldn't have said anything else. Hakee doesn't need me to coddle him. But I also don't want to go back to where we were before today. I take a deep breath and head into the kitchen.

"Sweetie, if it makes you upset, why do you watch?"

"Because it pays to be informed. I'm surprised at how naïve you're being right now."

I bristle at his choice of words. I'm no fan of the lecturing tone he's opted for. "Why am I naïve? Just because I choose not to fill my head with all of that political crap? As long as I vote Tuesday, that's all that matters."

Hakee selects another wine glass from the cabinet. He lifts the boxed wine sitting on the counter over the glass and opens the spicket. Cheap merlot fills the glass. He gulps a large swallow of wine, winces, then helps himself to another.

"Are you really that concerned?" The question sounds stupid considering my guest's reaction.

"Everybody is ready to pop the confetti and give her the election when nobody has voted yet."

I maneuver the glass away from him to wrap an arm around him, to be there for him in the same way he's been here for me. But something stops me from reaching out. I kiss his cheek, a woefully inadequate gesture. It won't make the political booboo go away. I try not to react to the distance Hakee puts between us. I say nothing else. I've probably said too much already.

# TWENTY-FIVE

The next day I walk into the hospital room. Ma is awake, sucking on ice chips. A Jamaican nurse on the opposite side of her checks her IV. Marva is also here, patiently holding out a small, plastic spoon with the next serving of ice chips.

Ma looks pitiful in her ashen skin. It's hard to stay angry with her, especially when her eyes flood with joy the moment she sees me.

"You came," she says, her voice thin and drawn out.

"Of course, I did." I smile, grateful to have Ma alive and for the second chance to repair our relationship. I reach for her, selecting the hand untethered to an IV.

"I told her you'd show up," Granddaddy says from a seat near the door. His gruff, boozy voice startles me. I didn't expect to see him here.

"Hey, Granddaddy."

His eyes are hostile, like those of straight homophobes whenever they're in the presence of faggotry. An uncomfortable silence passes between us until the nurse's ample bottom pulls his focus, which remains within his lustful crosshairs until she leaves.

"Lord have mercy," he exclaims, shamelessly adjusting the crotch of his pants. He cranes his neck long after the nurse has left the room. It's a flagrant display of hyper-heterosexuality for my benefit, a reminder that attractive women are God's gift to ogling men.

Marva isn't amused, either. "Mama ain't even been dead a whole month, and already you're out here chasing butt!"

"Don't lecture me about your mama," Granddaddy snaps. "I loved your mama!"

"I can't tell!"

Ma pulls her hand away from me and waves weakly. "Y'all stop fighting, please."

Both cease verbal fire, though their animus hangs still in the air.

"Where's Tyrell?" Ma asks.

I don't have the heart to tell her she might want to lower her expectation of a visit from him. Between Pastor and Granddaddy, I can't tell who's the bigger asshole. Neither of them would grasp the true meaning of the word respect if I threw it at them from across the room.

"I'm sure he'll be along soon," Marva says, though her eyes belie the sentiment. She offers Ma another spoonful of ice chips, but Ma refuses it.

Granddaddy clears his gravelly throat. "Say, uh, can someone take me home after this?"

"I've got to go to work right after I leave here, so I can't. Sorry," I reply.

"Fine. I'll do it," Marva says. However, the darkness in her voice does little to mask her hatred for her father.

I kiss Ma's forehead and promise to come back after my shift. The moment I step out of her room, my phone rings. Sameer's name shows on the caller ID. Relieved, I answer.

"Hello?"

"Hey, it's me. Just wanted to tell you that I'm fine and I got your message."

"Where are you?" I ask, barely able to hear past the cutting ambient street sounds blaring into my ear.

"I'm in India."

I'm hit with heavy guilt. What if this is my fault? Did my rejection of him make him hop on a plane? "What are you doing in India?"

The myriad sounds of city hustle and bustle intensify; cars honking and indecipherable, angry yelling fills the void where Sameer's response should be.

"I worked things out with my wife."

"I thought she put you on blast to your family."

"No. I begged her not to and told her I was coming to join her. She told her family she's pregnant."

"Umm, congratulations?" I say, confused.

"She's not really pregnant. She just told them that to put pressure on me to give her what she wants. I give her a baby and she will keep my secret."

"Oh, man. How do you feel about that?"

"Trapped."

"Then why are you going along with it? Tell her to go fuck herself!"

"And what happens after that? Are you going to be around to pick me up when everything goes to shit?"

I've already involved myself more than I intended. All I want to know is that he's safe. But who else is there for him to talk to about these things?

"Yes, I'll be here for you."

"Good," he says as if his own emotions were banking on my response, "because I can't get our kiss out of my mind."

The kiss appears at the forefront of my memories, causing my dick to spring awake.

Unfortunately, however enjoyable, it can never happen again.

"Listen, Sameer, about that…"

Loud crackling interrupts our connection. I attempt to push through the noise but to no avail.

"Hey, Lawrence, my reception is shitty where I am at the moment. Can I call you later?"

"Sure," I say, still stuck on his mentioning our kiss, but also confused by his decision to stay put in a marriage he never wanted to be a part of. It's none of my business, but how is he going to find freedom in such an arrangement? Will she have a baby and then ask for a divorce? Will they stay married and lead separate lives? Or will she rope him into staying married with the looming threat of her spilling his truth?

"Okay, I'll call you," he says before the call drops.

Behind me, the squeak of rubber soles on the tiled floor causes me to turn around. It's my grandfather jogging towards me.

"I changed my mind. I'm not goin' home. Think you can drop me at the Spruce?" he asks.

I glance at my watch. Almost ten in the morning. "Can't Marva take you?"

"I ain't goin' nowhere with that crazy bitch!"

"Why?"

"Because she hates me. Both of 'em do!"

"No, they don't. Marva's just frustrated. And Ma is in no condition to hate anybody."

"Either way, there ain't nothin' I can do for your mama. She's in expert hands," he says.

"So, will you run me over there?"

That Granddaddy would rather pass the day in a bar than be at his daughter's side is offensive, but then again, this is the same man who ordered his terminally ill wife out of bed to make him something to eat. Hell no, I don't want to drive him anywhere. But it's too hard to say no to an elder.

"Fine."

He zips up his coat and slides on a skullcap. "Thank you," he says, dropping his face sadly. "Just as well that I go. Nobody wants me here, anyway. Can't say I blame 'em. I was a lousy father. The less they see of me, the better."

"I think you're imagining things," I reply, trying to downplay the sting of truth in what he said. Truth is, I really don't care. I'm so annoyed with him that I'll say anything to stop him from talking. I push the down button on the elevator.

"The hell I am. I know when I'm not wanted. Matter of fact, wouldn't surprise me none if folks wished I would trade places with your grandmama."

I don't answer because I know the level of hatred he's experiencing. I feel that very hatred towards my biological father, Diallo Washington. He threw me away twice. The first time was when he refused to be an active participant in my life. I was sixteen when he came back, presumably to make things right. But he only stayed long enough to realize I was gay, and took off again. When Ma told me someone in Rhode Island stabbed him to death, I waited until she was out of earshot... and I laughed.

Through the years, I've wondered whether men who cast their children aside like littered garbage ever quarrel with themselves over such a choice, or do they close their eyes at night unburdened, expecting the sun to rise the next day? From what I know, Granddaddy is different. He found time between booze and chasing women to raise his daughters. From the eye daggers thrown at him earlier by Marva, he must've done a bang-up job.

By the time we arrive at the Spruce, the first flurries have begun to fall. Unbuckling his seatbelt, Granddaddy reminds me to vote tomorrow. I tell him I will.

"I mean it," he says in a tone the elderly use when they're about to impart wisdom. "I'm old enough to remember when they had us swinging from trees because we wanted our right to vote."

"I promise you; I'm voting tomorrow." I appreciate the sacrifices made by those who walked before me. When I was in high school, I read a book called *We Are Not Afraid*. It was the story of three civil rights workers named James Chaney, Michael Schwerner, and Andrew Goodman, murdered on June 21, 1964, in Mississippi after attempting to register black Americans to vote. There are countless others who contributed, but I hold that piece of history close whenever election season comes around.

However, Granddaddy eyes me skeptically. "Aiight," he says, unsatisfied that I'll make good on my word. "Thanks for the ride."

He's out of the car before I utter, "You're welcome." He crosses the street with an old-school stride in his step, like someone who was the shit back in the day and holds on to that fading glory with everything he possesses. Watching him, I think about the times before I realized he's an asshole. Like when I was a kid and used to jump on his bed like it was a trampoline while he watched football. Or how Granddaddy kept my brother and me stocked up with notebooks, snack cakes, and candy bars for school. A part of me wants those memories to stoke in me a fondness for the old man. Sadly, they don't. But I continue to wait until he disappears behind a dark, tinted glass door and there's nothing left to see. Then I drive away.

# TWENTY-SIX

After a hectic day at work, I receive a text from Hakee telling me to hurry home because he's cooking dinner for me. I let him know that I'll be home after I check in with Ma.

I return to the hospital. Ma is asleep, and Marva is at her side. She peers up from her Bible and smiles. I'm almost honored because it's the first smile I've seen from her in years.

"I suppose it's too early to ask if there's been any improvement."

"Not really. She's been sleeping most of the day." Marva pauses, her mouth twitching. "At one point she woke up and asked about our Mama. But then she realized Mama is dead and gone. It was like she found out all over again. She cried herself back to sleep."

I'm glad I wasn't here to see that. "Had to be rough to watch."

Marva nods; tears glimmer in her eyes. "I should be glad Mama's not suffering, and I know she's in a better place, but nothing prepares you for losing someone."

Her raw vulnerability draws unexpected tears from me. What if Ma hadn't come through surgery and all I had left of her were text messages I never answered?

Strangely, I'm glad my aunt is here. We're actually making progress. Our longtime frozen relationship can finally thaw, however slowly.

"Do you remember when you were little, and you showed up at your grandma's house crying because you'd lost the twenty dollars your stepdad had given you for a haircut?"

The memory pushes through my sadness. I crack a smile.

"She said she'd give you the replacement money, but you'd have to come over one day and help her do yard work, remember that?"

"I sure do. Both me and my brother were getting haircuts that day."

Marva considers this for a second. "Yes. Junior was with you."

"He was. But you're right, Grandma saved me from an ass whipping."

Marva's loud, youthful laughter softens the hard lines on her face. "It feels good to laugh," she says. "I almost forgot how."

"Hey, if I can remember how to pray, then you can remember how to laugh."

"Good point."

"I knew you two would make up," Ma groans from her bed.

"I'm sorry, did we wake you?" I ask.

"Yeah, but don't worry." Despite the pain, she props herself up. "Has Tyrell been in?"

Marva and I exchange a look.

"Yeah," Marva lies. "You were sleeping. He said he'll come back another time."

Ma drifts back to sleep, her faint smile still intact.

"A little white lie never hurt anyone," Marva whispers.

"No judgment here," I say, glancing at my watch. "I should go. Can you tell her I'll come back tomorrow?"

"You've got plans tonight?"

"Yes, as a matter of fact, I do."

"With that man who showed up here the other day?"

Is this a trap? Is she going to quote Leviticus? "He's the one."

"Nephew, please believe me when I tell you I never meant you any harm. My concern has always been with your soul. If it wasn't for your soul, I wouldn't care who you sleep with."

I sigh loudly. "Do you have any idea how many years I've had to listen to people like you give their opinion about where I'm spending eternity? No one cares whether I've got a pot to piss in, they only care that I put dicks in my mouth. Now, if you don't mind, will you please tell my mother I'll be back tomorrow?" I leave her standing there, forcing her to swallow her rebuttal. I couldn't care less if she's mad. I'm tired of always being placed into the position of having to explain and justify my life. For once, I just want to live my life, and with the same peace afforded everyone else.

Heading towards the elevator, I receive a text from Hakee: *Hope you like salmon! Is Bok choy okay for the veggie?*

Waiting by the elevator, I quickly tap out a reply. The moment I hit send, the elevator bings, and the doors open, placing me face to face with a man who appears unsure whether he's on the correct floor. His right arm is in a sling. He eyes me with a panicked familiarity.

"What happened to you?" I ask, giving Ma's ex-boyfriend, Dino Taraborrelli, the once-over as he limps out of the elevator.

He doesn't speak right away, though his expression offers a bleak prologue of what's on his mind.

"Were you in the car with my mother" I ask. Dino stares at me through bruised eyes. I don't care that my question catches him off guard. If I need to continue digging until I strike gold, so be it. "You were, weren't you?" I prod accusatorily.

"Yes," he says, his face reddening. "I was driving her back to her car."

"Back from where?"

He looks at me the way parents look when children forget their place in the authority dynamic. "We had some things to talk about."

"Like what?" I ask, awaiting some tawdry secret to unfurl from his moustached lips. Instead, he regresses into stubborn silence. "Do you know what I think? I think if my mother wasn't in that car with you, she wouldn't be hurt right now."

Dino narrows his deep-set, Pacino-like eyes. "Look, she called and asked to see me."

"Really?"

"Yeah, really!" he snaps. "What the fuck do I look like explaining myself to you?"

If I don't tread carefully, any goodwill he once held towards me will evaporate before we part company. "You're on your way to visit her, right?"

"Yes."

"Now's not a good time."

His face changes to worry. "Jesus, did something happen?"

"She's asleep, and my bible-banging aunt is there with her. Why don't we go somewhere to talk?"

"Wanna grab a coffee?"

"Fine."

An elevator arrives at the left of us, too crowded for my comfort level, but Dino is already going inside. Reluctantly, I follow, stepping into someone's passed gas. The stench lingers over the cramped space. A black woman sucks her teeth, muttering, "This don't make no damn sense!" She pulls a travel vial of perfume from her purse and squirts the air. Soon, the mystery flatulence clashes with the sickeningly floral scent of the fragrance. No one else speaks. I focus on the side of Dino's face to keep from laughing. Someone behind me coughs. The elevator stops.

Dino and I are the first to exit when the doors open to the lobby.

"There's a place in uptown called Uncommon Grounds," Dino says.

"Fine. I'll meet you there."

We luck out finding spots on a graveled parking lot behind a converted Victorian country house that is now a coffee joint. Inside, I ask Dino what he wants to drink. He says he'll have whatever I'm getting, then goes to find a place to sit.

Waiting in line, I send a text to Hakee informing him I'm running late. When my turn at the counter comes, I order two cappuccinos. The pungent aroma of espresso beans reminds me of a time back in my twenties when Kenyatta asked me here to check out a coffee date he met online. When the date excused himself to use the restroom, I warned Kenyatta of the bad vibes I was getting, then returned to my seat before the man returned. Kenyatta declined the man's offer to go home with him. Months later, cops arrested that same man in connection with a snuff film murder.

Dino waits in the rear, staring out the window at the parked cars. I set the beverages down. He groans when reaching for his mug.

"Didn't they give you anything for the pain?"

"Yeah, but I wait until I go to bed so I can sleep through the night," he replies, ripping open the corner of a sweetener with his teeth, and pours the granules into the heavy froth topping his mug.

"Makes sense."

Dino blows on his cappuccino before taking a sip. He lifts his face to reveal a foam-coated mustache. "So, where do I begin?"

"I have plans, so how about the abridged version?"

"All right. Long story short, I ran into your mother at the grocery store two weeks ago. You could say I was happy to see her. She's always been the one bright spot in my life. I told her to call me if she ever wanted to catch up. And she did."

"I'm going to be honest. I don't care if the two of you are having an affair. It serves that asshole husband of hers right."

"I'm gonna stop you right there," Dino says sharply. "We just talked. Nothing else happened. Got it?"

"Okay." I believe him because he's too worn out to lie. However, I'm also a tad disappointed. An affair would've been music to my ears.

"I was driving her back to Wilder Park. It's the in-between point from where we live. Anyway, we were talking, waiting for the light to turn green. As soon as I pulled into the middle of the intersection, we got sideswiped. She got the worse end of it."

"Who did it?"

"Some kid who was texting while driving. Thankfully he didn't flee the scene. I can't tell you how sorry I am. Believe me, I wish I could switch places with your mom."

Dino's selflessness doesn't surprise me. He's a good man. After Ma's divorce from Plez, she was in an awful place because of the financial burden he left her with. Dino stepped in and offered to help in any way he could. She refused to accept money from him, but he was quick to make himself available to me and my brother while Ma worked double shifts and did what she needed to do to dig herself out of debt. I knew then how much he loved her. And while Junior acted antisocially by sequestering himself in his bedroom, I enjoyed the uplifting conversations I had with Dino. He encouraged me despite the bullying I faced in high school and tutored me to help me raise my D in math to a B.

"I wish she would've married you when you asked her. I miss having you in our lives."

Dino grins, then puts a hand to his cut mouth. "Aww, buddy, you don't know how nice it is to hear you say that. I've missed you guys too. Even Plez Jr. How's he doing, by the way?"

"Following in his father's footsteps."

Dino bows his head. "Damn shame."

"Tell me about it. Maybe his wife taking off will teach him a lesson."

"Oh, she split?"

I enjoy my first sip of cappuccino. "I just hope she doesn't go back to him. I mean, not unless he gets some help first."

"Do you think he's capable of seeking help?"

"I doubt it. He didn't seem to own any of the responsibility for her leaving in the first place."

Dino laughs. "They never do."

# TWENTY-SEVEN

"Welcome home, baby," Hakee says, greeting me at the front door with a spoonful of creamy risotto and a kiss. He's wearing my white cooking apron with red-lettered *Best Chef* on the chest. It embodies every bit of the fantasy floating inside my mind.

"Yummy."

"Which, the kiss or the risotto?" he asks.

"Both," I reply, entering the house and removing my shoes. Stepping into the living room is like entering an idyllic scene that I'm delighted to come home to. Minor touches have transformed my living room into a cozy, welcoming space. Dust bunnies are gone, and throw pillows have been fluffed and situated on the sofa in a basic formation I'm too embarrassed not to have thought of myself. The small stack of books I keep promising myself I'll read are returned to their home on the shelf, and my magazines are artfully fanned across the width of my coffee table.

"How was your visit with your mom?"

I sit down, relieved to be off my feet. "She was asleep for most of it. But the good news is I found out who was in the car with her."

Hakee's inquisitive eyes twinkle. "Oh yeah? Who was it?"

"Her ex, Dino."

"Dino? Yo, she got down with an Italian dude?"

"He's a good guy."

"I didn't know your moms was down with the swirl. I ain't mad at her."

"Well, ultimately she wasn't quite so down. She couldn't handle people's opinions."

"So, what, were they hooking up or something?"

"No, they were just talking."

"Yeah, right."

"I believe him."

Hakee laughs. "And what did you expect him to say exactly? 'Yeah, me and your mama are fuckin'. In fact, we've been fuckin all this time.'"

"Eww!" I say, frowning.

"Hey, mamas need lovin' too."

"I guess."

Hakee moves behind me, wrapping himself around my waist. "Come to think of it, *I* could use some lovin' myself."

I swing my ass suggestively. "That can be arranged."

Before melting into a pool of lust, he leads me through the living room, past the election coverage he's been watching on TV. We end up at the dining room table. Like a gentleman, Hakee pulls out my chair, and I take a seat. Sometimes the simplest gestures are the most romantic.

"Okay, you sit tight while I bring out the fish."

I smile, taking in the lovely spread Hakee has set up. There are two plates with intricately folded napkins for each. Forks placed to the left and knives to the right. A bowl of risotto and a large plate of bok choy with slivered almonds are at the center of the table between flickering candles.

"Wow. This looks nice," I yell to him.

"Thanks. Those Home Ec. classes came in handy," Hakee yells back from the kitchen. He returns with a pan of lemon-peppered salmon filets and a spatula. Both of which are placed to the right of the other dishes.

My mouth waters, anticipating the culinary treat Hakee has prepared. "This looks delicious."

"Thank you," he replies, taking a seat himself.

Sitting together at the dinner table is the perfect way to unwind. As I plate our food, I envision future meals together, maybe even entertaining other couples. My fantasy moment changes when I catch Hakee glancing at the TV, and the subsequent look of concern on his face.

"Something on your mind?" I ask, passing him a plate of food.

"Can't stop thinking about this election."

"All we can do is do our part. Everything else will work itself out."

"Yeah, I know we're going to vote tomorrow, but I spoke to a gang of folks who said they aren't voting because they don't think it'll do any good. That makes me uncomfortable. That means anything can happen."

"Try not to let it worry you."

Hakee won't even look at me. He devotes his full attention to the TV. His increased distress is worrying. "Can we eat this in front of the TV? I wanna check the different cable news shows and see what they're talking about."

"But won't that just upset you?"

"Nah, give me an hour and I'll be straight." He picks up his plate and goes into the living room and turns to Fox News Channel. The food on his plate goes uneaten. I eat everything on mine. Though the food is great, Hakee robbed me of the full romantic dining experience.

"Why are you watching this if it's going to bother you?" I ask, picking up Hakee's plate to take into the kitchen. But he's too focused on the coverage to respond. I excuse myself and retire to my bedroom to read a book. *Maybe he'll show up to make good on his sexual promise.* But the more I think about it, the less sex is going to make me feel any better about what's happened with my mother or being attacked by Byron. In fact, if I'm being completely honest with myself, busting a nut is the farthest thing from my mind. But it still would be nice to spend the night in Hakee's embrace, where I can dream of us waking up together with the sunlight in our eyes.

But Hakee has chosen the TV as his companion for the evening. He never makes it to bed.

# TWENTY-EIGHT

November 8, 2016

Election Day

Hakee is gone by morning. I'm convinced he left in the middle of the night. I blame myself. Maybe I should've given him a piece of ass the moment I walked in the door. It might've taken his mind off the election coverage.

But then, the more I think about it, why should I care? He knows I'm going through a hard time. In fact, he's supposed to be here to support me, but all he cares about is this damn election. Is this indicative of what I can expect in a full-fledged relationship?

A medley of sounds draws me to my living room: keys jingling and the crinkling swish of plastic bags. I enter the room as Hakee bumps the front door closed with his ass.

"Morning, babe," he says cheerfully, He sets down the bags of groceries on the credenza to remove his shoes. I gather up the bags. He rewards me with a quick peck on the lips.

"I was hoping you'd still be sleeping when I got back. I wanted to surprise you with breakfast in bed. Figure after the way I acted last night, it's the least I can do."

And just like that, I'm a fool again for having doubted him. His gesture renews my faith that Ma is wrong when she complains that all men are dogs. Maybe just the hounds she fools with. Hakee is proof that some good men still exists in the world.

"What, you thought I dipped out on you?"

It's best not to answer even though that's exactly what I thought. The fear of rejection has to be written all over my face, so I flash him a wink and head towards the kitchen with the groceries.

"What do you think you're doing?" Hakee asks, taking the bags back.

"I'm helping you cook breakfast." Saying it has a nice ring to it. I imagine the two of us trying out different recipes. The fantasy allows Hakee to be bare-chested, with a dishtowel slung over his trapezoid and a dusting of flour on his forehead and the tip of his nose.

"No, I got this," he says, popping my dream bubble. "Go freshen yourself up. I'll call you when the food is ready." He sends me off with another peck on the lips.

Midway through my shower, the house fills with delectable aromas. Once I towel off and dress, my nose summons me to a breakfast of Eggs Benedict and corned beef hash.

"I'm starving!"

"Good. I hope you like it. By the way, after we eat, I've got to split. I wanna beat the voting lines. Want me to come over tonight to watch the polling results?"

Despite a full mouth, I answer yes. After swallowing, I suggest Hakee keep a positive outlook. He suggests we eat our breakfast before it gets cold.

*****

Hakee arrives a half-hour before the cable stations report the first results from the precincts. I proudly thrust my chest forward to show off the shiny red I VOTED sticker on my shirt. I'm proud of partaking in my civic duty. I could almost smell my grandfather's aftershave this morning, as though he were in the voting booth with me, looking over my shoulder. When I slid the completed ballot through the machine, I knew Granddaddy no doubt would be proud that his grandson kept his word.

Hakee brought Chinese takeout and a bottle of sparkling wine to celebrate Clinton's possible win. I put the bubbly into the fridge and open a bottle of merlot. While I grab the plates and cutlery, he assists me with the bottle and glasses.

I eat the vegetable Lo Mein. Hakee eats from the shrimp fried rice. We both ravenously attack the egg rolls. Hakee commandeers control of the TV remote to flip between the cable news channels. It's the home life I've visualized with him. Over time, I would love to bring him frosty, cold beers on warm, hazy days, or a glass of cheap wine poured from out of a bag-n-box.

This time, Hakee at least attempts to split his attention between me and the TV, but ultimately, I lose out to a panel of political analysts giving their predictions of tonight's results.

He notices the disappointment on my face and mutes the TV. He even puts down his fried rice as further proof that I have his undivided attention. I test my appeal by putting my feet on Hakee's lap. He dutifully massages them.

"How was your day?" he asks.

"Work was okay. I'm grateful Quish allowed me to change my schedule to accommodate voting this morning." I don't mention the call I received from Sameer.

I reciprocate the question. Hakee tells me someone offered to pay his balance owed on his studio time if he sleeps with them. I almost choke on my wine, surprised by his candor.

"Your gig at First Avenue wasn't enough to take care of it?"

"No, it wasn't."

"But you'd seriously consider it?" Technically, I don't own Hakee's heart, but it will break mine if he says yes.

"Nah," he says after too long of a hesitation. "He's just some white dude I used to kick it with."

"Used to?"

"Yeah. Well, I cut him off when he told me he was letting me smash because he knew it would piss off his racist parents if they found out my black dick was sullying his whiteness."

"Did his folks ever find out?"

"Yo, this dude secretly recorded us fucking, and sent his parents the tape. Then, his daddy sent someone to my apartment to intimidate me. I wound up beating his ass."

"Whose? The father?"

"Naw, the dude he sent over to fight me."

I'm strangely titillated by his answer. I drop between his open legs and rub his strong thighs. Subservient and practically begging, I want desperately to make up for the other night. There's nothing to be gained from withholding from him.

"Oh, you want some of this?" Hakee asks, nodding to his crotch. He slowly unzips his fly.

I swat his hands away and yank down his pants with a force that surprises both of us. The stark white fabric of Hakee's briefs expands against his stiffening dick.

"Oh shit," he says, assisting with the unwrapping of his package, jutting forth like a python on alert. He reclines back into the sofa; his arms raised behind his head. "You wanted it, go on and take it."

I need no further instruction. I take Hakee's girth into my mouth, slobbering down to the base. Hakee's pubic hair is aromatic with the slight funk of man… just enough to not be offensive. His balls taste herbal and mildly salty. Hakee winces, enjoying my deep suction and tongue play. I keep my eyes on him, paying attention to how his body responds to me.

He slowly outstretches his arms, which span the length of the sofa. His head tilts back, revealing a pronounced web of muscles in his neck, before popping forward again like the retracted cartoon head on a Pez candy dispenser. I recognize the goofy grin on Hakee's face as the same I put on Byron's face multiple times. Hakee opens his eyes, looking dazed but not confused. We stare down at the brick between his legs.

"Wanna go into the bedroom?" I ask, revving to take the action further.

"Naw, let me hit it here," Hakee replies, slapping the cognac-colored leather seat cushion.

The request lacks the romantic hues of our first night together, but I jump at the opportunity. "I'd better go shower up."

Hakee slaps my ass. "Yeah, go in there and get that thang ready for me."

The first spray of shower water is refreshing. I waste no time cleaning my vessel. Hakee deserves my best. Every taste of me will be memorable.

The shower curtain opens. Hakee steps in to join me, his dick vibrating like a tuning fork finding a perfect pitch. I use soap to lather it. The bathroom acoustics capture his deep-baritone moans. Hakee turns me around before I fall into his hypnotic gaze.

Soon he is lathering my back better than I ever could. He is unbothered by the dimples and zits. However, my old insecurities rise to the fore. I tense under his touch.

"Relax, baby. You're perfect," he sings into my ear before descending to my southern regions. He washes my ass with the care he probably washes his own. Afterwards, he slowly spins me around to face him again. Suddenly, I'm tasting his tongue inside my mouth. We stand chest to chest, our jousting erections swelling to full alert as shower water rains upon us.

"My turn to clean you," I offer.

"I got a better idea. I know you're more comfortable in your bedroom. Why don't I finish up here, and you go get everything ready for us? I won't be too long."

I leave Hakee alone in the shower, toweling myself off before tying it around my waist. I stop off at my linen closet to get a brand-new candle to replace the one we burned down to a nub the last time we had sex.

After the jasmine candle is lit, I get the lube and condoms ready on the nightstand. Then I wait. When Hakee arrives, he's dripping wet. He climbs on top of me and weaves his fingers between mine, all the while grinding his manhood against mine.

"I want our makeup sex to be like fire, you hear me?" he asks, suddenly forcing my legs apart.

Our sexual inferno rages on. I lose track of time. All I know is that when our burning rapture is finally extinguished, the candle has melted to its mid-point. Hakee rises from the bed, leaving me cradled in sheets, my insides blissfully invaded and my legs twitching from being over his shoulders for so long.

He kisses my temple. "I'm gonna watch a bit of the election results."

"Okay. Don't be surprised if I'm knocked out when you get back."

"I bet I wore that hole out, didn't I?" he says, blowing out the candle.

"Yes, and then some. Do you want some company?"

"Nah. You get some sleep. I'll be back in a little bit."

Those are the last words I hear. Like the candle, I'm out.

# TWENTY-NINE

I almost sleep through my phone alarm. My eyes open to a torrent of sunlight coming through the blinds. I look to my right. Hakee should be there.

I reach for my phone to scroll the newsfeed. I click on an electoral map of the country. The red metastasis covering it alarms me.

I sit at the edge of the bed, knowing Hakee won't be in the best of moods. The somber voices of cable TV news personalities coming from the living room confirm what Hakee warned me about.

I presume he hasn't slept at all. I don't go to him immediately. Frankly, after hearing him throw a late-night fit by smashing my wine glasses against a wall, I'm not interested in a morning confrontation.

I shower, then dress for another day at the hamster wheel. It's a new day, and yet another mid-shift to get through. No idea what work has in store for me. I cross my fingers and hope the day passes quickly and without incident.

I go into the kitchen to grab something quick to eat. I'm greeted with broken glass and burgundy wine droplets splattered on the wall and counter. I step around the mess to the cupboard. Inside is a box of granola bars I had forgotten about. Guess I've just found breakfast.

I go to Hakee in the living room. He's sitting on the sofa, disheveled and stewing in residual anger from last night.

"I'm going to work. Are you going to be okay?" I ask.

He stares blankly at the TV. "No, I won't be okay. We're doomed." He turns to look at me with an expression that suggests I should already know this.

I regret asking the question. I'm already running on empty, barely slept from worrying what else he would destroy in my house. It's too early to dive into how either of us is feeling after the election. "I'm going to be late. Will you be here when I come home?"

Hakee shrugs and turns back to the TV.

I sigh exasperatedly. "Fine. Text me what you decide to do. And please clean up that mess you made."

Hakee doesn't respond.

Driving along 35 W is like being trapped in a slow-moving funeral procession. I pass the time counting Clinton/ Sanders/ Trump bumper stickers.

At work, a post-election fog of disbelief has befallen the restaurant. Solemn-faced employees go about their duties. I haven't seen people look so defeated since the OJ Simpson verdict.

Quish is barely holding it together at the fry station. She's on the brink of tears.

"How's everything?" I ask, knowing the answer. Her eyes spill over with tears. Her hand trembles to the point she's about to drop the fry scoop. I take it from her.

"How could America get it wrong?" is all she says.

I don't have an answer. Nothing any of us can do about it anyway except put on our game faces and move forward.

Later, after a busy lunch rush, Doug texts me concerning an emergency post-election get-together at his house. Seven o'clock. I reply that I'll be there. The expensive booze being served is worth the drive to Edina within and of itself.

I call Hakee to hear his voice, but his phone goes straight to voicemail. I text him my after-work plans: a quick visit to the hospital and then hang with the other Freed Church Boys to talk about the election. There's no response, which doesn't bode well for my need for instant gratification.

Quish is getting off the phone when I walk into the office with pulled tills from the lunch shift.

"Thanks for holding down the fort today. Needless to say, I'm not in the best of moods," she says.

"Neither is half of the country. We still have a job to do," I say with more heat than I intended.

Quish blinks; her mouth opens slightly. I'm sure she doesn't appreciate my tone but I don't give a shit. She should've had her ass on the floor like the rest of us, not hiding out in the office because she's angry over the election.

I begin to sort currency from one of the tills. To make nice, Quish begins sorting from another.

"Why don't we knock these out together so you can get out of here at a decent time," she says.

A notification chirps from my phone. It's a reply from Hakee, asking what time I'm going to the hospital. I smile, grateful to have a positive morsel on an otherwise crappy day.

"Who's that?" Quish asks, staring at my phone.

"Just Hakee asking what time I'll be at the hospital."

"Oooh, who's Hakee?" she asks teasingly.

"Someone I'm seeing."

"Is he cute?"

"Disturbingly so."

"Huh," she says, and looks again at my phone. "You know what? You did an outstanding job today without my help. Why don't you take off? I got this."

"Are you sure?" I ask, not knowing whether she's just being helpful or I'm being punished.

"Yeah, go enjoy the rest of your day."

"Thanks." I grab my belongings and head out, texting Hakee that I'm leaving now. He replies that he'll meet me at the hospital entrance.

*****

Hakee is waiting by the automatic sliding doors at the entrance. He flashes a sexy yet contrite smile. I'm happy to see his mood has improved from the storm cloud I fled this morning. Once I'm close enough, he greets me with a peck on the cheek.

"Before we go in, I want to talk about this morning," he says.

"Okay." I'm open to hearing what he has to say, but if there isn't an apology at the end of his explanation, we're going to have problems.

"I'm sorry that you saw me in such a funk earlier today. I'm embarrassed that I've let this election make me crazy."

"I think the whole country is on edge."

"Yeah, but I'm only responsible for myself. Since Bali, I've tried really hard to get a hold of my emotions. I shouldn't have taken my anger out on your wine glasses. That's not who I am."

"Are you sure about that? I don't want to get emotionally invested in someone who turns out to be violent."

"I was afraid you'd think of me like that."

"So far you've smashed wine glasses against the kitchen wall. What's next, my face?"

Hakee steps away from me, a mix of alarm and sadness settling in his eyes. "I would never do that to you."

I want to believe him. My intuition tells me he's a good guy who had a bad moment. But then, I wonder how many times Junior and his father insisted they weren't the type to lay hands on someone. Or how many times they apologized after promising the first hit would be the last.

"I wish there was something I could do to make you believe that." His contrition speaks to my heart. He seems genuine enough. Coming to the hospital to show his support is definitely a step in the right direction.

"Maybe there is something you can do," I say with an idea towards lightening the moment.

"Name it and it's yours."

I eye his bulky army-green jacket. "Let me borrow that."

"What's mine is yours."

His willingness to share makes me beam. Some people are particular about loaning out their clothes. "Really? Already?"

"Well, it's not a kidney, but I think I can handle loaning you my jacket. What time are you going to your friend's house?"

"Right after this. I texted Doug to let him know you're coming."

Hakee does a double-take. "I am?"

"I mean, only if you want to. I guess I should've asked you first, huh?"

"Well… but it's cool. I have nothing else going on tonight, anyway."

Reading his face, I don't know whether he's really cool with it. In my excitement to show up with Hakee on my arm, I never asked him what he wanted to do. "Shit, I messed up, didn't I?"

"Don't worry about it. It's nice that you're including me in your plans. How were you planning on getting there? No sense in us taking both cars."

"We could park my car at the house and you can drive."

"I'm with that."

"You sure you don't mind?"

Hakee's lips curl devilishly. "Yep."

The entrance doors slide open. Pastor stomps out, exuding a hostility that I sense has nothing to do with me. I swallow my dislike for the churchman long enough to ask if Ma is awake.

Pastor stinks of his usual contempt. He glances at Hakee, then back at me before informing me that both Ma and I can burn in hell. It happens so fast that he's gone before I can retort. *I hate him.* Yes, it's a powerful emotion, but it's also accurate and honest. Hakee gently squeezes my arm. His hand remains there for the duration of the elevator ride up to Ma's room.

When we enter her room, Ma is sitting upright in bed, crying into Dino's chest.

"You did the right thing," he says, placing a protective arm around her. "You had to tell him the truth."

"Let me guess, Pastor doesn't like to share," I quip.

Dino's glare is quick. "Seriously?"

"It was a joke."

"Yeah, well, now's not the time!"

Suddenly, it's as though I'm in grade school again, being admonished in front of the class by my teacher. "What happened?"

Ma lifts her head. "I told Tyrell I just can't do it anymore," she cries.

"It's about time."

Hakee nudges my arm. "Babe, c'mon."

"What? I'm supposed to stand here and pretend to be sad? He can go leap his black ass off a bridge for all I care!"

"Don't say that," Ma croaks.

"Uh, he just told me he hopes you and I burn in hell. Frankly, if all he left here with is hurt feelings, then he got off easy. He deserves a lot worse."

Hakee whispers he's going to wait in the hall. Ma waits until he leaves to ask who he is.

"Someone I'm seeing."

"Does he have a name?"

I came to see how she's doing, not talk about my love life. I'm not ready for that yet. Dino rises from the edge of the bed and announces he's going to grab something from the cafeteria, which gives Ma and me some time to talk. He asks if he can bring either of us anything back. We tell him no. Dino pats my shoulder. Until now, I hadn't realized how much I've missed him as a father-figure, and what a difference my earlier life might have been had he remained a part of it.

As for Ma, I have so many questions, but with the rift between us, she isn't obligated to provide answers. Besides, she can make her own decisions.

"You look better. How are you feeling?"

"I feel all right. The doctors are telling me I could be out soon."

"Already?"

"They don't keep people around like they used to. Must need the bed," Ma says.

"I know, but still. Seems kind of fast, doesn't it?"

"I'm not complaining. Can't wait to be home in my own space."

Because of her progress, she's being released as early as the following week, Ma inches back into her stacked pillows but is uncomfortable. I fluff and re-layer them. Again, she leans back; this time she finds comfort. Relaxation warms her face.

"Listen, I have to ask, and you don't have to talk about it if you don't want to. What made you finally say enough?"

"I want my real family back."

I wasn't expecting her to say that, but the earnestness in her eyes is smile-worthy.

"So, are you looking to patch things up with Dino?"

She sighs; whether from exasperation or deep thought I don't know, but I remember how he rescued her from her first disastrous marriage. This will potentially be the second… history repeating itself. And while I don't have an issue with Dino stepping in as soon as possible, it must weigh heavily on her because it once again calls into question her choices.

Ma pauses, almost as if she thinks there is a right or wrong answer. But there are no wrong answers for what brings peace and happiness.

"What can I say? I love him," she allows herself to admit finally.

"Then maybe you ought to go where the love is."

"Yeah, but I'm not jumping into anything right away. Nothing becomes official until after the divorce is finalized. I owe Tyrell that much."

"You don't owe him squat, but okay."

The mention of Pastor draws out a long yawn from Ma. Whatever she needs to do to work through the situation is probably too taxing to think about. Perfect time for me to leave so she can rest. But she says...

"I'm happy you came to visit."

"And I'm happy you're making such excellent progress."

She chuckles. "Guess we both have reason to be happy, don't we?"

"I guess."

Ma pauses until the laugh lines fade, leaving her face serious once again. "Are *we* gonna be okay?"

"I'd like to think so... with time, we'll be good again."

"Good, because you know I would never deliberately do anything to hurt you, don't you?"

It's my turn to pause. I'm sure it would give her such joy to know that I've moved past things, but I refuse to be fake.

"Lawrence, look, I'm sorry for letting Plez throw you out. I should've fought for you. In fact, if it meant keeping my children with me, I should've left sooner, but I didn't. Now, I can't undo what I did or didn't do, and I'd like to think we can truly move forward. But you need to let me know now if you're gonna keep holding this over me because I didn't fight this hard to get through surgery just to go back to the way things were."

I exhale deeply. "As long as you're willing to do the work, I'll meet you halfway."

"If that is what it's gonna take, fine. But I'm also gonna need for you to believe that all I've ever wanted is for you to be happy."

I nod. "Fair enough."

"Good. Tell your friend to come here."

"Why?"

"Can't a mother see who her potential son-in-law is?"

"Uh, Hakee and I have a long way to go before that's even a thing."

Ma's face lights up. "Hakee's his name?"

"Yes."

"Well, tell Hakee to get his ass back in here," she says with a wink.

I poke my head into the hallway. He looks up from scrolling his phone. My eyes call to him. No words are necessary. He re-enters the room. Ma's face goes straight again. She gives Hakee the once-over. I brace for whatever embarrassing thing she's going to say.

"Hakee?" she asks, affecting a pretend stern expression.

"Yes, ma'am."

"You got a last name?"

"Mitchell."

"Okay, Mr. Hakee Mitchell, what are your intentions with my son?"

"Ma, come on!" I say, just as embarrassed as when she used to interrogate my school friends whenever they came over to our house. It was her way of sizing them up, to see what they were about.

Hakee fixes his posture and smiles warmly. "It's all right. My intentions with your son are noble, ma'am."

"Oh yeah? And how do I know that?' she asks, allowing the tiniest smile to form.

"Ma, seriously?"

Hakee reaches for my hand, but his eye contact with the woman lying in bed never wavers. "Well, I can't promise that I won't ever say or do something that may hurt him, because I'm human. What I can say is getting to know your son is a pleasure, and you have my word as a gentleman that I will never do anything purposely to cause him any pain."

Ma again puts on her pretend humorless face. She presses the recline button on her bed. "Fine. Now, if you'll excuse me, I need to get some rest. Hakee Mitchell, it was nice meeting you."

"Likewise, ma'am."

I give my mother a gentle hug. "Keep me posted on when they discharge you, and I'll come pick you up."

"I will."

Hakee holds my hand all the way to the elevator, ignoring the disapproving stares from a few passersby.

"Mitchell, huh?" I ask.

"Yep."

"Middle name?"

"Horatio."

"Hakee Horatio Mitchell. Very nice."

Once inside the elevator, Hakee's perfect affect crumbles a little as he sighs a breath of relief and wipes his sweaty hands against his pant leg.

"Man, your moms is tough."

"Don't worry," I say, giving him a quick peck on the lips. "I think she likes you."

# THIRTY

After dropping off my car at the house, I join Hakee in his vehicle. He informs me that he's happy to see me working things out with Ma, adding, he isn't sure whether he can become involved with someone who doesn't have a good relationship with their mother.

I'm quiet for much of the ride to Doug's place. He asks if I'm okay. I reply that I'm fine, although inwardly a little defensive over his remark. I don't owe him any explanations as to the fallout between me and my mother, nor do I want to rip the bandage from the healing wound I share with Hakee.

Parked cars line both sides of Annaway Drive, which is Doug's street. It's impossible to find a place to park. Ultimately, Hakee finds a spot one block over. Walking back to the house, we're all smiles, transfixed by the opulence of the neighborhood, an environment I predict Hakee will one day enjoy for himself.

"This is nice," he says as we backtrack to Doug's place.

"Yeah, it is," I reply, trying to ignore how cold it is.

"I can't believe ain't nobody tried to run a couple of gay black dudes from over here."

"This is Alvin's world. He wouldn't allow himself to be ran off from anywhere."

"Now, which one is Alvin?"

It's the perfect opportunity to warn Hakee that Alvin is Doug's bougie asshole partner, but I drop the bougie asshole part.

I don't recognize the luxury cars parked compactly in the driveway. Two BMWs, a Lexus and a Jaguar.

At Doug's front door, condensation rolls the length of the frosted-glass. After ringing the doorbell, we let ourselves in. Hakee follows my lead, removing his shoes in the foyer, then adds them to the line of guests' shoes.

We encounter Michael and Langston. Each has a drink in hand. Brown liquor… the hard stuff. Both men smile politely despite their otherwise forlorn expressions. I reciprocate and introduce them to Hakee. After pleasantries, we move on toward the sound of jovial voices coming from the living space. Several men gather around the kitchen island, helping themselves to a spread of food and booze set up there. I don't know any of them. Alvin leads the conversation, holding a glass of red wine. I avoid making eye contact with him, but after an accidental glimpse, he waves me over. I muster my most convincing smile and squeeze Hakee's hand for support.

"Alvin, so good to see you again!" I lie.

"And who might this be?" he asks, giving Hakee an inquisitive glance.

My plus-one steps forward to introduce himself. He extends a hand to Alvin. "Nice to meet you, man. The name's Hakee,"

Alvin shakes the offered hand. "Good to know you." He turns to me and says, "My, my, my. He's actually nice-looking. What's he doing with you?"

I roll my eyes at the dig. He's nothing if not consistent in his assholery.

Hakee puts his protective arm around me, shrouding me from the leering faces of strangers. That's when I realize many of them are there at the behest of Alvin. What better way for him to be his less than charming self than in front of a friendly audience.

"Yo, is this how you treat your guests?" Hakee asks gruffly.

Alvin lightly taps my chest. "Oh, I kid this one."

"It's all right, Hakee," I say, picking up a bottle of wine to pour myself a glass. "It's not like we're here to see him anyway."

"As true as that may be, you are in my house, about to drink my liquor."

I put down the bottle. "I don't need to drink that badly."

"You sure? From what I hear, you really know how to throw 'em back."

Hakee approaches, putting his face within inches of Alvin's. The two men can probably heat each other's faces with their breath. "Say something else smart!"

Alvin backs away, his palms out, a shit-kicking grin on his face. "Relax. We're all friends here."

I'm flattered by Hakee's valor, but there's no need to get bounced before I have the chance to see Doug, nor do I want to hand Alvin something else to take out on him later.

"Let's go over there," I suggest, eyeing a place to sit on the chaise lounge across the room.

There, standing in the middle of the room, is Doug, disquieted in demeanor and nursing his standard martini. As soon as our eyes connect, I take Hakee over with me. Doug and I embrace.

Already a few cocktails in, he slurs into my ear, "Can you believe this shit? She should've won." Doug breaks our embrace when he notices Hakee for the first time. "Oh, I didn't know you were bringing trade to my house."

I laugh. "This isn't trade. His name is Hakee, and I texted you he was coming."

"Chile, I've been so glued to the TV, I didn't bother to check my phone." He shoves his hand toward Hakee to shake it. "Anyway, I'm Doug. Nice to meet you."

"Same here," Hakee replies.

Doug looks down at our drinkless hands. "The world is going to hell and y'all aren't drinking?"

"We were over there trying to get a drink, but I don't think your man wants us here."

He looks in Alvin's general direction and rolls his eyes. "What did that motherfucker say to you?"

"You know what? It's not a big deal."

"No, fuck that! He needs to stop talkin' reckless to my friends! And besides, I'll be damned if I'm the only one getting faded tonight. What are the two of you drinking?"

"We don't want any trouble," Hakee says.

"Don't be silly. I'm playing hostess. Alvin can kiss my black ass!"

After we tell him our drink requests, Hakee suggests we move around. I spot Stephen finishing a conversation with Reese. We make eye contact but he doesn't look happy to see me. After the way I spoke to him the last time we were all together, I can't say I blame him. The same way I didn't appreciate Alvin's dumb ass judging me for the kind of work I do I have no business judging Stephen's decision to go back to church.

He veers off to the right, past a cluster of members, but I intercept him.

"You don't have to run from me," I say, putting on a smile that I hope conveys I come in peace.

"What's up?" Stephen asks, not fully committing to our reconciliation.

"Listen, I owe you an apology."

"For what?"

Now why is he acting like he doesn't know the reason he's just tried to avoid me? Why is he going to make me spell it out? "I had no right to give you grief over going back to church."

"What can I say, I had to do what felt right for me. I don't wanna burn in hell."

Hakee's observation of two versions of God comes to mind. Guess I can figure out which one Stephen believes in. But hey, to each their own.

"So, are we good?" I ask.

An ease comes over Stephen's face. "Yeah, man. We're good," he says giving me a fist bump. He holds up an empty glass to indicate it's time for a refill and walks away.

I head in the opposite direction. The house feels warmer than the last time I was here. I watch the strangers hanging on Alvin's every word. Dressed in Lacoste and Ralph Lauren, they wouldn't dare set foot in a place like Sparkles. They belong in a swanky wine bar I'm not hip enough to know about. I bet if I were hosting this get-together, they would take one look at my modest home and keep driving.

Hakee eases into an innocuous conversation with Brian and Colby, two members I haven't seen in a while. I half-listen. My mind drifts to a flyer I saw tacked on a restroom wall at the club, advertising Election Night two-for-ones.

*Where the hell did Doug go?* Was he picking the damn wine grapes himself? That settles it, I need to stop drinking so much. For the past year, I've promised myself I'll cut back on the booze, even threatening to start the next day… go all in… cold turkey. Anyway, I drink out of habit. It's not like I get "dope sick" like some junkie if I go a few days without a drink. Although, for as long as it's taking Doug to come back with the goods, maybe this moment is as good a time as any to quit. But, before I head over to change my drink order to a sparkling water, Alvin's buffoons migrate into the living room. Their festive verve belies the reason Doug has called us here today.

Alvin, of all people, appears with my wine and a Courvoisier for Hakee, a snide, knowing glint in his eyes. "I see someone's changed his mind."

"Hey, everyone… hello!" Doug yells. "Can we get started?"

We quiet down, and take seats wherever they are available. Alvin pushes the drinks at me to take from him, then joins Doug in front of the fireplace. I'm glad I don't have to come up with a response. Hakee returns to my side.

Doug clears his throat. "So, after last night, Alvin and I decided we'd have you guys over to talk about how we feel about the election result. Anyone want to share their thoughts with the group?"

Alvin raises his index finger. "Uh, allow me to say for the record, this is all for Doug's benefit. I'm cool with the outcome."

Hakee solemnly grips my hand.

"Yeah, and I'm still trying to wrap my brain around that one," Doug mutters.

"Why are you acting as though this is some monumental revelation? I told you who I was voting for," Alvin says in an irritated tone better suited for when the two of them are alone.

Guests exchange uncomfortable glances. Reese raises his hand to speak. Doug calls on him.

"On the way here, I was telling myself that I need to rededicate my life to Christ. Maybe start attending worship services again."

"Why?" Alvin asks.

"Because last night proves that we're living in the last days."

"How?" Hakee asks.

"I've begun reading my Bible again. Last night I was reading 2 Timothy chapter 3. It speaks on the different signs that will come to pass: love of self; love of money; religiosity without godliness; unforgiveness and cruelty towards one another. You mark my words, that demon that just got elected exemplifies *all* of those things!"

"You got all that from an election?" Alvin asks. "People have been misbehaving ever since Eve gave Adam fruit from the tree of knowledge. Hell, Cain killed his brother because he was jealous of him. And if you ask me, all politicians are crooked one way or another. So, in the end, it really doesn't matter who sleeps at Sixteen-hundred Pennsylvania Avenue. Life is going to continue just as it did the day before the election."

"Yeah, but this time feels different," Reese says, unconvinced.

"Don't worry, brother, I get you," Stephen says to Reese. "Nothing wrong with wanting to make things right with God."

Hakee raises a finger, but he doesn't wait to be called on. "I guess I'm struggling to figure out how you guys think going to church is going to change what's happened."

Stephen tosses an annoyed look in Hakee's direction. "What kind of question is that? Do *you* even believe in God?"

"Yeah, as a matter of fact, I do. Listen, I'm just asking a question. Not trying to be disrespectful."

Stephen side-eyes Hakee and sucks his teeth.

Reese clears his throat. "I don't think anyone is saying that going to church is going to change the outcome of last night. It's just, and I'm speaking for myself here, if this *is* the beginning of the end, I want to be right with God."

"Who's to say you're not already right with Him?" Hakee asks.

Everyone, except Alvin and Stephen nods. Judging from the smirk on Alvin's face, he probably thinks this entire conversation is silly.

Hakee continues. "I'm guessing at one point or another everyone here has accepted Christ as their personal savior. Do we still believe that?"

This time everyone nods, including Alvin.

"So, then I repeat, who's to say you're not already right with Him? If God put us here, knowing we're imperfect, and sent His Son to die for our sins, we're saved by His grace. There's no amount of right we can do to warrant salvation. So, what else is there to do besides try and be a decent human being to our fellow human beings?"

Stephen scoffs. "You think that's all there is to it?"

"I sure do. And it shouldn't be too hard. Because even though most evangelicals voted for his ass, there's nothing remotely Christian about him. Sorry, but you can't tell me he's a good person and say it out loud with a straight face."

"Look, Trump is a showman. All that blustering and chest thumping was to get people out to vote. Now he'll get down to business and give me my tax cuts," Alvin says to thunderous applause from his group of buddies.

"Tax cuts? That's what this is about to you all? Don't you care who he appoints to the Supreme Court?" Hakee asks.

"Actually, no, I don't care about the Supreme Court. None of those cases they've adjudicated affect me in the least. My only concern is how can I best protect my money. The tax cut Trump proposed to implement protects my money."

"Don't you mean your daddy's money?" Doug mutters louder than he probably intended.

Alvin passes Doug a dirty look. He leans in and whispers something in his ear before remembering there are others present. Alvin turns to offer us a smile, cartoonishly wide and all upper teeth, for our consumption. He says, "Whether it's my money or my father's money, you have no qualms about spending it."

"Aww, shit. Something's about to pop off," Hakee whispers to me.

I look into my glass of exquisite wine. It's almost empty. My sips must be massive. Yes, I need to lay off the wine. But what happens when it's too good not to enjoy? I glance at Hakee's snifter, which he's barely touched.

"I'm going to get myself another glass."

Hakee removes his arm from around my waist. I catch looks of envy from some of Alvin's friends which make me giddy. I carry it with me to the kitchen island.

There's a bounty of wine options. Too many options. Everything from a Sangiovese or a Malbec to Pinot Noir. I don't know which of them I've been drinking. Maybe I'm too basic to appreciate the differences. Give me a decent Cabernet or Merlot any day and I'm fine.

I grab a bottle of Stags Leap and pour into my glass. A heavy buzz hits me, unlike the kind that grows over time after a few drinks. My inner voice tells me to put down the glass. My liver is sure to thank me for it. Another voice, my saboteur, reminds me I can always cut back tomorrow. I acquiesce to mischief and pour the hearty glass like I pour for myself at home.

I maneuver back to Hakee without spilling a drop. I'm proud of that, too. Hakee gives the full glass a long, disapproving glance.

Someone asks to see a show of hands of Trump supporters in the group. More hands go up than I expected. All belong to Alvin's cronies, but a mix of groans and boos counter their smattering of applause.

I'm laden with disappointment and concern; trapped inside an expanding unease. This brotherhood I've relied on, however sporadically, is splintering before my eyes. And all because Alvin invited some of his hotshot buddies over to gloat.

While everyone argues amongst themselves, Alvin forcibly ushers Doug from the room. I knew it would be just a matter of time before Alvin unmasked himself as the bully I've always suspected him to be. His expression is the same ornery mask that most abusers display when they feel disrespected. Add alcohol to the mix, and there's no way Alvin is going to wait until everyone leaves to flex his intimidation muscles and remind Doug who's wearing the expensive trousers in their relationship.

I hand my glass to Hakee and excuse myself to use the restroom. I creep along the hallway, past the guest's bathroom, toward the master bedroom in the house's rear. A partially open door gives way to angry whispers. I press my back firmly against the wall, cocking my head far enough to listen.

"What did I tell you about your mouth?" Alvin yells suddenly.

"Will you keep your voice down? People can hear you!"

I peer through the crack of the open door. Alvin grabs Doug by the scruff of his shirt, pinching the skin along Doug's sternum. "Who the fuck do you think you're talking to?"

"Ow! You're hurting me!"

"Tough shit!"

The two men fall into the wall with a loud thud.

"Let go of me!"

Alvin regains his footing while maintaining his grip on Doug's shirt. He pushes him back into the wall. A framed picture of the two of them drops off the wall and shatters on the floor.

"Then you do what I tell you to do," Alvin says, his hand rising to his partner's throat.

"I can't breathe!"

"Shut that shit up! You wouldn't be able to talk if you couldn't breathe!"

It's disconcerting to witness my friend cowering under Alvin's psychotic gaze. Who knows what Alvin would do to him if no one else was here. I take a deep breath for courage, knowing the moment I enter the room there's no going back. By involving myself in something that's none of my business, I will be shaking the proverbial hornet's nest. I should turn my tipsy ass around and go back into the living room and listen to everyone fuss. At least Hakee will be there. But I can't leave Doug alone. Against my better judgment, I push open the bedroom door and charge into the room.

"What the hell is going on here?"

My presence startles both men. Doug staggers from Alvin's weakened grip. Straightening his shirt, he smiles feebly, the way Ma used to when my brother and I would walk in on Plez Sr. giving her a wallop across the face. "We're just talking," he says.

"Yeah, this doesn't concern you," Alvin says.

"If you're hurting my friend, yes, it does concern me!"

Alvin approaches me, his eyes deathly serious. "I advise you to take your lumpy ass back in that room with the others."

Doug positions himself between us. "Sweetie, just do what he says. I promise you, we're good."

"You are *not* good. You're terrified of this man! There's no way I'm leaving you alone with him!"

Stress lines run the width of Doug's creased brow. Despite trying to verbally discourage my involvement, his wide, stoned eyes plead for help. I know he lacks the courage to utter the word. Nothing more than a gasp escapes his trembling mouth. He's too shaken to move. I guide him into the massive walk-in closet. Designer luggage is stacked in the far corner. I take the lead and select the Louis Vuitton case with wheels on its bottom. I open it.

"Douglas P. Joyner, you leave this house, don't expect to come back" Alvin threatens.

"Start packing," I instruct Doug, ignoring Alvin's bluster.

Whatever is in Doug's path gets tossed into his suitcase. Each time he emerges from the closet, another clothes hanger swings bare. Next, he rifles through dresser drawers for underwear and hidden jewelry. He stops to put on a pair of oversized "celebrity" sunglasses.

Once Doug has everything he needs, we head back into the living room. None of the other guests seem to care that the homeowners are MIA. It isn't until we pass through, and they hear the stiff squeaking of Louis Vuitton luggage, that they lift their noses from their drink glasses. Doug announces that he and Alvin have just had a fight.

Some idiot (most likely one of Alvin's friends) asks if this means the get-together is over. Not to be embarrassed in front of his friends, Alvin shouts, "Fine! Take your funky ass on if you're going! You'll be selling it by the end of the week!" He follows Doug to the garage, screaming, "Oh no you're not! The car stays here!"

Doug silently gets into his black 2015 Mercedes. Hakee and I wait at the foot of the driveway as Alvin's diatribe continues. The other Freed Church Boys are leaving as well. Alvin's friends gather behind him to watch the drama unfold.

"You're dead to me, bitch!" Alvin booms. "Good luck finding someone who will put up with your useless ass!" He goes on and on until finally, he loses steam and retreats into the house and slams the door.

Doug offers to drive us the block over to Hakee's car. We accept. En route Doug asks if anyone minds stopping off at an Arby's.

"I'm hip," I reply.

"I always think better on a full stomach," Doug says.

"What's to think about?" Hakee asks.

"Where I'm sleeping tonight. I'd better start checking hotel availabilities."

"Ha ha. Hilarious. You're staying with me," I say.

"I don't want to intrude."

"You won't be."

At the restaurant, we order takeout to bring back to the house. Hakee orders nothing, deciding at the moment to go home.

"Are you good?" I ask.

"Yeah, I'm cool. Just thought you might want some time to help your friend figure things out."

"You don't have to go on account of me," Doug says.

"Naw, seriously, I'm good."

I lower my head. "Maybe one day you'll let me see where you live."

"Funny, you should ask. I was thinking about cooking you a nice birthday dinner at my place."

I smile, elated I'm not the only one thinking about it.

"Alrighty, y'all have a good night. Doug, it was nice meeting you, man. Sorry it wasn't under better circumstances."

"You and me both."

I walk Hakee to his car to give him a kiss goodnight and promise to call him before I go to bed. Two straight guys get out of their vehicle to go inside the restaurant. One leers in our direction, nudging the other. Hakee flashes them both a venomous look, and they hurry along.

*****

At home, I open a bottle to go along with our order of regular roast beef sandwiches and potato cakes.

"Well, aren't you going to say, 'I told you so?'" Doug asks.

"I don't need to be right. I'm just glad that you left his ass."

Other than the sound of our chewing, we're silent for the duration of our meal. Doug's been through enough. No need to press the issue. I assume he'll talk about it when he's ready.

"Let me know when you need me out of here tomorrow," he says later.

"You're welcome to stay as long as you like. Hell, you can move in for all I care."

"Seriously?"

"Sure, why not?"

Doug leans back into the sofa and sighs his relief. "As long as I can pay you rent."

"I wouldn't have it any other way."

For the next few hours, we enjoy *Two Can Play That Game* and *Waiting to Exhale*, taking turns reciting dialogue. I stopped drinking after my glass of wine with dinner. However, Doug kills that bottle and another all on his own.

We take a break to use the bathroom. Doug goes first. I gather up fast-food garbage to bring into the kitchen. An explosion of glass sprays the living room floor. A large brick lands on top of the broken shards. I race to my front door, my heart pounding through my fingertips. I open the door just as a dark vehicle screeches away.

I quickly close the door. My panic is fully ignited, and my imagination wheel once again churns vividly. What If scenarios leap across my mind? What if whoever threw the brick comes back and shoots up my house with an AK-47? What if they kick in my front door and murder us as we sleep?

Doug runs into the room, alarm splashed across his face like cold water. "What in the hell happened? Who did this?"

"I don't know," I reply, absentmindedly touching the back of my neck. "You've never told Alvin where I live, have you?"

"Are you, crazy? Of course not."

I step around the broken glass and pick up the brick. A gust of cold air blows in through the large break in the bay window.

"If it isn't Alvin, then there's only one other person it could be."

"Who?"

"Byron's punk-ass!"

"What reason would he have to do that?"

I don't want to say it, but the need to do so bubbles inside me like bad gas. I often find myself sideswiped by memories of that evening. They're inconsiderate visitors, manifesting while I'm driving or walking to the fry station, or being chewed out by a customer at work. I can't forget the coarseness of Byron's jeans against my thighs or the dewiness of sweat on his face. I even remember the staleness of his boozy breath.

"Last time he was here, he was drunk and tried to sexually assault me," I say.

Doug's eyes widen. "Oh my god! Did he rape you?"

"Like I said, he tried. But don't worry, I broke his nose for his effort."

"Good! That's what his ass gets. And it's too bad there wasn't a knife around."

"I didn't get off scot-free, though. He promised me he'd get me for what I did to him."

"What you did to him? Bitch, please! What about what he did to you?"

"Well, I thought maybe since he'd been drinking, he'd calmed down. Guess not."

"You are going to call the police, right?"

"Not if I'm not sure he did it."

"You said yourself, who else could it be?"

Doug doesn't wait for my reply. He's on the phone with the cops, and the night air chills my face the longer I stare from the damaged window.

"What did they say?" I ask when he's ended the call.

"They're sending someone." Doug grabs the broom from the kitchen to sweep up the glass, but just like with Hakee, I'm not in the right frame of mind to assist. My heart tells me Byron is the culprit. But what if he was only talking shit out of anger?

"Let's not wait until the New Year to make our resolutions. I declare here and now, no more trifling-ass men," Doug says. "Are you with me?"

I nod as a cop car slows down in front of the house and pulls into the driveway. Its high beams are blinding.

The cops take my statement, but besides Byron's name and a description of him and his silver Bentley, I'm unable to answer questions regarding his whereabouts. He's always been careful not to divulge any personal information that would be detrimental to whatever he has going with his wife. Still, the cops are professional and appreciative of what little info I offer. I still feel useless.

We stand at the window to watch the cops drive away. The lack of resolution is infuriating. Damn shame I let what I thought was good dick impair my judgment. Instead of asking Byron whether he preferred boxers or briefs, I should've asked better questions, like, was he a possessive asshole? Did he have the propensity towards sexual assault, or chucking a brick through my damn window?'

"I should've been smarter. I should've seen this coming," I say.

"Meh! Shoulda, woulda, coulda. You did the best you could at the moment... we both did."

"Yeah, well, our best wasn't good enough."

We get to work patching the hole with cardboard, a black garbage bag, and duct tape. Afterward, as we admire our handiwork, we listen to the wind rattle the plastic. The fix is shabby and makeshift, but at least it keeps the cold air outside where it belongs.

"Tomorrow call a window specialist," Doug says.

I scoff. "And pay with what? I didn't include vandalism into my budget this month."

"I'll pay for it."

"I can't let you do that."

"You're just going to leave it like this? That patch job isn't going to hold up forever."

He's right, but that's a problem for another day. My pressing concern was naming Byron Ross to the police. I have to be sure because if I got it wrong, the hole in my window will be the least of my problems.

# THIRTY-ONE

I just woke up from a nightmare of Byron standing at the foot of my bed, stroking himself with one hand, while brandishing a large kitchen knife with the other.

Doug sleeps unbothered. His snores are like sputtering lullabies, sung from the distance of the living room.

The intense overnight gusts of wind continue to flap and rattle the affixed garbage bag against the window. I lay awake wondering how in the hell is Doug sleeping through all that noise. Maybe being away from Alvin has given him peace of mind. Meanwhile, I'm in here tossing and turning despite needing to be up in a few hours to open the restaurant for the breakfast shift.

Eventually sleep comes. I'm able to squeeze four meaningless hours from it. Later, I awaken sluggish. Doug is awake, slurping down the last of cereal milk from a bowl. Without prompting, he announces that the rattling plastic bag eventually got to him too.

"What do you have planned today?" I ask, checking the refrigerator for something to eat and half-expecting different options to have magically materialized since yesterday.

"I need to figure out a way to get the rest of my shit," he says. He runs a stream of warm water into the now empty bowl, swishing it around, and pours out semi-milky water before putting the bowl into the dishwasher.

"Maybe you should take a police escort."

"Or we could use that soldier boyfriend of yours."

I chuckle, smiling my first smile of the day. "Okay, first, he's not my boyfriend. Second, I'd like to keep him out of this. I don't want him to think he's got to be my protector all the time."

"Mmm hmm. All that man... I bet he beats it up in the bedroom, don't he?"

This is the first we've discussed Hakee. My cheeks warm from the newness of it, like a teenager's first experience with blossoming love. Because Hakee and I are giving it another go, I want to keep our relationship secret for risk of jinxing it. "Isn't it a little early in the morning to be having this conversation?"

"All right, all right. when does your shift end?"

"I should be finished after three. Why?"

"I was thinking, if you're serious about me being your roommate, you could come with me to pick out a bed for my new room." Doug holds up his phone, displaying a variety of beds on the screen.

"Sure, we can do that. Do you want me to meet you somewhere in particular?"

"Calhoun's Bed World in Uptown."

"Okay. When I'm ready to leave, would you mind moving your car so I can get out?"

"Sure. Let me know."

After a hot shower, I'm delighted to find a travel cup filled with piping hot coffee waiting for me on the counter, next to a brand-new coffee maker I never got the hang of using.

"So glad you know how to work the machine. It's been just sitting there collecting dust, which is a shame because it's top-rated for its coffee. Be a dear and teach me how to work it, won't you?"

Doug executes a low, dramatic curtsy. "I am but a faithful servant." He grabs his keys and heads outside to his car, halting in front of mine.

Etched with a knife in large letters onto the top hood of my car is the word *faggot*.

"Who did this?" he asks.

"The same asshole who threw the brick into my window. Fuck, one more thing to worry about."

"You're going to file another report, right?"

"Oh, you better believe I'll be paying the police a visit after work. Anyway, I'll keep you posted on my progress."

*****

My shift goes smoothly. Doug texts me the name of an auto body shop he uses. I make an appointment for an estimate later in the week. I'm unhappy about driving around with a pejorative scrawled on my vehicle, but at least I have a potential fix to the problem.

After work, I file a complaint at the police station, then join Doug at Calhoun's Bed World, although it's clear he wants me here more for the sake of companionship than helping him pick out bed frames. He selects a nice low-rise, platform. I ask which mattress has he picked out. He tells me he's already ordered the mattress from another vendor, the company that makes the mattress he used to share with Alvin. When I ask won't that just remind him of Alvin, he announces he's ready for lunch.

We eat lunch across the street at Figlio's. I order cavatappi pasta with grilled chicken, broccoli, and diced tomatoes. Doug orders a mixed-greens salad with grilled portobello mushrooms.

"Why aren't you drinking?" he asks me, noticing the sparkling water I've been nursing, while he's already onto his second glass of Sauvignon Blanc.

"I think I need to take it easy on the booze."

"Does it bother you that I'm having wine with my lunch?"

"Not at all. Do you."

Doug looks thoughtfully at his salad. "Do you think maybe you have a problem?"

I shrug. "Maybe. Anyway, better I deal with it now on my own than one day be court-ordered to."

A server I recognize from the club walks past. One of those bitchy queens who think he's a ten, and on the lookout for a twelve. It's too late to avoid eye contact. He rolls his eyes, then drops an entire tray of food. Serves him right.

"Lunch is on me," Doug says, stifling a desire to laugh.

"Don't you think you ought to be careful spending your ex-partner's money?"

"I'm good."

"Not if he freezes those accounts, you aren't."

He chuckles. "He can't freeze what he knows nothing about. I have my own money."

"Really? I thought he took care of you."

"Alvin needs somebody he can control, so he insisted on paying for everything. But while he did that, I was making a pretty penny writing erotica fiction."

I almost spill my water. I'm not the only one withholding information. "I didn't know you wrote."

"Technically, I don't. My nom du plume, Brandon Nutts, does. Alvin didn't want any of his friends to know I write smut, and he didn't think it would amount to much. He forbade me from telling anyone. But, while he thought he was calling the shots and paying for everything, I was at Starbucks writing on my laptop. And just to show you how little faith Alvin had in me, he didn't realize I was having my silly little stories edited, and independently published on Amazon."

"Wow, and here I thought you wanted someone to take care of you."

"At one point, I did. But I hated how judgmental people were. I was his kept boy and made to feel inferior. One day I said no more, and I began squirreling away money. Thank goodness I'm able to make a sweet living doing what I love."

I raise my glass and clink it against Doug's wine, happy that my friend is way ahead of me in realizing the type of man Alvin revealed himself to be.

"So, what becomes of the Freed Church Boys club now that we've lost our luxury surroundings?" he asks. "Is there any way we could host it at your place?"

"After seeing your place, I doubt anyone will want to come to my modest dwelling."

"You sell yourself short. I think the group is a necessary brotherhood. Although we sometimes veer from its original purpose, I still think we ought to continue."

Once again, I raise my glass. "I'm in if you're in."

Later, when I pull into my driveway, I'm treated to a lovely surprise... the sun reflecting beautifully off of a brand-new bay window. From the way Doug is beaming, it's no secret who's responsible for the good deed.

"You know, you didn't have to do this," I say as he gets out of his car.

"I felt bad. You shouldn't have to tolerate a broken window, Lawrence. You've been a real friend to me. It's the least I can do for you."

I open my mouth to contest the gesture.

"Just say thank you."

I can't help but grin. "Okay. Thank you."

# THIRTY-TWO

November 20, 2016

It's beautiful to wake up in Hakee's bed on my birthday. His apartment isn't what I thought it would be, not that I had any clear idea. It's a new development, ultra-modern with the usual sharp angles and minimalism. The sparsely decorated apartment could serve as a model unit shown to prospective renters. Hakee likes it this way, and told me it's easier to move from place to place with fewer possessions.

Hakee has a well-paying gig tonight at a club called the Fine Line Music Cafe, so we celebrated my birthday last night. At first, he feared offending me by celebrating a day early, but when he mentioned the appearance would pay the remaining studio balance with mad money to spare. I thought he'd be a fool not to accept, and it actually works out that Hakee's performance is tonight because Ma has something special planned for my birthday.

However, Hakee made sure last night was special, too. For dinner, he made spaghetti aglio e olio and garlic bread. For dessert, we had chocolate mousse and each other.

"I could be way off track here, but I know how important your Church Boy group is to you. I got you something. Hopefully, it'll help you find some direction." He handed me a Barnes and Noble bag. Inside was a book called *Overcoming the Spiritual Bully*. How thoughtful. My face warms with a smile.

"Did I do okay?"

"You did very well, mister. Thank you. I can't wait to read it."

Afterward, we watched *Paris Is Burning*, another movie he hadn't seen but figured it had to be something special if I had a movie poster of it on my bedroom wall. It touched me when he cried towards the end when Anji Xtravaganza revealed someone murdered her house daughter, Venus, and left her under a bed in a sleazy hotel. That scene brought tears to my eyes as well the first time I watched it.

A morning text pulls me from my reverie. It reads: *Happy Birthday, Kiddo! I miss you!* Only LaSaundra calls me "Kiddo." We haven't spoken since she told me exactly what she thinks of me. I thought there was nothing left to say. Apparently, she does, but I'm going to file that conversation away as yet something else needing resolution. My first priority is finding out who in the hell threw a brick through my living room window and scratched the hood of my car. The cops are good for nothing. I doubt they even take my complaints seriously. I'm partly relieved, because if they aren't taking this seriously, I don't have to worry about the potential of blaming an innocent person. Then again, I recall the hatefulness in Byron's eyes after I broke his nose. I'm pretty certain he's behind it.

"Happy birthday, birthday boy," Hakee whispers, treating my shoulder to kisses.

"Thank you," I say, reclining into his spoon.

"Checking birthday messages?"

"Just one. You won't believe who it's from."

"Who?" he asks, still flecking his velvety tongue over my shoulder.

"Ex-roommate," I moan, snuggling my back against his warm chest and my ass into his crotch.

"Oh, somebody wants morning dick, huh?" He rolls on top of me with a swift pounce, the platform bed creaking beneath us. "Hmm, you want some of this dick?" he asks breathily as he rubs his mightiness against me. He catches me in mid-nod, with a stroke of his hand along my neck, gently raising back my chin. He sniffs the back of my head, which still smells of his shampoo I used during our shower together last night. Thinking about our lathered, wet flesh coming together causes my dick to spring awake.

My phone rings. The number is familiar, though no longer included in my contacts.

"You wanna get that?" Hakee asks, wrapping his arms around my waist to pull me away from doing just that. I'm more than happy to let the phone ring, and give into what he has in store for me.

After our wake-up sex, we stare into the featureless, white ceiling, our chests rising and falling in unison.

"It's funny," he says, breaking the silence. "When I bought that book, I wondered whether you'd ever step foot in a church again."

The thought rarely crosses my mind anymore. Too many modern-day pharisees have hijacked Christianity to control and divide people, I don't know where I fit in with organized religion. This current incarnation of Christianity is nothing more than a spiritual roux of self-righteousness, judgment, and performative deeds. However, that isn't to say there aren't any decent, well-meaning Christians left. I know they're out there, spread all over the place.

"I don't know," I say wistfully. "I kind of miss the superficial stuff like potluck Sundays and checking out the fashion sense of the congregants. Other than that, I'm not sure I still have anything in common with the church. I do still consider myself a child of God, but I feel funny using the term, Christian."

Hakee gently runs his fingers along my stomach in up and down streaks. "I feel you. But you never know, maybe the right church is out there for you. A shitty meal at one restaurant shouldn't keep you from trying other restaurants."

Hakee's wisdom dazzles me. "Good point."

"And when you find a church you're comfortable in, maybe you can get your moms to go with you."

"One miracle at a time."

Hakee laughs. "Fair enough. I was just thinking it might be a good way to reach out to her. But what do I know?"

He makes perfect sense. A voicemail notification chirps from my phone, saving me from conceding that Hakee's idea is a good one. I listen to the voicemail.

"Hey, boo! Haven't heard from you since your disappearing act at the club. Anyway, it's your birthday, and I wanted to buy you a drink. Call me." Kenyatta also leaves a text saying the same thing. I delete both.

*****

My lunch shift is a breeze. Quish surprises me with a German chocolate cake. She proudly informs me she baked it herself. Crew and management gather around me to sing "Happy Birthday."

"How does it feel to get old?" an employee jokingly asks me as Quish slices into the cake.

I think for a moment then reply, "I'm not getting old, I'm getting better." For the first time in my life, I actually believe it.

As everyone enjoys a piece of cake, I receive another text from Kenyatta. Again, I delete it.

Later at Ma's house, Dino answers the door. He's dressed in jeans, a white dress shirt, navy blazer, and cognac-colored dress shoes. He's still sporting a cast, but appears less stiff and pale than when I saw him at the hospital.

"Where are you coming from, looking so handsome?" I ask him.

"Aww, just felt like dressing up. Happy birthday, man," he replies, allowing me entry into the house. The smooth sounds of Roy Ayers' "Everybody Loves the Sunshine" fills the house. With the aroma of Ma's catfish, it feels like old times.

"Is he here?" Ma yells from the kitchen.

"Yeah, Ma, I'm here."

She comes into the living room, holding fast to her cane. Whatever pain she's in, she's doing a credible job to hide it. She looks pretty in a cranberry-red cowl-neck sweater dress. She embraces me with her free arm. I carefully hug back, delicately handling her like a Faberge egg. Dino stands behind her, a shiny copper-colored gift bag in his hand.

"Give it to him," she instructs him. He hands it to me.

"Happy birthday," she says.

"Thank you. Shall I open it now?"

"Go on."

I dig through layers of dark-brown tissue. There's a small black box that says Kenneth Cole in white lettering. Inside is a watch with a black leather strap and a sleek, black, and silver face with white roman numerals. Someone already set the time to the current hour and minute. It's a beautiful, classic timepiece. One, I would covet from another man's wrist. But this one is mine, a bright spot in turning a year older. Ma says it's elegant-looking, and while I appreciate it, the cynic in me can't help but also see this gift as a peace offering.

"Thank you very much," I say, giving her another hug before swapping my old, beat-up watch with the new one. I rotate my wrist, allowing the face of the watch to glimmer beautifully in the light.

"Dino helped me pick it out."

"Thanks, Dino," I say, giving him a hug as well.

"You're most welcome."

"How old are you now?" Ma asks.

"I'm forty-two."

"You're getting old, boy."

"Someone at work said the same thing, and I'm going to tell you the same thing I told them… I'm getting better."

I assist Dino with bringing the food from the kitchen to the dining room. A year ago, I would never have thought Ma and I would be in such a great place to where she's making a birthday dinner for me. And yet, here we are, my prayer answered, and about to enjoy Cajun catfish, collards and sweet potatoes.

I also appreciate the way Dino looks at her, like a man who's grateful to be given a second chance with the love of his life. He values her. I never saw Plez or Pastor (the times I'd been in their company) look at her that way.

"You know your brother is in jail, don't you?" Ma announces out of nowhere. "He tracked Nadine down in Chicago. Beat her so bad somebody had to come take the baby."

It breaks my heart to hear this because Nadine was so sure he wouldn't find her. She didn't even want me to know where she was going.

Ma adds that Junior came over one day, crying the blues about missing his daughter. Ma told him it was his own fault Nadine left his ass.

"I'm sure that went over well," I say.

"No. He just kept calling around, asking if I'd been in contact with her. Eventually, I thought by telling him I had, it would calm him down. Later, he brought some Chinese food over and watched TV with me. He must've waited until I went to the bathroom to check my phone, because that's the only way I can think he could've gotten the number she called from."

"At least she pressed charges," Dino interjects.

"I mean, I don't know why Junior turned out like this. He saw what I went through with his daddy. You'd think he would've learned from my experiences."

"Sometimes life doesn't teach the kinds of lessons we think it will," Dino says.

I hate that Junior hurt Nadine, but it thrills me to find out he's in jail. I hope she doesn't go getting a case of the softies and bail him out. She needs to let him rot in there. And just maybe once and for all someone will stomp the dog piss out of him so he'll know what it feels like.

After dinner, I help take the dishes into the kitchen. Ma follows. As I organize the dishes to rinse before putting them in the dishwasher, she tells me Hakee is a nice-looking man.

"Yes, he is fine, isn't he?"

"I'm glad to see you've got good taste."

"It's funny that you bring him up. He suggested that maybe you and I could visit some churches together."

Ma's face brightens. "He's nice-looking and smart."

"Listen, I don't want to make any promises, but I'm willing to go to church with you every once in a while, assuming we can find a church where we can both be comfortable. Does that sound okay with you?"

"I'll take it." She reaches in for another hug.

Dino appears in the doorway as our embrace dissolves. Ma gives him an odd look to which he nods before disappearing around the corner. I hear the creak of the hallway closet door opening, then closing. He returns with a garment bag draped over his useable forearm.

"I saw it in the store window and I thought it would look nice on you," Ma says.

I unzip the bag and pull a black overcoat off the hanger. Dino takes both the hanger and bag from me, and I try on the coat. With my work button-down shirt and tie, the coat gives me a dapper appearance.

"Nice. Thank you."

"Leave it on because we have to get going," Ma says, putting her own coat on. Dino hangs the hanger up and folds the bag in half and puts it in the closet before retrieving his own coat.

"Where are we going?"

"Follow us and you'll find out."

I head outside, making my way down the walk when my phone rings. It's Kenyatta. If I don't answer, he'll just keep bothering me. Irritated, I pick up.

"Yeah?" I answer coldly.

"Why haven't you been answering my texts."
"I'm answering you now."
"What are you doing?"
"Living my life."
"I mean, what's been going on?"
"Not much. Just working hard," I reply, maintaining a flat tone.
"Are you gonna come down to the bar so I can buy you that birthday drink?"
"I don't think so."
"Other plans?"
"Yeah, I'm with my mom and her boy… uh, her friend. They're taking me somewhere."
"Where?"
"Why do you need to know?"
"Maybe I could come down and meet you."
"That won't be necessary."
"See, this is what I'm talking about."
Ma and Dino get into his black Lincoln Town car. I should hang up the phone now. "What are you talking about?"
"I'm talking about your funky-ass attitude."
"Well, maybe I don't like yours, either. So that makes us even."
"There you go acting all uppity and shit! You always think you're better than me!"
"No, I don't. I just don't have time for your nonsense."
"Boy, are you coming?" Ma calls to me.
"Yeah, I'm hanging up now."
'Don't you dare hang up on me!" Kenyatta snaps.
"Dude, I have to go."
"Fine. We'll talk later."
"I don't think so. Better still, lose my number!"
"Oh, so now you're showing your true colors, huh?"
"Better late than never."

"I see. Well, enjoy your fucking birthday, bitch!" Then, suddenly, with a burst of mischievous delight, he adds, "Oh, before I forget, sorry to hear about that brick thrown through your window."

I know when a game is being played, but decide to take the bait. "How do you know about that?"

Kenyatta laughs, and I put the phone on speaker and get into my car. Soon, I'm following Dino's car while attempting to understand how Kenyatta knows about the vandalism.

"Tell me how you know, Kenyatta!"

"My cousin's husband came home late one night with a broken nose. It took some coaxing for sure. I had to damn near threaten to tell my cousin that we slept together, but he eventually told me what happened."

Wait a minute! Kenyatta's cousin is married to Byron? And he not only slept with Byron, but knew about our affair? Yet he said nothing?

"What did Byron say happened?" I ask, testing how Kenyatta reacts to me mentioning Byron by name.

"That he went to your place to break it off, but you tried to seduce him. And when you failed at that, you became belligerent and broke his nose."

My using Byron's name sails right over his head. It strikes me how ridiculous Kenyatta's revisionist version is. Listening to his dumb ass, I find myself three cars behind Dino. If I don't pay closer attention to my driving, I'll lose sight of Dino's car altogether.

My mind is racing. I hate liars. And I hate being in the middle of a liar's lie. I have the feeling Kenyatta is playing with me. Now that I know Byron is involved, Kenyatta better get to who keyed my car and chucked a brick through my window.

Both cars in front of me turn left, and I'm back behind Dino.

"Who keyed my car and threw the fucking brick?"

"Wouldn't you like to know?" he says and hangs up.

Yes, I would. And so will the police. They're going to love to hear about this. And once they get to the bottom of everything, I look forward to watching Kenyatta (and Byron, if he's a co-conspirator) get what's coming to him.

My mood is crap until we pass the Fine Line Music Café. The marquee proudly announces Hakee Mitchell, but I discover TC Carson from *Living Single* is sharing the billing. Hakee never mentioned TC was doing a set too.

We park two blocks from the venue, but I don't care. Tonight, I get to watch Hakee do his thing after all. And Ma and Dino will soon find out just how talented Hakee truly is.

"How'd you know Hakee was performing tonight?" I ask as Ma and Dino get out of the car.

"I called her," a voice says from behind me. I turn to find Doug standing there, extending a white gift bag to me.

"You knew about this, too?" I ask, thrilled to see him.

"Hakee got my number from your phone. He asked me to call your mother and invite her to the show."

We soon approach a line of would-be spectators that snakes along the side of the building, extending to the end of the block. Before I join up with Ma and Dino at the end of the line, I pause until they're far enough ahead to let Doug in on what I found out.

"I think Kenyatta was the one who keyed my car."

Doug's eyebrows raise. "What about the brick?"

"That too."

"Did he say why?"

"He said Byron told him I initiated sex and broke his nose when he declined."

"And how would he know Byron like that for him to tell him that?"

"Are you ready for this? Byron is married to Kenyatta's cousin."

"Stop playin'!" Doug exclaims, stomping a foot on the ground. "Oh, my goodness! Are you serious?"

"Oh, that's not the best part. He and Byron have slept together at least once."

"Kenyatta told you that?"

"He bragged about it."

"So how are you gonna handle it?"

"I'll tell the cops and have them confront him where he works."

"Kenyatta works?"

"I know, right?" I reply with a chuckle.

"Serves him right. I never could stand that messy bitch!"

The show is electric. Once again, Hakee proves to be quite the showman, bringing his brand of neo-soul and jazz to his performance. Dressed in black leather pants and an open, white, flowing poet's shirt, he moves barefoot across the stage. His hard chest gleams under the stage lights. I'm surrounded by flocks of mesmerized women. Most of them are salivating, whistling, and cheering at Hakee. Even Doug is transfixed. Thankfully, unlike Hakee's show at First Avenue, this performance goes on without the manic screeching of a disruptive audience member.

"Ladies and gentlemen, before I do my closing song, I'd like to say that now more than ever, it's important for us to love one another."

Audience applause is immediate and full.

"I mean it. Black, white, straight, gay, Christian, or Muslim… it doesn't matter. If you think about it, there are so many ways we're the same. I choose to celebrate our sameness. We're all in this together. With love, we can change the world."

More applause. Hakee's speech is right on time. I'm filled with a sappy hopefulness that anything is possible. Looking around the room, it's nice to see others who believe in his message too.

"But I can't do it alone. I don't want to do it alone."

More whistling and cheering.

"There's someone special here tonight that I've gotten to know, and who I'd like to continue to get to know. In our brief time together, I feel like we click. This song is for us!"

A female backup singer starts the first run of their cover of Keith Sweat's "Make It Last Forever." Hakee sings with her but soon breaks from their duet to peer into the audience. Women wave frantically for his attention; each wanting to be the one he gives his affection to. But it's my eyes Hakee's locks onto.

At the end of the evening, I return to his apartment. He brings out a slice of coconut cake with a single candle in it from the kitchen. Upon lighting it, he cups his hand to protect the flame.

"Happy birthday, Lawrence. Make a wish."

"It already came true," I reply, giving my best Samantha from *Sixteen Candles* delivery.

Hakee snorts. "You're so corny."

I won't deny it; I'm a huge cornball. However, I don't think he gets the reference. Still, I close my eyes and wish for a happy future; one in which I have a job I actually look forward to going to, and a man I look forward to coming home to. Maybe Hakee is that man. Then I blow out the candle.

He winks at me, then stabs a fork into the cake. He tells me to open wide and feeds me. In between bites he dotingly wipes frosting from my bottom lip with his thumb before kissing me there. Soon the cake is gone, and our kisses turn ravenous.

We retire to bed. As we undress, Hakee says, "I'm excited."

"About what?"

"I dunno. This. You and me. I'm looking forward to spending a lot of time with you, Lawrence."

"Me too."

We climb into bed, but we don't have sex, and I'm okay with that. Our mutual enthusiasm to see where things lead more than compensates. And while I don't expect any miracles, I feel good about the man I'm lying next to. And for the first time in my life, I don't need to second guess whether I deserve the happiness he brings me. My insecurities aren't completely gone, but with some effort, they won't rule me, either. As Hakee wraps his arms around me from behind, I close my eyes and thank God for what's ahead, and for making it good.

## THE END

\*\*\* You've finished the book! Yay! I hope you enjoyed it! It would make me very happy if you could take a moment to leave an honest review where ever you purchased this book. Whether you liked the story or not, *constructive* reviews help other readers find my books, and also helps me grow as an author to continue doing what I love! Thank you in advance!

CPSIA information can be obtained
at www.ICGtesting.com
Printed in the USA
BVHW081149040123
655464BV00008B/800